BALO'S WAR

BALO'S WAR

A Novel About the Plan of San Diego

Alfredo E. Cárdenas

MCM Books, March 2015

This is a historical novel of what could have happened, based on what did happen. The central characters and what they say are not real, but they are based on true events and actual people. The interaction of these fictional characters and real people did not happen, but they are based on events the real people participated in or on actions they took.

Thanks to my wife, Genie and my children, Monica, Christina and Matthew, for all their support.

ISBN: 10: 0692318631

ISBN-13: 978-0692318638

Library of Congress Control Number: 2004118309

Dedication

To my parents, Aurora Esparza and Servando Cárdenas, for my life and their love, and to all our grandparents and great-grandparents for leaving us all with an enduring legacy.

Chapter 1

A loud cracking noise shattered Balo's sleep, and instinctively, he sat up in bed. He held the side of his bed with both hands as he tried to focus. The ever-present stench of human waste shook him into awareness of where he was. Another blast, and he jumped up and rushed to the window. He saw the carts of the *hieleros* at the ice plant making their early morning deliveries.

His first thought was that Pancho Villa and his army were attacking Carranza forces in Matamoros. As he stared through the steel bars of the third floor of the Cameron County Jail, he could see into México across the Río Bravo, just four blocks away. It was still dark, but he could see the outlines of buildings clearly, and all was calm.

At Fort Brown, on the American side of the river, all he saw was the silhouette of a man in the stables spreading out hay to the cavalry horses.

There was no battle on either side of the river. It wasn't time for that, he thought.

1

Suddenly he saw a flash of light coming from behind the jail, from the east. A rumble soon followed. Then rain started pouring down. The lightning, thunder and rain were unrelenting. All the souls in Heaven were lamenting and shedding tears for the plight of his people, he thought. All except for the *gringo* souls, if any had made it to Heaven.

Balo went back to his bed and sat down. He leaned against the concrete wall. The humidity caused his *camiseta* to cling to his hairless body. For the past two weeks, since the *gringos* had thrown him in jail on January 15, 1915, thoughts of his capture had kept him from sleeping most every night. The conditions were not the best, but he had been in worse *cárceles* in México.

***

He had started out a week earlier with great hope from Monterrey. Upon arriving in Matamoros he had sought a meeting with General Nefarrate, which was not granted until late in the afternoon. After extensive discussions with the general and his aides, Balo was exhilarated.

His mission was clear. His cause was just. His spirits were high.

He crossed the river into Brownsville at dusk, and quickly walked the length of the commercial district on Washington Street and made his way to the San Carlos Hotel on 10th Street and St. Charles, two blocks east of the downtown and two blocks north of the Río Bravo. The San Carlos was a sprawling wood compound with peeling white paint covering its two buildings. In the larger building were the office and a large parlor. Behind the office was a *café*. Behind the main building was a smaller, two-story structure where the guest rooms were located. At one time, Balo thought, this must have been an important social center, and it would be an important center for him as well.

Balo took a room on the second floor. He paid his four dollars and walked up the staircase. He only had one small suitcase where he carried a change of clothes and important documents. After getting a sound sleep on his first night back in Texas, he set out in the morning to look for old friends, whom he hoped to enlist in the movement. His short time in Brownsville had been very successful. Balo persuaded his old companion Salvador Sifuentes and a number of other friends to join. Balo's words fired them up, and they were ready for action.

Salvador offered to take Balo to McAllen in his wagon pulled by mules. Salvador was a big man, standing more than 6 feet tall — tall for a Mexican, everyone told him — and weighing more than 200 pounds. Despite his size, he was a gentle man and not prone to violence. With his bronze skin and slightly kinky hair, some speculated he was a mulatto, perhaps the product of one of the Buffalo soldiers stationed at Fort Brown years earlier. That always angered Salvador, who would tell everyone that his father was still alive and he was not a *negro*.

On the three-day trip to McAllen, the sight of his fellow *campesinos* on the fields, stooped over and picking vegetables for their *gringo patrones*, reinforced Balo's motivation. It is for the *gringos* to sell up *norte*, and the *Mexicano* will not even get a taste of his own labor, Balo thought. New vegetable fields were being planted everywhere along the road to McAllen. The *gringos* were building irrigation stations and pumping water from the Río Bravo to make the whole valley on the north side of the river green and rich. Who gave the *gringo* the right to take the water from the *río*, Balo asked himself. It belonged as much to México as to the *gringo*. But, so did the land on the north side of the river, Balo reminded himself.

When they got to the city of Donna on the second day of the trip, Salvador and Balo came to a restaurant on Miller Street, next to the post office, and a number of old *gringos* were filing out. Two of the *gringos* went into the restaurant, and Balo told Salvador to find another place to stop. They rode up Seventh Street to a pool hall on Hooks Street, and they stopped for some food and refreshments. Balo told Salvador that Donna, situated on La Blanca land granted to the Cavazos family by the king of Spain, was like most of the new *gringo* towns in the valley. The *gringo* had taken land from the *Mexicano* and made himself rich on the back of the poor *Mexicanos* who remained. Balo and Salvador each ate a *gordita* of *picadillo* and drank a Coca-Cola, before continuing their trip to McAllen, which was still 14 miles up the road. They decided to spend the night under the stars just outside of Donna.

Arriving in McAllen in mid-afternoon, Balo sought out a Mexican doctor whom the professor in Monterrey had said was sympathetic to the cause. Balo did not know the man, but the professor had vouched for Dr. Alvaro Villalobos. Balo and Salvador asked an old man on the street where they could find the doctor; they learned that his office was at the corner of 16th Avenue and 17th Street. The street grid in McAllen had always confused Balo. North and south streets were called "streets," and east and west streets were called "avenues." Or, was it the other way around? They were all numbered, and the numbers repeated themselves. One of Balo's favorite restaurants was on the corner of 17th Street and 17th Avenue, and that is where Balo and Salvador went when Dr. Villalobos told them he was busy with patients and asked that they come back at sunset.

At the Diez y Siete Café they sat at a table by the window, where a breeze and a couple of Pearl beers helped them recover from the taxing trip. Sitting on a wooden plank, bouncing up and down a bumpy road for three days, was not an experience Balo relished.

The cold beers hit the spot. After an hour, they walked to a print shop where Balo's brother Manuel had apprenticed several years earlier. The owner was an old *Mexicano* who loved to play pool, drink beer, and dabble in local politics. He fancied himself the *patron* of the *barrio*, but most of his neighbors thought he was a pompous ass who liked to kiss the *gringos'* behinds. Balo was careful of what he said around old Remigio but asked what kind of man Dr. Villalobos was.

The old man laughed and said the doctor still had his mind and heart in México and needed to get over it, because he was now in America. Dr. Villalobos, Remigio said, was always reading *Mexicano* newspapers and spouting revolutionary talk. The doctor was a fan of Pancho Villa and was sure his hero would soon become supreme leader of México.

As Balo and Salvador walked back to the doctor's office, Balo felt he was truly going to see a kindred spirit. Anyone who championed Villa was a true man of the people, Balo thought. He felt that the doctor would be receptive, as the professor had said. When they arrived at the doctor's office, the nurse who had greeted them earlier was locking the door. She let Balo in and told him to go to the back room, where the doctor was with a friend. Salvador waited outside. The doctor introduced his friend as Don Martin Gonzales, a leader of the *Mexicano* community in McAllen. Balo shook hands with the man, whose small hand with stubby fingers gave a firm grip. Even though Don Martin was sitting, Balo could tell that the man had a short, corpulent figure. He wore a suit and had a large, poorly manicured mustache. His green eyes had a distrusting look.

Dr. Villalobos, by contrast, was slight of build and had a thin mustache, perfectly manicured.

Balo pulled a letter of introduction from his inside vest pocket and handed it to Dr. Villalobos. The letter was from *profesor* Antonio Guerra. It said Balo had an important document to share with the doctor.

"*¿Y cual es ese documento?*" the doctor inquired about the papers.

Balo reached into his vest pocket once again and handed the doctor some papers folded in three parts. After reading silently for a moment, the doctor handed the papers to Don Martin and asked Balo how his good friend *profesor* Garza was doing. As they spoke for a few minutes, Balo could see Don Martin going through the papers with an odd look on his face.

"*Bueno joven,*" Don Martín said as he pushed on his chair to lift himself up, "we will have to put you under arrest for these anarchist and treasonous papers."

Don Martin reached into his vest pocket, revealing a sheriff's badge, and pulled out a gun and pointed it at Balo. He ushered him out of the doctor's office while the doctor shamefacedly sat down at his desk. Balo hoping to save Salvador from arrest, managed to signal him as he walked out. Salvador pretended not to know Balo, moved on down the street and prevented his own arrest.

***

"*El hijo de su puta madre,*" Balo sneered, sitting in his jail cell. The son of a bitch Villalobos had betrayed him and was not sympathetic to the movement. The *profesor* had been wrong to think the doctor was a friend. Balo lay down on the bed, trying to relieve his stress. His mother's words came to him, *"y qué culpa tienen las madres,"* she would say whenever anyone invoked anger on an adversary's mother. Mothers were blameless in such matters, she would say. Of course, she was right, but still Balo could not help but think that the doctor's mother had done something wrong to raise a man with such poor character. Balo finally dozed off thinking of his mother.

"Las madres son inocentes," he heard his mother's voice in his head.

Chapter 2

Captain Matthew Hoffman was at his chair behind an old oak desk that was pushed against the wall in the basement of the headquarters building at Fort Sam Houston. Someone had stored this large desk in a small room, and the captain thought it was the perfect place for when he wanted to get away to think and to write down his thoughts. As secluded as it was, its location was no secret to the men of his company.

"Captain Hoffman, the president wishes to speak with you!"

Hoffman put down his pencil and glanced up at an excited young soldier.

"Calm down, Corporal, and tell me all about it," the captain said. He swiveled around and rose from his chair. In a quiet, meticulous manner, Hoffman asked the corporal, who was out of breath after his run down the stairs, for details.

"The president of what institution? What is his name? Is he here or is he on the telephone? Is it urgent or can it wait?"

"No, sir!" Corporal Schaefer shouted in exasperation.

"No, sir, he's not here or no, sir, he's not on the telephone. Or no, sir …"

"You don't understand, Captain," Schaefer interrupted. "It's the president of the United States. It's President Wilson. He's on the telephone in the company room."

"Oh," the captain responded, so quietly the word was barely audible. The unexpected surprise should have evoked a more forceful reaction, but a sudden onset of nostalgia muffled it. Hoffman sat back down for a moment of contemplation, before the corporal snapped him out of his daze.

"The president is waiting, Captain!"

Hoffman stood up, grabbed his papers in uncharacteristic haste, and rolled down the top of his desk. He quickly set out for the telephone. Earlier, a strong urge to write down some thoughts and observations overcame him and he went to his hideaway in the basement. He marched double time to the company room clear across the expansive old fort. He had arrived at Fort Sam Houston in San Antonio a few months earlier. As he rushed through its beautifully landscaped grounds with soldiers running all about, Hoffman suddenly thought of himself on the grounds of Princeton University. How many times had Professor Wilson admonished him?

"Matthew, the intellectual spirit needs solitude to grow."

Every time Hoffman approached the professor of political economics with a political question, Wilson would sent him off to some secluded place on campus to develop the thought or idea. When Hoffman thought he had a good case, he rushed across campus to the professor's office to discuss his ideas. Hoffman grew fond of this gentle man, but time and circumstance had pulled them apart. What quirk of fate had led the president to call him now, Hoffman wondered, as he came back to reality?

As Hoffman rushed up the wooden stairs and into the company room, for a moment he thought he would see Professor Wilson at work at his desk. But instead he found the room in unrestrained suspense. Three enlisted men stood behind a young private who held a telephone tightly in his hand. The captain stared at the four recruits, who stared back, but no one spoke. Finally, Hoffman turned to the private with the telephone.

"Is that for me, Soldier?"

"Yes, sir," the youngster stammered. "It's the President, sir."

Hoffman regained his composure.

"That's fine, son. Now do you think I can speak with the president?"

He disengaged the telephone from the young man's hand and spoke into it.

"Mr. President, Captain Hoffman at your service."

"At ease, Captain," came back a sensuous voice from the president's secretary. "The President will be right with you."

"Pardon me, ma'am, of course."

Hoffman remained calm but was unsure of how to act when the president would come to the telephone. He had not spoken with Professor Wilson in years. Now Professor Wilson was the president of the United States, his commander in chief.

"Matthew, are you there?"

The familiar voice struck his consciousness, as though time and circumstance had never intervened. Hoffman paused for half a moment to regain his thoughts. The emotion overpowered him. He was happy to hear that friendly voice. Still, he was apprehensive, unsure what motivated the president to call him.

"Yes, sir, Mr. President, at your service."

"Why so formal, Matthew? You can call me professor."

"Yes, sir, Mr. President. I mean, uh, Professor."

It was early March and the weather had been chilly. It did not compare to a winter at his home in Maryland, but somehow Hoffman was sure he should not perspire under these conditions. He changed the telephone to the other hand and wiped his wet palm on his greens.

After some brief pleasantries, the president got to the point.

"Matthew, what do you know about this Plan of San Diego business?"

The question sounded familiar, yet it elicited a blank. Hoffman realized that it was not the question that was familiar, it was the interchange. How many times had the professor posed other questions in the same fashion, and how many other times had he drawn a blank?

"The San Diego business, Mr. President?"

"Yes, this whole business of a Plan of San Diego, and a Mexican insurrection in South Texas."

"Oh, that, sir; well not much, Mr. President, just what the local newspapers have reported, which has not been much. I haven't gotten a good measure of them, so I don't know how reliable they are."

Hoffman knew that was a poor excuse. His commander in chief expected more from his officers. Still, the question confounded Hoffman, and he had no better answer.

"Well, Matthew, I need for you to take on a special assignment for me. I have cleared it with your commander, General Funston. I want you to come to Washington as soon as possible. Leave tomorrow."

"Yes, sir, Mr. President. Right away."

"All right, Matthew, I'll see you soon. And, Matthew, it is Professor Wilson, remember?"

"Yes, sir, Mr. President."

"A special assignment," Hoffman murmured to himself.

Hoffman slowly put down the telephone as he came to grips with what had just happened. A special assignment—it sounded like Princeton all over again.

He walked out the door and down the stairs into the courtyard, hoping that he would be able to handle this assignment and not let his professor down.

***

A look of severe worry spread over Hoffman's face as he sat at attention in his hard train seat. The train was already near Washington, and Hoffman did not know how to face the president. He stared at the newspaper headline before him.

BORDER CITIZENS
PATROL IN VAIN

How close to his failure that headline had come, Hoffman thought. As soon as he had gotten over the shock of the president's call, Hoffman researched his assignment.

His orders were to leave for Washington immediately, so he had not had much time. Hoffman visited the Carnegie Library in San Antonio and perused the local newspapers from the start of the year. His search, like that of the border citizens, was in vain. The *San Antonio Express* had run two brief stories on the alleged plot. The *San Antonio Light* had done no better.

From these accounts, he had learned that a group of men in South Texas had concocted a revolutionary plot to overthrow the U.S. government. The alleged perpetrators were Mexicans, but not much more was clear.

His early journalistic preparation in his father's newspaper prompted him to ask the obvious questions. He ran through them quickly. Who were the revolutionaries? The best he came up with was that they were Mexicans.

It was unclear to him whether they were Mexican nationals or Texas Mexicans.

What was their mission? They proposed to overthrow the government. Hoffman thought it was a preposterous idea, but that was what he had determined from the newspaper accounts. The other three W's — why, when and where — were complete blanks. The big "how" was an equally big question mark.

Unprepared as Hoffman was by these skimpy reports, he still had to face the professor. This was not the first time he encountered this type of situation. On many other occasions, Hoffman had reported to the professor unprepared. The realization that he no longer was a student and the professor was now the president filled him with apprehension. Grim as the prospects appeared, that is all he knew. Resigned to this fact, he tossed the newspapers on the empty seat next to his.

Hoffman slid down on his seat and laid his head back, and massaged his tired eyes. The tension built up by the past 24 hours invaded his body and mind. He had to relax and release the anxiety from within him before he met with the president. He found no room to make himself comfortable. It was impossible to cram his six-foot-three-inch body into such a small space, so he got up in search of an area to relax for the remainder of the trip.

After a brief walk of the length of the train, he stood before the glassed-in portion of the observation car in the rear. As he watched the scenery roll along in an endless panorama, he was reminded of his father's presses as they rolled out sheet after sheet of newsprint. He made his way back to his seat and subconsciously began to recount his association with the president.

***

He had enrolled in Princeton in 1899 at the age of 17 to pursue a Liberal Arts education, which his father felt was essential if he was to one day take over the family business. The Hoffman clan had come to the United States in the early 1800s from an area around Cologne, Germany. They had fled from Napoleon's armies and his abolition of the Holy Roman Empire in Germany. They sailed from Bremen to Baltimore, and upon their arrival in the United States, they settled in Allegany County in northwestern Maryland. They soon set up a print shop and published a German-language newspaper, the *Allegany County Republican.*

The Hoffmans prided themselves as learned, so when they arrived in America, they had found the idea of slavery despicable. Although they had not seen the practice up close and had no firsthand familiarity with this abhorrent practice, its existence appalled them. What made it unacceptable to them was that it existed in this haven of Democratic ideals and independent spirit. Quite naturally, when Abraham Lincoln and his young Republican Party advocated an abolition-ist program, the Hoffman family embraced the cause. Ever since the first Lincoln presidency, the Hoffman men and their newspaper proclaimed themselves as Republican.

Matthew Hoffman was born into this political atmosphere in 1882, and his father inculcated Republican thought into him from early childhood. In 1899, upon graduation from high school, his father sent him off to Princeton to further his education. Editor Hoffman had no idea that his son would come under the influence of a future Democratic president. Young Hoffman, blessed with a quick mind, had a strong desire to learn. He soon caught the attention of his popular professor who befriended him and took him in as his research assistant.

When Professor Wilson became president of Princeton in 1902, he took young Hoffman along with him as an aide. Throughout their association at Princeton, Hoffman had admired Wilson for his incisive mind. It was from Wilson that Hoffman had acquired and improved his ability of deductive analysis. Logical thought had been the hallmark of their relationship. Wilson often admonished young Hoffman to investigate the facts, consider the angles, and weigh the evidence before he made a decision. It was ironic that with the guidance provided to him by this fine man, Hoffman reached certain political conclusions that eventually created a distance between them.

Hoffman stayed at Princeton until 1906, when he received his doctorate. His dissertation on "The Republican Legacy" won him wide acclaim and so impressed President Theodore Roosevelt, that he offered Hoffman a minor position in the government. Wilson knew of Hoffman's family background and encouraged him to accept the position as a means to study firsthand both American politics and government. Reluctantly, Hoffman left for Washington. While the opportunity excited him, he nevertheless felt remorse at his departure from Professor Wilson's side. Wilson had been his teacher for many years and now the umbilical cord was cut.

Washington was a great place to live and work. His job at the State Department offered Hoffman a new area of intellectual development. The complexities of foreign relationships and the delicacies of diplomacy presented a new challenge. Moreover, it provided him with an opportunity to broaden his education. While he and Wilson had not often discussed their political beliefs, they knew enough to ascertain that the professor was a progressive in regards to social programs and a pacifist in foreign affairs. Hoffman only partially agreed with this philosophy. While the excesses of business demanded some governmental intervention, Hoffman was not in total agreement with Wilson as to the extent of that control. His experience at State had further convinced him that Wilson's foreign policy views were somewhat naive.

With the departure of Roosevelt from Washington, Hoffman had wanted to return home to Maryland, but the new Taft administration prevailed upon him to remain. He quickly grew to respect and admire

President Taft as a man of genuine concern for people
and a devoted disciple to principles. It was ironic that
his administration was to suffer because of these traits
in his personality. The progressives did not understand
his adherence to principle and the conservatives dis-
dained his actions against their specific interests in
favor of the common man. It was precisely this dogged
pursuit of principle, despite the consequences, that so
impressed the young student of government.

When Wilson announced his intention to run for governor of New Jersey as a Democrat, Hoffman was not
surprised, but he was concerned. Frankly, he was not
sure Wilson had the toughness required of a politician.
Although they had corresponded from time to time
while he lived in Washington, from the time of Wilson's
entry into politics, their relationship ended. It was difficult to say what caused their correspondence to stop,
whether their contrary political views or the nature of
their new lifestyles. Nonetheless, Hoffman had not had
any communication with Wilson since 1910.

In the presidential election of 1912 in which his
three mentors vied for the presidency, his triangular
loyalty tore Hoffman apart. He was more closely akin
politically to Taft, so he stuck with him. Upon Taft's
defeat, Hoffman accepted an Army commission. He
reasoned that the world situation would inevitably lead
to war, and Germany was to be at the center of the
conflict. His German ancestry provided him an irksome

apprehension. He was certain that eventually the United States and Germany would face each other on the battlefield, and all German-Americans would have their loyalty severely questioned. To allay his qualms, Hoffman had joined the Army as an outward manifestation of devotion to his country.

Chapter 3

A barking dog snapped Balo out of his reverie. He rose from the jail cell cot, looked out the window bars and saw a plump woman, her hair in *trenzas* and an apron covering her ankle-length dress, come out the back door of one of several board-and-batten houses across the county jail on Van Buren Street. Years of exposure to the sun, dust, wind, and rain had turned the house's natural wood to a somber gray.

As the woman carefully stepped down the two wooden steps, trying to avoid a puddle at the foot of the steps, a midsize black mongrel dog with white spots on his forehead and back snipped at her heels and jumped at her legs.

"*Quítate, perro,*" she said, trying to shoo the dog away.

The dog persisted, jumping up and down as he followed her to the *gallinero* in the rear of the *solar*. The woman kicked at the dog to get him away. With each jump, the dog splashed mud on the woman's dress. She entered the chicken coop in the rear of her backyard and quickly shut the mesh wire door to keep the dog from getting to the chickens. She gathered some eggs for the day's breakfast in her apron.

She went back to the house, slipping out off her muddy *huaraches* on the wooden steps and went into the house barefoot.

Balo could see her work in her small kitchen that was lit by a kerosene lamp. She put some *leña* in a wood stove and placed a *sartén* and a *comal* on the stove top. Using her *palote*, she rolled her *testales* into nice round *tortillas*. The woman reminded him of his *tía* Cuca back at the *rancho* in Piedras Pintas. The thought of *tía* Cuca's flour tortillas made Balo's mouth water for a moment, but memories of *tía* Cuca had always brought on his worst nightmares. He always tried to shake those thoughts of so long ago out of his head but they were what had defined his life — a life that had amounted to disappointment to his mother and father and near ruin for himself.

***

His mind once again trailed off into recollections. Balo had found that he had been doing a lot of day-dreaming in jail. There was not much else to do. But in reality he had not been doing much with his life until recently. Even before reaching manhood, he had begun to drink heavily to erase the fear, guilt, and anger that consumed him. His father often yelled at him that he was no more than a *borracho* and a *viejero*, who drank too much and had no respect for women. In truth, he had lost track on the number of women he had bedded and the number of jails in which he had slept off a drunken night of carousing. Balo remembered trying to escape the life of one who, as his father would often tell him, "*no sirves para nada.*"

After a particularly disturbing drunken episode in Monterrey three years earlier, when he was 36, Balo awoke in a pool of his vomit. He knew he had to change, or his life would come to an early end. He decided that the best way to clear his mind and his memories was hard work. Balo jumped on the first train to San Diego in Texas, where his brother Manuel lived. When he arrived, Manuel told Balo he was just in time to join a friend and his friend's family in their annual journey to the *piscas*. Desidorio Arrieta and his family regularly migrated north to pick cotton and produce in various locations in Texas and beyond. That year they packed their belongings into a horse-drawn wagon and joined a caravan headed for Yoktown, east of San Antonio on the way to Victoria. Yoktown was the Mexican way of pronouncing Yorktown. The *gringos* found this funny and attributed it to ignorance. Balo would smirk at this, since these were the same *gringos* who called Refugio, Refurio.

The farm owner rented the family a one-room shack by the banks of the Coleto Creek, on a grove of pecan trees. It was one of six shacks that were made available to workers with families; single men like Balo lived under the sky and usually slept under wagons. The *patron's* two-story stone mansion was set up on the *barranco* overlooking the fields on the other side of the creek. The farm owner was in his early sixties, but he had a wife who was not more than 30. Shortly after Balo arrived, the pretty *huera* with *ojos azules* began to cast her eyes toward Balo. He ignored her, not wanting to have anything to do with women, and most certainly nothing to do with a *gringa*.

Since Balo spoke English, one day Desidorio, who was the *mayordomo,* sent Balo up to the house to tell the *gringo* owner that *gusanos* were eating the cotton plants. As he walked up the hill to the back door, Balo noticed that the *gringo's* automobile was not at its usual location in front of the house. He knocked on the door, and the *señora* came to the door and smiled.

"I have a message for Mr. Givens from Desidorio," Balo told the woman, who had cracked open the screen door and motioned him to enter the house.

"Mister Givens has gone into town, and I'm all alone in this big old house," the woman teased Balo, waving her arms and her long, flowing blond hair as she turned to gesture how big the house was.

"Why don't you come in and tell me all about it while we have some coffee?"

"There is nothing to tell, only that the cotton plants are infested with worms," Balo said.

"Oh, my," she feigned, "how dreadful." She then came up on Balo suddenly, grabbed his crotch area and whispered, "but not all worms are bad."

Balo had met many *viejas ofrecidas*, as his mother often called the easy women he dated, but this *gringa* was certainly bold. She looked up at him and told him to kiss her. He grabbed her and kissed her.

"What if your husband comes back?" Balo asked.

"The old fart isn't coming back until after lunch," she said. "We have plenty of time, don't worry."

She led him by the hand to her upstairs bedroom.

Afterward, he learned her name was Bonnie and she had married old man Givens in New Orleans, where she had been working in a whorehouse. The old man had money and wanted a wife to brag about, but he was a lousy lover and she yearned for someone closer to her age. When Balo would see the old man leave in his car, he would go up to the house.

One day, the old man, who had grown suspicious, returned to the house on horseback and surprised the lovers. Balo heard Givens come up the stairs and quickly grabbed his jeans and shirt and jumped out the window onto a ledge. He worked himself down to the ground and made a quick escape down the large pecan trees along the creek. All hell broke loose.

***

The rattling of a horse-pulled wagon snapped Balo out of his reminiscence, as it headed toward town on 12th Street. The horses were blindfolded to keep them heading in the right direction where the men wanted them to go. The two men wore denim shirts, jeans and fur-felt

hats to protect them from the rain. They were carrying
a load from the rice mill on Harrison Street to the Río
Grande Railroad freight depot. The sacks of rice in the
back of the wagon were weighing it down, making it
hard to maneuver on the *barro* that had formed from the
mixture of the rain and clay streets. The mud was nearly
a foot deep and the horses struggled to pull the wagon.
The men whistled and yelled directions at the horses to
keep them pulling. As the wagon made its way down the
street, it reached the creosote-paved part of the road at
the intersection of 12th and Adams Streets, where the
market square was located and the horses seemed to be
relieved as their load suddenly became lighter.

The day was beginning to gray as the sun began to creep
out over the eastern horizon. Balo saw *vaqueros* — dressed
in jeans, fading shirts, worn and scratched boots, and
floppy *sombreros* limped from years of sweat — enter the
café behind the bank for their breakfast or morning coffee.
A few *catrines* in suits and ties who probably worked at the
bank were also eating breakfast at the restaurant.

Balo sat down on his bed again, which was a wooden
box on legs with a spring and a thin sheet as cover. He
placed his elbows on his knees and cradled his head in
his cupped hands. He realized he was not going to be
able to get any more sleep, as the rest of the world was
now busy taking advantage of the daylight. His *ojos
borrados* followed a *cucaracho* as it crawled from behind
the lard can on the cracked cement floor in the corner

of the cell. The guards provided cans for the inmates to use as urinals, and their spray often went errant, creating ideal conditions for the cockroaches. Two other of the brown flat insects followed with hurried movements, much like a gang of juveniles emerging from dark alley after committing a crime, looking in all directions to see if they were undetected.

Balo rose to his feet and walked toward the window to see the *cucarachos'* journey. As he approached the window, the last of the roaches flew out between the iron bars into freedom.

"*Córrele cuate,*" Balo said to the *cucaracho*, with a crooked smile. At least one of us has his freedom, he thought.

"Hell," thought Balo, "we've never been treated any better than animals on the outside, why should the *cucarachos* take second seat to us here?"

Thirty days earlier, federal agents had thrown Baldomero Reyna into the roach-infested Cameron County Jail. He still had not been able to get used to the filth and urine stench that permeated his cell. With each additional day in jail, Balo grew angrier. He was ready to get the hell out of this hellhole.

Chapter 4

Baldomero Reyna was looking forward to the day with mixed feelings. He knew the *gringos* were going to question him again and he thought it was a waste of time. On the other hand, it would get him out of the jail, which he detested more with each passing day.

"Reyna!" a jail guard yelled. "They want you downstairs for more questions."

"*Otra vez?*" Balo snapped. He despised having to answer questions yet again.

"How many times do these *gringos* have to ask their stupid questions?"

"Just move your ass, greaser, and do as you're told," the guard yelled as he pushed Reyna with the butt of his rifle.

"You're very brave with a rifle in your hand, eh *gringo*?"

"Just move it, Meskin," the guard growled.

As Balo and the guard moved down the jail corridor, the other prisoners shouted encouragement at him. Balo's toughness had endeared him to fellow inmates, poor *Mexicanos* jailed mostly for getting drunk on a Saturday night. Reyna did not put up with any of the guards' crap and preached to the others about their rights. They admired his guts as well as his smarts.

"*Raya les la madre Balo*," shouted a mustachioed prisoner with a jerking clenched fist, urging Balo to tell his questioners to go to hell.

They called him by his nickname because they felt as close to him as a member of their families. Balo's charisma had quickly taken hold with his *paisanos* in the Cameron County Jail.

As Balo and the guard reached the bottom of the narrow stairs, two officers from the Immigration Service met them. They informed Balo that they were taking him to the office of the Inspector in Charge for a hearing on his case. The inspectors had already interrogated Balo on numerous occasions. He did not like it the first time and he grew more recalcitrant each time they subjected him to the same questions. About the only thing he enjoyed about the whole affair was the opportunity to go outside and breathe some fresh air.

The interrogation required the officers to take Balo to the Federal Courthouse, several blocks from the county jail. As Balo and his two guards exited the jail, the mid-morning hustle and bustle was well underway in Brownsville's business district.

Across the street from the jail, Balo noticed his old friend Poncho Torres fooling around with a local prostitute. Torres twirled her around as they danced on the sidewalk. Torres winked at Balo. The friend had visited with Balo the day before and the two had worked on a plan to execute an escape. Guards had told Balo that he had another appearance before immigration inspectors the following day, so he advised his friend to hang out in front of the jail and wait for the right time to spring him free. Balo did not know what his friend had worked out so he kept his eyes on his friend for some signal.

"*En la vuelta, nos salimos del baile,*" his friend mocked in song as he twirled his lady companion again. Balo got the message. The jail break would be executed on his return.

They arrived at the Inspector's Office, and the inspector told Balo to sit at the middle of a long table. Sitting opposite him were Immigrant Inspectors P. R. Adams, acting as examiner; Ronald J. Almond, interpreter; and A. N. Wright, stenographer. They wasted no time in getting started. Adams opened the hearing.

"This is a hearing before the Immigration Service, Mexican Border District of the Department of Commerce and Labor. It is a hearing in the matter of Baldomero Reyna Jr., alias Baldomero Reyna García, alias B. H. García, arrested pursuant to a departmental formal warrant. The alien is charged with being a person likely to become a public charge at the time of his entry into the United States."

Balo rolled his head pretending to be massaging his neck. He appeared very bored by the proceedings. He could not really understand the purpose of this hearing. He was sure that in the end they would do whatever they wanted anyway. He supposed that it must be some pretense to satisfy their alleged judicial system. At least in México the authorities did not go through this kind of charade to trample your rights, he thought. Adams, in the meantime, went on with his charge.

"That he was an anarchist or person who believed in or advocated the overthrow by force or violence of the government of the United States, or of all government, or of all forms of law, or the assassination of public officials at the time of his entry into the United States and that he entered without the inspection contemplated and required by the Immigration Act."

"Guilty as charged," Balo thought to himself. "Oppression in any form needed to be wiped out. After all, had not this country's revolutionaries advocated the overthrow of government? The only difference between him and them was that he would not replace one overbearing government by another." A direct question from Adams snapped Balo out of his self-indulgence.

"The amount of bail set in this case is $3,000. Do you wish to avail yourself of this right of bail?"

"Where would I get that kind of money, *gringo*?"

Adams had grown accustomed to Balo's remarks and pretended not to hear them. The first hearing had been no better than a series of racially splattered charges. Adams just wanted to get this hearing over with as soon as possible, a wish equally shared by Balo. Once sworn in, the chief interrogator directed Balo to introduce himself for the record. By this time, he could recite what they wanted to hear by rote.

"My name is Baldomero Reyna. I am 39 years of age and a citizen of México. I embarked for the United States from Matamoros, México, and landed at the port of Brownsville, Texas, about January 8, 1915."

He went on to give the names and addresses of his parents and other members of his family. When he was done, Inspector Adams read into the record a description of Reyna. He described the "alien" as a single male, age 39, height 5 feet 11 inches, 175 pounds, light complexion, flaxen hair, light hazel eyes, with a black mole in the upper left corner of his mouth. He finished his portrayal by noting that Reyna had an intelligent-looking face. He then continued with his questioning.

"Where were you born?"

"In Linares, Nuevo Leon."

"Where were you raised?"

"In Linares."

"Are you a citizen and subject of Mexico and of the Mexican race?"

"What do I look like to you, *gringo*? Yes, I am a citizen of México."

"Have you ever been married?

"You just finished reading into the record that I was a single male. Next thing I know you will asking me if I'm a male. No, I have never been married."

"In what schools were you educated?"

"I attended the public schools of Linares for several years, and I finished high school there. I was also briefly enrolled in a school in Rolla, Missouri."

"Can you speak English?"

"*Si, Señor, un poquito,*" Balo mimicked.

"Where did you learn to speak English?"

"In Rolla and along the border."

"What kind of work have you been engaged in?"

"As an office clerk."

"When did you last come to the United States?"

"Again with that one? I crossed from Matamoros, México, to Brownsville, Texas, about the 7th or 8th of January 1915."

"Were you manifested or registered by any immigration officer at that time?"

"Some officer asked me a couple of questions and let me pass."

"Where did you cross the river at that time?"

"At the bridge. Where else do you have officers asking questions? I crossed in a taxi."

"Is it not a fact that you never crossed the international bridge at all, but crossed in one of the illegal boats up in the bend of the Rio Grande?"

"No, that is not a fact, *gringo*."

Inspector Adams then called as a witness Customs Officer Cummings, who testified that he was the officer in charge through the month of January, and he did not recall ever seeing Reyna. Furthermore, he reported that it would have been impossible for immigration officials to allow Reyna to cross the bridge and that he probably crossed the river illegally at Freeport Bend. Adams then continued his questioning of Balo.

"Were you ever employed by the Mexican customs officials in Reynosa, Mexico?"

"Yes, I was secretary and clerk at the customs house in Reynosa, México?"

"You are more or less familiar with the procedure required of aliens crossing the frontier, are you not?"

"Yes, I am, but so are you *gringo* — but that doesn't mean you cross illegally, does it?"

"You have entered the United States a number of times previous to January 8th last, have you not?"

"Many times."

"Have you ever been regularly inspected and manifested at any immigration office along the border?"

"Never."

"At the time you entered the United States from Mexico during January 1915, did you have in your possession a number of treasonable and anarchistic documents, which were typewritten, and in the Spanish language?"

Balo leaned back in his chair and exhibited a wide grin. "They are now getting to the heart of the matter," he thought. His interrogation had been mundane up to that point, but now they were going for the guts. He thought for a while of just going along and getting the whole thing over with—but then he figured he would have some fun. He relished the idea of exercising his mind, although he did not feel he had much of an interested audience. At the very least, he would buy a few more minutes outside of the cesspool.

"Well, *gringo,* that is an erroneous question on two counts. First, treason implies disloyalty or treachery to one's country or its government. I am a citizen of México and have nothing but love for my country. We meant the documents you mentioned to refer to the Yankee imperialist state that now occupies this land through fraud and thievery. Second, you describe the documents as anarchistic. What we propose is not the absence of government, but the restoration of the reins of government to the governed. Now that should not be too novel an idea even for you, should it?"

"You do admit crossing with these documents then?"

"I acknowledge carrying the Declaration of Independence from Yankee tyranny for my brother Mexicans living in the occupied lands of Northern México, which you insist on calling the United States. Yes, I do."

"Among these documents was the one described as the Plan or Plot of San Diego, Texas?"

"Yes, it was," Balo said.

"Was your signature attached to that document known as the Plan of San Diego, Texas?"

"No I did not sign that document."

"Did you read that document and thoroughly understand the meaning?"

"Of course I read it, *gringo*. I not only understood what it said, I understand perfectly what it means."

"Then did you yourself personally sign the document with pen and ink?"

"No, but I would have signed it in blood if I had been asked."

"Who were the signers to this document?"

Balo did not answer that question immediately. He thought for a long moment about the implications of his answer to his comrades in the movement and finally determined that their names appeared on the Plan anyway so he would not betray them if he named them. He went on to name the signatories to the Plan but decided at the same time to be more careful with his future answers. After all, he might have inadvertently jeopardized others. The questioning continued.

"Who prepared the document known as the Plan of San Diego?"

"I do not know who wrote it. He was some friend of the signers, but I do not know his name."

"Were you commissioned or appointed as an organizer of juntas or lodges, under the Plan of San Diego?"

"Yes, I was."

"At the time you last entered the United States, did you have a typewritten commission, duly signed, appointing you as an organizer or deputy of the treasonable and anarchistic movement known as the Plan of San Diego?"

Balo had the urge to play word games again but he decided against it. He felt he needed to remain calm or even subdued in order not to reveal too much. Still, he decided to get in one last jab.

"It is my contention, *gringo*, that I never crossed into the United States but merely crossed from one side of México to the other. More to the point of your question, however: Yes, I was appointed as an organizer."

Adams then introduced into evidence the copy of a letter commissioning Reyna as an organizer for the Plan of San Diego. He then continued with his questioning.

"At the time you last entered the United States, did you have in your possession a number of other documents and recommendation letters, pertaining to the same movement?"

"Yes, I did."

"At the time you entered the United States, where did you carry these incriminating documents?"

"In my pockets."

"Did you come to the United States for the purpose of spreading the doctrines contained in the Plan of San Diego and for the purpose of organizing juntas, in pursuance of that plan?"

"Yes, I did."

"How long did you remain in Brownsville after you arrived here?"

"Six to seven days; I do not remember exactly. I arrived about the 7th or 8th and went to McAllen about the 14th of January."

"Did you converse with anyone in Brownsville in regard to your mission here?"

"No, I did not."

"Where did you stop here in Brownsville?"

"I stayed at the San Carlos Hotel."

"Didn't you carry a recommendation letter to Ignacio R. Rodríguez, Post Office Box 5, Brownsville, Texas, in reference to your mission here?"

Again, Balo feared that he would disclose too much, so he took his time answering the question. He spent six to seven days, by his admission, in Brownsville. Surely, they would wonder what he did all this time. How foolish he had been, he thought, for telling so much. There was no way of avoiding the question; they had a copy of the letter.

"Yes, I did, but I did not go to interview Mr. Rodríguez."

"Was that the only letter of recommendation you had addressed to people living in Brownsville?"

"Yes."

"What was your objective in going to McAllen, last month, about the 13th or 14th of January?"

Reyna could not believe that was all they were going to ask about his stay in Brownsville. They had only two lousy questions to account for six days. He quickly decided that the best way to put them off was just to give them enough information to satisfy them. He would give them the information he already knew they had.

"Whom did you go to see in McAllen, Texas?"

"Dr. Andres Villalobos."

"Did you approach Dr. Andres Villalobos in McAllen, and present your documents to him, and make an appointment for a meeting with him?"

"Yes, I went to see Dr. Villalobos and introduced myself, and showed him my documents, telling him I wanted to have a private talk with him in reference to same, but Dr. Villalobos told me he was very busy just then, and someone called him out, and he made an appointment with me for later that day."

"Did you ever fill that appointment to go see him?"

"Yes. I was arrested during my visit with Dr. Villalobos."

"Who else did you approach with your documents in McAllen, Texas?"

"No one else."

"Among your other documents, did you have a passport signed by General E. P. Nefarrate of Matamoros, Mexico, and also a letter signed by him?"

General Nefarrate was the Carrancista commander in Matamoros, and Balo had to be very careful not to compromise him. General Nefarrate was sympathetic to their cause, and Balo had to take care to conceal his position so that he could continue to assist the move-ment. Nevertheless, he had to acknowledge the known.

"Yes, I had those documents."

"Who was furnishing you with the money to upkeep this propaganda, as outlined in the Plan of San Diego?"

Balo could not believe his luck or the stupidity of his questioners. One solitary question was all they had about Nefarrate.

"I had about $50. I wrote some of the organizers to send me more money, but they did not send it. They wrote me a letter saying that they could not send me any just then, but would send me some when they got it."

"You were expected to secure plenty of funds and other valuables at the time the uprising took place along the frontier, and at the same time these small unpro-tected towns were captured, were you not?"

"That was the idea, but I was not counting on that very strongly."

"How many times have you been arrested in Mexico?"

The questioning was beginning to get so haphazard that Balo began to relax. Just as he was bracing for some heavy follow-up questions, they changed the subject. He decided on a new tactic. He would start giving longer answers where possible—maybe this would confuse them even more and end the whole thing.

"I was arrested twice in México; once in Nuevo Laredo, where I was kept in prison for a month. Then they ordered me to leave México and never return.

At that time, I crossed the river to Laredo, Texas and remained in Laredo, Texas, for two months, during which time I had no work. Then I went to San Diego, Texas, as a salesman for a beer distributor and I remained in San Diego, Texas, for five months. Then I left San Diego, Texas, on the 28th day of December and went to México through Piedras Negras. My destination at that time was Monterrey and Tampico. When I got to Monterrey, they arrested me again and kept me in prison for about five days. It was while I was in prison in Monterrey that I was given the documents that were taken off my person in McAllen, Texas."

The tactic apparently worked. It was getting on to the lunch hour, and Inspector Adams informed everyone in the room that he had only a few more questions and then they all could go to lunch. Balo was relieved and quickly decided to shorten his answers again. He had been through these questions twice before and they were not only boring, but he was beginning to feel that his answers might start contradicting and that he may be divulging too much. Adams continued.

"Were you arrested on January 14th last, in Brownsville, on a complaint filed by Special Agent Beaman of the Department of Justice, charging you with seditious conspiracy against the United States?"

"Yes, I was."

"Were you given an examining trial before the U.S. Commissioner here in Brownsville, in January 1915?"

"Yes, I was."

"What action was taken at this examining trial before the U.S. Commissioner?"

"My bail was placed at $3,000, and I was sent back to jail, as I could not give bond. I was told that my case would be tried in Federal court here in Brownsville during the month of May," Reyna responded, showing exasperation.

Adams showed Balo a copy of the warrant for his arrest and the evidence used to secure the warrant. He also advised him of his right to legal counsel, which Reyna thought rather curious since he had already been in jail for more than a month. He informed Adams that he had no money to pay a lawyer and would have to waive his right to legal counsel. Adams then wound up the hearing.

"You are now informed that translations of all the treasonable and anarchistic documents that we found in your person at the time you were arrested have been forwarded to Washington, D.C., with the application for warrant of arrest in your case. Have you any further statement to make to show why you should not be deported in conformity to law?"

The temptation to lash out at his interrogators one last time occurred to Balo, but he shook it off. It was best to get the whole thing over and done with.

"I have nothing further to say."

Adams turned to the stenographer and asked him to enter one additional observation into the record.

"This alien is rather stubborn and evasive in his answers and gives the impression of not desiring to tell all that he knows in reference to the charges against him."

Balo broke into a big grin. "*Gringos pendejos*," he thought, "how easy it is to fool them by mixing in a little truth into one's story."

With the hearing over, the deputies took him back to his cell. As they approached the jail, Balo quickly eyed his friend Poncho in front of the door to the jailhouse. As the two guards escorted Balo across the street, a horse and buggy raced in front of them. As the buggy passed them by, Balo's friend and his companion were crossing the street and were on top of the guards in the center of the street. The woman with Poncho pretended to bump into one guard.

"*Ay papacito, que grande estas*," she flirted with one of the guards, who let go of Balo and embraced the woman.

At the same time, Balo's friend pulled a gun, placed in the gut of the other guard and ordered him to hand over the keys to the handcuffs that shackled Balo. The guard complied, Balo's friend slapped the guard with the revolver, and Balo and Poncho ran off, quickly catching up with the horse and buggy and jumping into the buggy to make their escape.

Chapter 5

A bright full moon illuminated the sky as a group of men rode along a deserted country road in complete silence. Only the occasional snort of a horse could be heard. Even the hoofs were silenced by the sandy trail they were following. There were about 15 men, led by a tall, lean man astride a white spotted brown mare. As they approached the sleepy town of Sebastian on the railroad track 40 miles north of Brownsville, the leader pulled gently on his rein and brought his horse to a stop. All the others did the same and waited for his instructions.

"*Muchachos*," the sinewy man spoke in a whisper, "we only need some supplies, so we do not want to create a disturbance. We are not ready for a major battle so hold your enthusiasm and ammunition for a later time. *Bueno vámonos*."

They strode quietly into town. They knew the man who now led them only as *El General*. His name was Anacleto Peña, or Cleto for short. *El General* had recruited this unlikely company of militia in the *ranchos* of the fertile valley. He had spoken to them in fiery tones of the injustices that the *gringo* had committed against him personally. The *gringos* had stolen his land, which had been in his family for generations. It was land given to his forebears by the King of Spain before the *gringo* had even heard of this great region. Not only had they stolen his land, they had stolen the land of his many neighbors. He urged his fellow *Mexicanos* to join him in the struggle to wrest from the dirty *gabachos* the land that was rightfully theirs.

He told them of the revolution that was being organized by wise and brave men, such as Baldomero Reyna, whom authorities imprisoned in Brownsville. They had all heard stories of this young and defiant man. The whole countryside was filled with the stories of Balo and his ambitious plan to rub the *gringos* faces in the ground and kick them out of *el Valle*! Although they had never owned anything but the clothes they wore, these humble *campesinos* were easily swayed by the rhetoric of a man like *El General*. Surely, they thought, "their victory will also be ours; we will be able to get some land for ourselves once we get rid of the *patrones*."

As they entered the town, they came upon a *tienda*, which they could see through the window was well stocked with food and supplies. *El General* motioned to them to dismount, leaving two as guards outside. The rest pried open a window and climbed into the store. They grabbed some nearby oak sacks and filled them up with sugar, beans, rice, flour, coffee, and a variety of other staples. *El General* moved behind the counter and discovered a cache of ammunition. He quickly got several men to load up all they could into some saddle-bags, which they also took from the store. Behind the counter they found some fine rope and other materials they could use in crossing the river into México, where they planned to meet up with other groups to form a larger company.

Despite their efforts at silence, the prowlers awakened the storekeeper and his wife, who were asleep in the back room. The storekeeper quickly rose, putting on only his pants and grabbing a rifle while his wife held a lamp for him. The couple tiptoed toward the store and pushed open the door leading into the back room from the store. Although the door was only slightly open, a ray of light filtered into the totally dark room. The intruders quickly noticed it and one of them panicked and with a fast reflex fired into the door. Two others reacted in the same manner and the rapid blasts from all three weapons slammed into the storekeeper, throwing him backward into his wife. *El General* shouted orders to leave the store immediately and mount their horses to ride off. As the men hurriedly ran from the store and made for their mounts, lamps began lighting up throughout the small community. In a flash, the men were all on their horses racing out of town in the same direction from which they had come. Meanwhile, the store had caught fire from the lamp that had flown out of the hands of the storekeeper's wife when her husband was thrown against her. The townspeople rushed to the store to try to put out the fire, but it spread so quickly and all they could hear were the wild screams of the wife, who was trapped within. The raiders made a clean escape with nobody in pursuit.

After riding out of town, the group of raiders circled around and continued their track toward the border. They traveled 40 miles in two days before they came to the banks of the Río Bravo, where they sought out a shallow area and easily crossed over. On the other side they decided to make camp at night. They spread their *serapes* on the ground but left their horses saddled in case they had to make a hasty exit. Most of the men were ranch hands and had acquired many useful horsemanship traits from the older *vaqueros*. During a night when the *vaqueros* were rounding up cattle, they often slept with the reins tied to their ankle, and if the horses were alarmed by something in the dark — either the cattle or Indians — the horses' movements would wake the sleeping *vaqueros*. In this manner these ranch hands now slept.

As the sun began to rise, the reflections of the muddy river water blinded the horses and they started fidgeting, waking up the men and *El General*. They had ridden hard all through the night and had only gotten three hours of sleep. Nonetheless, they rose and began preparing for another hard day. Someone started a fire for the *brasas* needed to make coffee and cook breakfast.

Just as the men were settling down, a rider approached at full gallop. They all rose to their feet and went for their rifles.

"*Esta bien, muchachos,*" *El General* said calmly, "*es un amigo.*"

The rider pulled on his reins bringing his gasping horse to a stop at the center of the camp. The men surrounded him as he dismounted. *El General* stood behind him ready to welcome him.

"Luis," *El General* said, "welcome to our camp."

The rider turned and both men embraced in genuine affection.

"*Mi general,* I bring good news. Balo has escaped from the *cárcel* in Brownsville."

"*Viva Balo! Viva Balo!*" came the chorus response from those in earshot. The men shot their weapons into the air and let out a series of *gritos* of joy.

"He has escaped?" *El General* asked incredulously.

"*Si, mi general,* yesterday. He is making his way to Villa Hermosa and wants you to join him there."

"*Bueno!*" *El General* said, trying to restrain his excitement. His face expressed a strong conviction. He sensed the war was to begin in earnest. He slowly turned toward his men, pulling Luis along with him by the arm.

"Let's give our friend some breakfast, for we have to ride again. Eat well, men, for today we begin our war of liberation!"

"*Viva la revolución! Viva la libertad!*" the men shouted.

As the men ate a simple breakfast of *pan de campo* and coffee, *El General* went off to a side of the camp. He had been waiting for this day for a long time. He remembered clearly 10 years back as if it was only yesterday. The *gringo* sheriff had come to his house along with several other men. His father was dead and his mother was in charge of *el rancho*. He was 30 years old, but as long as his mother was alive she would be in charge. That's the way his father had wanted it, to keep the family from feuding over the land. They owned a big *rancho* of five leagues. It was a land grant made to his family by King Carlos in 1767.

The sheriff did not care about those things. He had papers that said that the land had been sold at auction for delinquent taxes. His mother had not been able to understand clearly what the sheriff was talking about. She was sure her husband had always paid *los impuestos*. They had forced them off the land and into squalid poverty. Within months, his mother had withered away in grief and despair. He had vowed to atone her death and regain their land.

"*Hoy se le llega la hora a los gringos,*" he muttered through clenched teeth. The hour of reckoning was at hand.

After breakfast they gathered their belongings and mounted their ponies for the 10-kilometer ride to Villa Hermosa. The country south of the *río* was as different from that of the north as were the people. The land on north side with its irrigation ditches was rich and fertile. So were its people. The south side was almost desert like with only an occasional prickly pear breaking the monotonous dusty trail. Its people were as barren.

The men covered their mouths with their handkerchiefs to keep from choking on the dry dust rising from the horses' hooves. After slightly more than an hour's ride the men came upon the small town of Villa Hermosa. It lay there as an almost cruel but natural part of a bad painting. Contrary to its name, it was desolate and ugly. The few homes were no more than thatched huts. Those with more sustenance were merely adobe mud structures. The people went about their business with dispassionate faces. The only life that could be heard was the barking of dogs chasing the horses as they trotted into town. At the center of town they came to the *plaza*, which was surrounded by the business district. There was an old church, a *café*, a general store, a *cantina* and an assortment of other small shops. As the troop drew closer, they could hear a general excitement coming from the *cantina*. *El General* dismounted his horse and his men did the same. They were tired but were anxious to take only a few more steps to reach their destination and satisfy their thirst.

They tied their horses and stepped into the *cantina*, where they saw about 20 men drinking and talking heartily. As they walked in, the men inside the *cantina* turned to Balo, who was sitting at a table next to a makeshift bar of a plank on two wooden barrels. Balo jumped to his feet with a wide grin.

"Cleto," Balo shouted as he strode over to *El General* and gave him a strong *abrazo*.

"It's so good to see you again, *amigo*."

"*Mano*, it was tremendous news that we got his morning of your freedom. The men have been pushing their horses to come meet the great Balo."

"Cleto," Balo said to *El General*, "if I am special for being caught, then your men are greater for eluding the *rinches* and remaining free."

Balo and *El General* turned toward the men who were standing still by the door. They were smiling, waiting for acknowledgement from their hero.

Balo walked over to the men and picked up a bottle of *tequila* from a nearby table and stood before the men.

"I drink to the soldiers of liberation," Balo said as he took a swig of *tequila* to a chorus of "*vivas*."

Balo invited the newly arrived recruits to join his own men in food and drink.

"Eat and drink all you want, *muchachos,* for soon we will need you at full strength."

He pulled *El General* along to a corner table where they could talk. The two men sat down and faced each other with a sense of anticipation. They could hardly veil their eagerness to pursue their dreams.

Chapter 6

The train hissed to a stop and jolted Hoffman out of his daydream. Beyond the steam clouds coming from the train he could see the hustle of people coming and going. He had not been in Washington in three years and had forgotten what a busy city it was. He often wondered whether the bustle of a big city was not due to mass neuroses rather than to productive activities.

He made his way back to his car and retrieved his bag. Because of the sudden nature of his departure he had brought along very little clothing. Hopefully, he would not have to stay long and would not have a need for more than a few changes of clothes.

He stepped off the train and walked into the expansive area of Union Station. With over a quarter million people, Washington was twice the size of San Antonio, and the contrast became immediate in the numbers and intensity of the people. Making his way through the crowded station, Hoffman stepped out Massachusetts Avenue and hailed a taxi. Although he had not been in

Washington for some time, he quickly became adjusted
to its familiar surroundings.

"Where to soldier," queried the driver as the captain
jumped into the back seat.

"The White House, please," was the sedate response.

"Pretty fancy address Capt'n, if you don't mind me
saying so. Don't get too many people wanting to go directly.
Usually they prefer to go to a hotel and freshen up."

Hoffman remained oblivious to the cabbie's chatter,
concentrating instead on the sights and sounds that had
been so much a part of his life only a short three years
before. Noticing that the driver was to turn left on North
Carolina Street and take him up Constitution and then
Pennsylvania Avenue, the normal route to the White
House, Hoffman interrupted his nonstop conversation.

"Please go up Massachusetts to New York Avenue."

"You know your way around, do you Capt'n. You
going up there to see Mr. Wilson?" the cabbie continued.

Captain Hoffman's reverie in the observation car
had served its purpose well. The chaos of Washington,
however, quickly snapped him out of his slackness and
he began to contemplate on his dilemma once again.
He began to think that perhaps his driver had a point
and he should stop off and freshen up. Before he could
make up his mind, the cabbie made it up for him.

"Sixteen-hundred Pennsylvania Avenue, Capt'n."

He walked up the sidewalk to the entrance gate where
he had no trouble clearing his business with the guard.

Once inside the White House, a Mrs. Hubbard met Hoffman and asked him to follow her. The guard must have called ahead. Hoffman was impressed by the efficiency of the operation, but at the same time he hoped that somewhere along the way he would have some time to sneak into a restroom to freshen up a little.

Mrs. Hubbard explained to him as they walked that the president was tied up in a meeting with a visiting dignitary but would be free within the hour. Once outside the president's outer office he was instructed to sit and wait.

"Excuse me, ma'am," Hoffman inquired, "but where could I find the men's room? It's been a long trip and I'd like to straighten out a little if I have time."

"Certainly, Captain," Mrs. Hubbard replied with a coy smile, "just go out the door to the left at the end of the hall, and it will be the last door on the right."

"Thank you."

Upon his return, he ran into an old friend coming out of the president's outer office.

"Jim," Hoffman exclaimed, "what a coincidence running into you here. He was about to ask him what he was up to when he realized it may have put his friend in an awkward situation.

Jim Brite was a career State Department man and was an expert at protecting any sensitive involvement. Coming out of the president's office was intrinsically a confidential matter.

"Matthew, how the hell are you?" Brite asked. Lowering his voice, he informed Hoffman that he had just given the president and the secretary of state a briefing on a highly sensitive matter. He dismissed the need for going into detail inasmuch as Hoffman himself was going in next and would be made aware of any details the president wished to share with him.

"The president will see you now, Captain," the secretary interrupted. Hoffman bid his friend good-bye and followed the president's secretary into the Oval Office.

"Matthew, it's so good to see you after such a long time," the president exclaimed as he walked toward Hoffman and extended his hand. His handshake was rather limp, which was truly characteristic of this kind man. Wilson had never had an overpowering physical presence. His personality, though warm, was not pervasive, either. It was with his intellectual powers with which he overwhelmed those who came into contact with him.

"It's a real pleasure to see you again, Mr. President."

"Please, Matthew, don't let me remind you again not to be so formal," the president pleaded as he swung around and led Hoffman into his office.

"Of course, Professor. I'll try to remember to forget my formality, although it will be difficult not to pay deference to your office, sir."

"Remember to forget, ha, I must remember that one," the president chuckled.

"Matthew, I want you to meet Secretary of State Bryan, whom I'm sure you are familiar with."

Indeed, who was not familiar with the "Great Commoner" who had been the titular head of the Democratic Party for so many years? Hoffman had almost met him once before, when he had been chosen to be on the briefing team for the incoming secretary of state, but he had secured his Army commission before Bryan took office so he had not performed this task. It had not been too much of a disappointment, for although Bryan was a political legend, Hoffman had not been impressed, as others, by his demagogic oratory. He did not particularly relish this meeting, but he assumed it must have something to do with his assignment.

"Indeed, I am, Professor. It's a genuine honor to meet you Mr. Secretary."

"Likewise, I'm sure, Captain."

The secretary's manner was aloof, and almost disdainful, which puzzled Hoffman, for he had always heard of him as a jolly sort of fellow.

"Woodrow tells me you were at state during the previous administration under the Republicans," the secretary injected, with a contemptuous emphasis on the word "Republicans."

So that was the rub on Mr. Bryan's wound. "Mr. Democrat" was insulted at having to deal with someone he no doubt considered a brash Republican. "So be it," Hoffman thought, "we're on mutual ground, Mr. Secretary."

"Yes, sir. I had the honor to serve my country at State just as you are honored, I'm sure. Now as you can see, I'm serving my country in the military, where I hope to be of assistance to our president in whatever assignment he has for me."

Hoffman likening himself to his service to the country agitated Bryan. Moreover, he was not at all comfortable with military men, and it helped little that this military man was an insolent young Republican.

The president came back into the room after having stepped out momentarily to give some instructions to his secretary.

"Well, I hope you two have gotten acquainted."

"Yes, sir," Hoffman replied, "the Secretary and I have gotten to know each other."

"Good, good. Now let's get down to business. Well, Matthew what have you learned about this matter since I last talked with you?"

Hoffman shifted uncomfortably in his chair and resigned himself to the fact that his ignorance was going to be exposed no matter what he reported.

"Frankly, Professor, not much. The local press has carried very little on it. Only a couple of short reports that treat the whole matter rather flippantly. There isn't much talk about it among the citizenry of San Antonio, although there are some reports that the folks in the Rio Grande Valley are quite stirred by the whole thing."

"The Secretary," the president explained, "has some landholdings in the area and corresponds regularly with some friends there. Go on, Matthew."

"There isn't any more to report, Professor. That's all I could find out…"

"That's all you can report?" Bryan asked on a growing contemptuous tone.

"As I was about to say, Mr. Secretary, before being interrupted." Hoffman had never been one to play second fiddle to anyone, much less to someone whose disdain was based on something other than intellectual superiority. Certainly, not to one whose contempt was a result of some self-perceived righteousness. The president sat back, with a crack of a smile amused at this somewhat David and Goliath battle unfolding before him.

Hoffman slowly turned to the president and continued his report in a testy mood.

"Frankly, Mr. President, I did not have enough time to look into the matter, as you requested me to leave for Washington immediately. Since I am no longer at the State Department, I am not privy to government communiqués on sensitive issues of this nature."

The last statement was intended as another verbal shot at Bryan. Wilson leaned forward, about to say something, when his secretary walked in to announce that General Burleson had arrived.

Hoffman quickly got up and stood at attention. The president broke into a mild laugh at this reaction.

"Relax, Matthew, it's not a general. Its only Postmaster General Burleson."

Hoffman felt a flushing heat wave rush through his head. The president noticed his embarrassment and tried to lessen the awkwardness.

"You see, Matthew, my closest adviser is Colonel E.H. House. Now, Colonel House is a Texan, and so is Mr. Burleson. Since Colonel House is not a real Colonel, Mr. Burleson not wanting to be outdone, insists that we call him "General" as a one-up on Colonel House. Now I know all that sounds frivolously complex, but its all part of an inside joke around here."

Hoffman eased out of his rigid stance and slowly regained his color, although he was not totally recovered from the embarrassment. Before he knew it, "General" Burleson stood before him with a wide grin reaching for his hand.

"Finally, I get the respect that my title entitles me to," Burleson roared as he clasped Hoffman's hand with both his hands in a masculine show of friendship.

"At ease, Captain," he continued with his ruse. "I hear you just arrived from the great state of Texas, and more particularly, the fair city of San Antonio de Bexar. I've recently returned from God's country myself. I was in San Antonio visiting my dear sister and darling daughter."

"General Burleson is from San Marcos, a short distance from San Antonio," the president volunteered.

Albert Sidney Burleson was the grandson of Edward Burleson, a vice president of the Republic of Texas, and had served five terms in the Congress before being asked by the president to serve as postmaster general.

"I am familiar with San Marcos, a fine little community," Hoffman responded as he felt Burleson turn loose of him.

"I've asked General Burleson to sit in on our conference inasmuch as he is our resident expert from Texas," the president explained.

"Don't let your Colonel House hear you say that, Mr. President, or he will be offended."

"Well, General," the President returned, "for the moment, you are our expert, seeing as our good colonel is off in Europe."

After everyone was again seated and Hoffman had returned to normal, the conversation turned to more serious business. Despite the brief embarrassment, Hoffman was glad for Burleson's addition to the group. He seemed an open and honest fellow, a welcome contrast to Bryan.

"As I was saying, Matthew" the President continued, "I asked you to come to Washington so that you could take on a special assignment for me in Texas. A couple of months ago, some local law enforcement officials in McAllen, Texas, apprehended a fellow who had in his possession a rather curious if preposterous document entitled "The Plan of San Diego, Texas." This manifesto was allegedly drawn up in the small South Texas community of San Diego by a group of Mexican radicals or revolutionaries. The culprit who was arrested was a Mexican national, but we are not totally satisfied as to the nationality of his fellow conspirators. Several individuals from San Diego have been apprehended but their involvement ..."

"Excuse me, Professor," Hoffman interrupted, "but what exactly was the nature of this plan?"

"Well, the whole thing is rather bizarre. It proposes that the Mexican population of the Southwest rise in revolt against the United States government and carve out their own country. It provides for raising a revolutionary army, establishment of local juntas and so forth. Additionally, it invites the coloreds, Indians and Japanese to join the revolution, after which they will be rewarded with land. The coloreds are to get their country, and the Indians will get their original lands back. I tell you the whole thing is untenable."

"I agree, Professor.," Hoffmans said, "but why our continuing interest?"

"Well, Matthew, for a number of reasons actually. First, it now appears that Reyna — he's the fellow who was apprehended in McAllen but who has now escaped custody — appears to be trying to carry out the Plan. There have been several incidents along the border that suggest to some that he and his followers are actually into the operational part of the Plan."

The president went on to explain that Texas Governor James Ferguson was badgering federal officials to assist the state in quelling the disturbances.

"Colonel House tells me that the governor is a peculiar character and will be a thorn on our side until we yield to some of his demands," the president said.

"A peculiar character, indeed," Burleson jumped in. "The man is a complete horse's ass. The colonel has gotten too damn diplomatic of late, and you, Mr. President, are too much a gentleman. We in Texas don't like to play free and loose with fancy words. A man who puts out nothing but horse manure is no more than a horse's ass."

"Well, General," the President said, "I will not contradict you, but in all fairness to Colonel House, his diplomacy I'm sure comes from not wanting to malign such a fine species of animal by comparing him to your governor. As for me, I simply don't want the ire of the ASPCA to fall upon me."

Burleson roared with laughter at the president's dry wit. Hoffman himself had to chuckle, not so much at what the president had said, but at the contrast and yet similarity of the two men. Here were two genuinely honest and warm individuals with totally disparate personalities. Yet it was their mutual sincerity that undoubtedly brought them together.

During this whole time, Bryan continuously fidgeted in his chair and grew more agitated. Finally, as if to put a damper on the relaxed mood, he volunteered an opinion.

"This whole thing is ridiculous and does not merit all this attention. The fact of the matter is that the Mexicans in South Texas are a gentle and harmless people content with their lives. I know them well. To suggest that they would be a party to a revolution is completely absurd. For us to take that possibility seriously is equally asinine."

"The Mexicans are as happy with their situation as a hog in a trough," Burleson said. "Because they're forced to live in such conditions does not mean either one of them likes it. If there is a blot in the Texas character, Mr. Bryan, it's the way we treat our Mexican citizens. And let us not forget that they are citizens."

"Well of course I am not a native Texan, Mr. Burleson, but my impression is somewhat different," Bryan said.

"Different and wrong, I might add," Burleson replied.

"I agree that the situation is somewhat ethereal," the president pointed out, trying to drive a wedge between his two Cabinet officers. Hoffman was quite bemused by the whole thing. At least he was glad that Bryan's attention was directed elsewhere.

"The fact of the matter is that no matter how pre-posterous this matter seems to us, the folks in Texas are concerned about it. Now the governor wants money from us for his Ranger force to help contain any more violent outbreaks. He supports his argument by the fact that the border is being used as a sanctuary and thus it is an international problem, and therefore our problem. I'm not too keen on providing any aid of a military nature, nonetheless the governor may have a legitimate request if in fact this thing is related to a foreign source; which brings me to my second reason for concern, Matthew.

"As you know, the unstable Mexican revolution has had an impact on our policy positions. We cannot hope to realistically provide leadership in our hemisphere unless some order is brought to Mexico. The vying Mexican factions handcuff all of Latin America. That in turn ties our hands. The fact of the matter is that none of the factions are satisfactory to me personally."

"Begging your pardon, Mr. President," Secretary Bryan implored, "but perhaps we are going beyond the purpose of this meeting. The Mexican situation after all is highly classified."

"Mr. Secretary," the President replied in a weary tone, "perhaps I did not make myself totally clear about Captain Hoffman. He has had at least six years of diplomatic service at the State Department. He has served exceptionally and honorably in the United States Army for an additional three years. Finally, he is a dear personal friend in whom I have complete confidence. I have no reservation in revealing any information to him, and you shouldn't either. In fact, if he is to perform his assignment for me adequately, I feel he should not go back uninformed and unprepared."

Hoffman felt a swelling joy within him. The whole insecurity caused by him not being prepared and the embarrassing "General" incidents were washed away immediately by the president's vote of confidence. Bryan's effrontery had been cleanly laid aside, but at the same time Hoffman could not help but feel a little grateful to him. After all, Bryan had unwittingly set up Hoffman's reaffirmation with the president.

"Now, as I was saying, Matthew. Carranza has control of Mexico City and claims to be the legitimate head of the Mexican state. Large areas of the country, however, are still in the hands of other revolutionary leaders, namely Villa and Zapata. I find Carranza a deplorable opportunist. The other two, while not so opportunistic, are not totally acceptable either. Our concern as it relates to the problem before us, is that this whole Plan business may be a device of some Mexican revolutionist to somehow influence our decision on their internal problems. At the least, if it is not of their origin, they may try to take advantage of the situation. Whatever discontent may be present in our border regions may offer them an opportunity to extract concessions from us. We understand that Reyna was a Huertista and may have been part of Huerta's scheme to re-enter the revolution."

"But Huerta has been removed from the scene, has he not, Professor?"

"Yes, but the Reyna association is still troublesome. We need to determine for certain what relationship, if any, exists to the Mexican conflict. The fact that some of the troublemakers in the Rio Grande Valley take sanctuary in Mexico lends credence to the Mexican connection theory. Moreover, it substantiates Governor Ferguson's claims as to the international nature of the problem.

"We have been able to hold the governor at bay by insisting that the source of the border troubles is local bandits and cattle rustlers. Unfortunately, even your commander at Fort Sam Houston is beginning to agree with the governor, and he, too, is appealing to us for more troops. General Funston is a good man, but I cannot bring myself to trust a military man. They're too quick to the draw, if you forgive the expression."

"I am not one to question your reasoning, Professor, but I am a military man, ipso facto, how can you trust me?"

"Matthew, since when do you not question my or anyone else's reasoning. I thought I taught you better than to accept anything at blind faith. In point of fact, what I mean to say is that I do not trust a career military man. You, Matthew, are no more a career military man than Secretary Bryan is a card-carrying Republican."

At that metaphor they all burst out laughing, even Secretary Bryan, who could not refrain from observing that at last he agreed with something that had been said in that whole meeting. After they all regained their composure, the president went on.

"There is one other concern we have, Matthew. This one is almost as implausible as the Plan itself, yet we have to consider it seriously. Aside from the Mexican influence in the area, we have reason to suspect that German agents are also operating there."

At the mention of the word German, Hoffman cringed in his chair. "Dammit," he thought to himself, "the president just finished bestowing you full confidence so why continue to persecute yourself." His German heritage had continuously bothered Hoffman since he had concluded that war with Germany was inevitable. His family had been in America for 100 years and he still felt suspect. After a short daze, he gradually tuned in to the president's continuing explanation on the German connection.

"There are those who hold to a theory that the Germans are highly concerned that we are ready to jump into the fight in Europe. Personally, that is the last thing I want us to do. Nonetheless, the theory goes that the Germans' preoccupation with our potential involvement has led them to seek means of keeping us busy on this side of the Atlantic. They are reported to be very active in Mexico, and through Mexico may be involved in the Plan of San Diego. The extremists of this theory propose, in fact, that the whole thing was hatched in Berlin."

The president leaned back in his chair. That, Hoffman knew from experience, meant that he was through with his presentation and was inviting comments from the participants. He looked at the Cabinet officers on either side of him to see if they were taking the cue. After a short silence, he finally responded to the president's opening.

"What exactly is going to be my mission, Professor," Hoffman asked.

"To get to the bottom of this whole crazy business and report to me as soon as possible," the president quickly responded.

"It's as simple as that, Matthew."

"At the risk of contradicting you, Professor: It sounds anything but simple to me."

The president smiled back. He was confident he had made the right choice in Hoffman. He had trained him well, and in the long years of their disassociation, Hoffman had honed his skills further.

"Do I have any deadline on this assignment?" Hoffman asked.

"I will get with you on that and other details in a minute, Matthew. First I would like to hear if Secretary Bryan or General Burleson has any comments to add. Mr. Secretary?"

"None, Mr. President," Secretary Bryan responded, still being uncooperative.

"General?"

"All your theories are fine, Mr. President. They're all possible and should be investigated fully so as to deal with them properly. But I can't help but suggest to young Hoffman here, keeping his mind open to the possibility that this may be locally inspired. I tell you, our Mexican citizens have enough reason to consider this type of action. After all, they were in the area long before us, and many have always held to the idea that we stole their land."

"That is a good point, General. We cannot dismiss the possibility that the whole thing may be an irredentist movement," the president added.

"If that's what you Princeton fellows call it, Mr. President," said Burleson, "it's fine with me. The fact of the matter is, those folks down there may be wanting their land back."

"Exactly," the president smiled.

"The revolutionary oratory coming from across the river is also bound to have an impression on those on this side who find themselves in somewhat of an unfavorable social, political, and economic position," Hoffman added.

"I mean to tell you," Burleson said, mockingly shaking his head, "you Easterners sure have a way of saying a mouthful."

"Well, gentlemen," the president directed, "if there is nothing else, I believe we are through here. Matthew, please stay on awhile for more directions and a personal visit."

"Certainly, Professor."

"Mr. Secretary, General, thank you for your contributions," the president said as he dismissed the two men.

They rose and bid the president a good day. Bryan curtly hastened off with hardly a word to Hoffman. Burleson heartily shook his hand and invited him to come by his office before leaving Washington so he could give him some names and addresses for his return to Texas. The president saw both men to the door and then returned to Hoffman, instructing him to sit down.

"Matthew, how have you been," the president asked in an almost parental tone.

"Very well, Professor. And yourself?" Hoffman answered, somewhat awkwardly, remembering that he had not sent condolences upon the recent death of the president's wife.

"I cannot complain, Matthew. After all, I asked for this job, so I have to put up with the headaches. Matthew, whatever made you ask for a commission?"

"Well, Professor, I saw it as my patriotic duty as an American. I am convinced, whether we like it or not, that war with Germany is unavoidable."

"Not if I can help it, Matthew."

"I'm not sure that any of us will be able to prevent it, Professor. The Germans are dealing the cards in this game."

"Maybe so. You know I had hoped to ask you to come work for me after the election. I knew you were on the Taft team, but I also knew that your political choice was made as a result of logical reasoning. Your experience in Washington would have been invaluable to me. Before I realized, though, you had gone off and joined the Army. Frankly, I'm not sure much reasoning went into that decision. You're holding something back on that one, but, no matter, the thing is done."

Hoffman merely remained uncomfortably silent. The professor was partly right. There had been some real thinking put into the decision, but by and large, it had been an emotional one.

"Who knows," the president said, interrupting Hoffman's thought, "it may have been for the best. It certainly put you in a position to help me now."

The president pulled out a folder from his desk and handed it to Hoffman.

"This contains some helpful information, Matthew. You will find a copy of the Plan. Actually, it's a translation, as the original one was written in Spanish. You will also find a list of some of the principals involved and a narrative that contains essentially what we covered today."

Hoffman took the materials and laid them on his lap. He had not been wrong in his initial assessment. Although he had been unprepared, the president, like during the days at Princeton, had educated him thoroughly on his assignment.

"You do not have any particular deadline, Matthew, but obviously the sooner you report to me, the better. I have secured an indefinite leave of absence for you from your regular duties. While this is not a particularly secretive mission, I know you will use your discretion in conducting yourself."

"You can be sure of that, Professor."

"Now then, Matthew, there are only two things I want you to do before you embark on your journey. First I want you to have dinner with me tonight."

"Thank you Professor, it will be a real honor."

"Second," the president said as he put his arm around Hoffman and led him to the door, "I want you to take a week and go to Maryland to see your family. And that is an order."

"One that I will have no qualms about obeying, Mr. President. I have not seen the folks in some time."

Hoffman left the president's office a different man than when he had entered it. All the tension and apprehension had been subdued by the very meeting that had created them. His fears, in the final analysis, had been ill founded. Professor Wilson had been a good and decent friend before, and President Wilson was no less.

Chapter 7

B alo lay on the hard ground in the open air of Villa Hermosa. There were no hotels in this small village, and though Balo's hero status could have easily gained the bed of any of the local ladies of the night, he preferred the solitude of a *vaquero* camp. He chose instead to join his comrades in arms in their bare surroundings; it would prepare him for what was ahead.

He tried to get some sleep, but the chirping of the *grillos* and the hooting of the owls kept him awake. Besides, his own thoughts prevented him from sleep. He kept rehashing over and over those days long ago when as a very young boy he was first exposed to the vicious way of the *gringos*.

***

As a boy of 10, Balo would go to San Diego with his mother to visit his *tía* and a couple of *tíos* who had established *ranchos* in the area. San Diego itself had begun as a *rancho* in the early 19th century. Balo's ancestral roots on his mother's side of the family were in the settlements along the Río Bravo founded by Spanish *empresario* Don José de Escandón. His mother's family was from Agualeguas. For decades, all throughout the 19th century, families from Agualeguas, Mier, Camargo, Guerrero, and other Escandón villages had been making the trek northeast to the *ranchos* around San Diego, such as Los Ángeles, La Amargosa, Concepción, Realitos, Rosita, Palo Blanco, and Casa Blanca. They settled and tamed this wasteland that had for centuries been left to the Coahuiltec and other Indians. In addition to the roaming Indian tribes, the area had been populated by herds of wild buffalo and mustangs. Other threatening animals such as coyotes, mountain lions, and javelinas also called the area home. As if the Indians and the wild creatures were not enough, the *nopal* and thick brush made the region unreceptive to folks who had been living a more peaceful existence in the established towns along the *río*.

His *tíos* Salome and Ildefonso had been invited to the area by their *cuñado* Rómulo, who was his *tía* Cuca's husband. They had come in the late 1870s and bought some small tracts of land from an old timer by the name of Julian Saenz. They settled close to the community of Piedras Pintas and slowly began to acquire some sheep, a few cows, and some wild horses. They were not rich men like Balo's father, they often told Balo's mother, but they owned their own *rancho* and were comfortable in this new and strange place. They had even begun to learn English.

Balo liked to visit his *tíos* and *tía* in Texas. It was an adventure for the young boy. It was exciting to travel on the *carretas* over the dusty plains of northern México and into the prairies close to the gulf. They would run into merchants carrying all sorts of goods, to and from. *Vaqueros* could be seen throughout the region herding their cattle with the longhorns. Shepherds tended to large flocks of sheep. And, although the area had settled somewhat, there was always the threat of meeting up with a band of Comanche coming down from the north in search of food and taking it, any way they could, from whomever they ran across.

Balo's mother made this trip annually. Her own mother had given all her children a charge that they must remain close and stay in touch after she died. And so, after her mother died, Genoveva—who had gone south to Linares with her husband—made the pilgrimage north every year, taking her unmarried sister, Lucinda, with her. Thanks to her husband's *huertas*, she could afford it more so than her siblings could. Besides, they were all together in one place; it was easier for her to come to Texas. As the oldest, she saw it as her duty to honor her mother's last wish.

In 1886, when Balo was only 10 years old, they made one of these trips. His mother and sister always stayed with *tía* Cuca, whose christened name was Refugia. *Tío* Poncho, as Ildefonso was called, had children close to his 13-year-old brother Manuel's age, so he stayed with those *primos* at their house. Balo was partial to his *tío* Salome, who was the youngest and more entertaining. Salome liked to sing and tell jokes. He had many friends. Since his own children were still infants, he, too, liked to have Balo around so he could teach him the ways of the *vaqueros*.

One windy April morning, Salome went off with a friend to a *rancho* called Los Indios to see about a horse that his friend wanted to sell. Salome told Balo to watch over some horses that were grazing in an open pasture.

"Make sure they don't run off or get stolen," Salome had instructed the young Balo, tussling the boy's hair.

After a hearty breakfast of *machacado con huevo*, Balo went out to perform his duties as a *vaquero*-in-training. He hoped he had a horse to sit on, at least. Instead, he walked back and forth and squatted, much more like a shepherd watching sheep. His uncles all had sheep as well. Everyone in this part of the world raised both sheep and cattle. Many preferred the woolly animals because the market was good and they could be sheared twice a year.

As Balo sat squatted, two men rode up. Balo quickly got up to make sure they would not take his *tíos'* horses. There was nothing particularly different about these men as any other cowmen he had seen in the area, except that they appeared to be overly armed, each with two six shooters and a rifle. One other thing Balo noticed was a badge on their coats. They appeared to be lawmen.

"*Hola, muchacho, donde esta el dueño de estos caballos,*" one of them said in patchy Spanish.

Balo told him that the horses belonged to his uncle Salome Molina but that he had gone to Los Indios to see a man about a horse he was interesting in selling.

The man then asked Balo if he knew who owned the sorrel mare he had seen in the drove. Balo had not seen that mare before but assumed that it was his uncle's, since he bought and sold horses and mares all the time. He told the man with the badge and armament that it, too, belonged to his *tío* Salome.

"*Bueno,*" the man said, "tell your uncle that Ranger Boyd came by and wants to talk to him about that mare."

"A *pinche rinche,*" the boy thought to himself. That was the way his *tíos* and most men in the area referred to this type of lawmen who were hated by the Mexicans and loved by the *gringos*.

This hatred, Balo would learn in time, was not without good cause. The *rinches* were believed by the *gringos* to be taming this wild area by bringing in the lawless *bandidos* who were a menace to the development of the region. Banditry had been a common occurrence through the early years of settlement in this section. First, the Indians raided *ranchos* and villages in search for food. Later, bandits from México, as well as misfit *gringos* who had come with the Army during the war with México, raided the same isolated *ranchos*. There was, at that time, a brisk trade open with the Eastern markets for hide and tallow. These bandits would make forays into the area, kill the cattle and skin them in the open range. Oftentimes, they would simply leave the carcasses in the brush for the buzzards to feast on. Their interest was the hide.

To the *rinches*, all bandits were Mexican. It thus followed, in their barbaric logic, that all Mexicans were bandits. They were suspicious of anyone who was not like them. They would most often shoot a Mexican they suspected of being a thief and ask questions later. They were supposedly lawmen, but in reality, they were men without the slightest concept of the law. The Mexican population viewed them as hired guns of the *gringo* land grabbers.

The *rinche* Boyd had gained a special reputation for savagery. He was widely known by the Mexican community of the region, from Río Grande City to Corpus Christi, as a ruthless, uncivilized thug. He had already killed and maimed a number of men who, as he would tell everyone, were trying to escape justice. He himself administered his brand of justice — without, judge, jury, evidence, witnesses, or representation by an attorney.

***

"And they call the Mexicans uncivilized," Balo reflected as he lay there going over in his mind the past 30 years of his life that had prepared him for nothing else but to seek revenge, or as the *rinches* saw it — justice.

***

When his *tío* Salome returned from Los Indios, Balo told him about the visitors. Salome thought it best to go quickly into town and clear up the matter. His wife, Juanita, balked at the idea, fearing the worst from the brute Ranger. Even the Mexican women, who by custom stayed at home in the isolated *ranchos*, had heard about this man who disrespected life and law and lacked human decency. They heard their men talk about Boyd and the *rinches* over the open fires when they gathered for family or church celebrations.

Salome overruled his wife and decided to go and face the *rinche*. The matter would be cleared up quickly, he told his wife. Juanita who was still fearful and asked a neighbor to go to Los Indios to bring Poncho. He asked her brother, who lived in a nearby *rancho*, to ride to Piedras Pintas and fetch Rómulo, who was the elder of the family and could provide his brother-in-law with wise advice in these matters.

When Salome arrived in San Diego, he rode over to the courthouse, a two-story wood-frame building just north of the creek. It appeared to have been recently painted, as did the jail behind the building. He tied his horse in front of the courthouse and walked in and asked the first person he saw for the office of the sheriff.

After finding the office, he asked the man in the office if the *rinche* Boyd was around.

"I'm Boyd," the man answered as he rose and reached for his sidearm at the same time. With his right hand resting on his six-shooter, he asked, "Who are you, and what do you want, Meskin?"

"I am Salome Molina," Salome answered. "My *nieto* told me you were out at my place looking for me."

"That's right," Boyd replied, "I didn't think you would show. I sure-'nuff thought I was going to have to go hunt you down once you learned I was lookin for ya."

"I have no reason to run, I have done nothing wrong," Salome said. "I would like to clear up any questions you may have so that I can return home for supper."

"Well now," the Ranger said, growing agitated with what he perceived to be a hot-tempered Mexican. "I'll be the one who will say whether you've done anthin wrong, boy."

Boyd asked Salome about the sorrel mare in his corral. Salome explained that the mare had strayed into his place the day before and he believed it belonged to Efraín Martínez, who lived north of San Diego near La Amargosa ranch of Don Encarnación Pérez. Salome said that he had sent word to Martinez to come take a look to see if the mare was his. In the meantime, he was caring for it and providing it with food and water.

"Well, as it turns out, that mare was stolen from Mr. Wright in McMullen County and you are holding stolen property," Boyd said.

"If you believe that to be the case than I can return to my *rancho* and bring the mare to you so you can feed it and care for it until you find its rightful owner," Salome responded. "It is not mine, and you can do with it as you please."

"No, I don't think we'll do that, *muchacho*," Boyd said as he approached Salome. He grabbed him by the right arm and pulled his pistol pointing it at Salome's face.

"I think I'll go get the mare and we'll keep you in the hoosegow, until we clear this up," Boyd said menacingly.

"Let me go, *rinche*," Salome yelled. "I have done nothing wrong. You can't put me in jail."

At that last perceived insolence, Boyd swung his pistol across Salome's right temple and knocked him down. Salome was stunned and bleeding but did not lose consciousness. Boyd pushed him toward the door and another Ranger grabbed Salome and dragged him to the jail cage behind the courthouse.

"Let's go fetch that mare," Boyd told the other Ranger. The two mounted their horses and rode off toward Salome's place.

As the *rinches* rode up to the ranch, Juanita came out and frantically asked what had happened to her husband. Boyd told her he had tried to resist arrest and had been thrown in jail. He informed her that they were there to take the sorrel mare into town because it had been reported stolen. The Ranger with Boyd went into the corral that was made of mesquite wood tied with leather straps made from dried hide. He lassoed the mare with a *reata* and led her out of the corral. As he pulled the mare along, Juanita came up to him and demanded that he leave the mare where it was, that it was not stolen.

"My husband can tell you it is not stolen, if you let him come here," Juanita cried.

"Get away from me, woman," the Ranger said, shoving Juanita to the ground.

At that moment, Poncho Molina rode up. He raced his horse toward the Ranger, pulling the reins and bringing his steed to a quick stop. Poncho jumped off his horse and ran over to his sister-in-law and picked her up from the ground.

"*Gringo cabrón*," Poncho yelled as he charged the Ranger who had pushed Juanita.

At that very moment a shot rang out and Poncho crumpled to the ground. He rolled around groaning in pain and reaching for his knee. Boyd sat on his horse with a pistol in his hand looking down at Poncho.

"Boy, I should have killed you for attacking a peace officer that way," Boyd said with a fiendish grin.

"Give that rope with the mare to me and tie the Meskin up so we can take him in for an examining hearing before Judge Whitman," Boyd told the other Ranger.

While Poncho was tied with his lariat around his chest, Juanita rushed to him to examine his gunshot wound. She quickly removed a bandanna holding her hair in a bun and applied it to the wound, soaking the bandanna in blood. She removed her apron, and using the strings that tied it on, she applied a tourniquet above the wound. She yelled at Balo to get her some water. He ran to the house and came back with a pan of water that Juanita used to make a mud pack that she spread over Poncho's gunshot wound. The bleeding seemed to stop.

"He needs a doctor or he will bleed to death," Juanita hollered as she rose and faced Boyd.

"That's no concern of mine," Boyd sneered back at her. "We'll get him a doctor when we get him into the jail."

Poncho was pushed onto his horse by the second Ranger, who then pulled him behind his horse. The three men and the sorrel mare headed for town. As they pulled out, Balo came out from behind a tree where he had been hiding and rushed to put his arms around his aunt's legs. The two stood terrified and in tears. It was a scene that Balo would never erase from his mind.

Unfortunately, the nightmare that would hunt Balo for the remainder of his life was only now beginning to unfold.

Shortly after the Rangers took off with Poncho, Rómulo arrived with several *vaqueros* from around his *rancho.* Juanita relayed to him everything that had happened. The older man listened quietly. He had been in this section many years and he knew the way of the *rinches.* He was not surprised by what he heard.

It was already dark. Rómulo asked his companions to feed and bed the horses and get some rest themselves. He told Juanita not much could be done this late at night but he would go into town just the same to make sure the boys were all right.

In town, meanwhile, Poncho had been thrown into the same cage with Salome and some 10 other men being held on suspicion of various crimes. They were all Mexicans. Boyd had sent one of the locals to get Dr. Whitman, the brother to the justice of the peace who was scheduled to hold the examining hearing for the Molina brothers. Judge Whitman was off in Corpus Christi and would not return until mid-morning the next day.

Dr. Whitman was in the jail tending to Poncho's wound when Rómulo rode up to the jail. It was very dark. Only a few candles here and there were visible inside the tiny houses in this small and poor town. Rómulo recognized Boyd in front of the jail. He asked to see his *cuñados.*

"Who would they be," Boyd asked.

"Salome and Poncho Molina," Rómulo said. "The ones you dragged in here for no good reason."

"I have my reasons," Boyd responded. "Don't you get huffy with me or I'll throw you in jail as well."

"If that's the only way I will get to check on them, then so be it," Rómulo said as he sat defiantly on top of his beautiful palomino horse.

Boyd was angry at the insolence of the Mexican but hesitated in pulling his gun because it was dark and he was not sure how Rómulo was armed. He sat down on a wooden chair in front of the jail and lit a cigarette.

"Dr. Whitman is in there now seeing to their wounds. You can ask him how they are doing when he comes out," Boyd told Rómulo, who was unaware that Salome, too, had been hurt.

The Ranger had reason to be leery. Rómulo stayed atop his horse and held on to his pistol, which he held cocked in his hand but out of sight from someone below him in the dark. The two men sat, one on his chair and the other on his steed, facing each other for nearly half an hour before Dr. Whitman emerged. The aging doctor walked with a stoop and almost imperceptible limp, and looked very tired.

"Well, doc, how is the Meskin?" Boyd asked.

The doctor turned around and angrily looked at Boyd.

"He'll be all right, no thanks to you," the doctor told Boyd. "He lost a lot of blood. It was a good thing the girl placed that tourniquet on him; otherwise he may have bled to death. Taking care of your messes is getting old Boyd."

"Hell, we's all just doing our jobs, doc, no need to get snooty about it," Boyd responded.

The doctor looked up at Rómulo on his horse and asked who he was. Boyd explained he was there to check on the Molina brothers. The doctor told Rómulo that they would be fine but Poncho needed to stay off his feet for a couple of weeks.

"*Gracias,*" was the only word Rómulo spoke to the doctor as he swung his horse around.

"I will be back in the morning for the hearing," Rómulo said while sitting on his horse, his upper torso turned back to face Boyd.

"Sure, we'll have coffee for ya," Boyd said with a laugh.

Early the next morning, Rómulo, Juanita and several of the men in the surrounding *ranchos* prepared to go into town to see what was to happen to Salome and Poncho. Balo, who had hardly slept all night, insisted that he wanted to go, too. Being as he was too young to stay alone at the *rancho*, Juanita took him and her babies along. They all rode in a hardboard wagon pulled by a mule.

As they approached San Diego they could see quite a hubbub. People were scurrying around on horse, buggy and on foot. They all seemed to be headed in the same direction, to the *plaza* at the center of town. As they entered town they asked someone what all the excitement was about.

"There are two *Mexicanos* hanging in the *plaza*. They appeared there this morning," the man said as he hurried down the road on foot.

"Who are they?" a frightened Juanita asked.

"I don't know," the man answered. "I just heard about it myself and am on my way to find out."

Rómulo's face reddened with anger. He had the strong suspicion that it may be his *cuñados*. He imagined that Boyd did not take kindly to his own and Dr. Whitman's tone regarding his treatment of Poncho. The *rinche* was vindictive enough to take it out on the innocent. It would not be the first time for him to do something like this. Rómulo knew of several men Boyd had shot supposedly trying to escape. He was unable to do that with Poncho because Juanita had been there to witness the event. Rómulo also had heard of another incident in which two men Boyd had captured had been killed while in custody. Shot to death in the jail itself.

Rómulo instructed Juanita to go with the children to the courthouse and he and the other men would go see about the men found hanging. Juanita insisted that she wanted to go make sure it was not Salome. Rómulo told her it would not be good for the children to see such a thing. Juanita was insistent.

"They are young, they do not know what is going on and will forget it, that is the way children are," Juanita said to Rómulo, as she continued to follow along in the direction of the *plaza*.

Balo, who was seated next to Juanita on the buckboard seat, never forgot it. He held on to her with his two small arms as she directed the mule along. As they

approached the central *plaza*, overgrown with weeds,
they could see the two men hanging. It was an eerie sight,
with the Catholic Church's cross steeple behind the
men. Juanita immediately recognized them as Salome
and Poncho. She hurried the mule as she screamed out
cries of despair. As soon as the mule was able to get to
the outer edge of the town square, Juanita jumped out
and ran to Salome. She grabbed on the feet, pushing
them up, trying to get him down.

"*Ayúdenme*," she shouted at the men around him.
"Help me get him down. Why do you just stand there
gawking at them? Don't you see they are dying and
need help?" The truth was that the two were already
dead. They had been since the first resident of the
town, the *hielero*, had come across them while he made
his daily deliveries of ice. There was nothing anyone
could do to help them. Rómulo rode up with another
of his companions, and they placed Salome and Poncho
across their horses and cut the rope, and the two fell in
unison, draped over the horses.

When Juanita leaped from the wagon, Balo had
jumped to the back of the wagon and held on to his
two smaller cousins. The children watched in horror
as their *papá* and *tío* were taken down from the tree
where they hung. They would not move. The children
kept calling out to their "*papá*" but he would not, could
not, answer them. Tears begin to roll down Balo's
cheeks. The two little ones may not understand, but

he understood clearly what had happened. He began to shake as the thought entered his mind that it was his fault for having told the *rinche* about the sorrel mare. That had triggered the whole matter that had resulted in this ugly scene. He began to cry uncontrollably, and the children got scared and they, too, wailed at the top of their lungs.

Some women in the crowd went to Juanita and began to comfort her. They led her back to the wagon and Rómulo directed one of his *compadres* to take charge of the wagon. The man tied his horse to the back of the wagon and helped Juanita up to the wagon seat. He climbed after her and took the reins. He followed Rómulo and the others.

Balo would never forget that gruesome scene, and he also would forever remember what happened next.

His uncle Rómulo rode to the courthouse, and with his Winchester in his hand, the butt of the rifle resting on his dead brother-in-law's shoulder, he called for Boyd to come out. No one moved inside the building. Rómulo then swung his rifle and fired a shot shattering a window to the courthouse.

"Tell the *rinche* Boyd that we will be back," Rómulo hollered at whoever was inside to hear him. "We will be back."

With that he swung his horse around and led the group out of town. He took Salome and Poncho to their family. The women were shocked at what happened and cried wildly. The two brothers were buried the next day in Piedras Pintas. People came from all the surrounding *ranchos*. Rómulo was well respected in the area, and Salome and Poncho were two young men everyone liked because of their courage, energy, and love for life. That night, after the funeral, presided over by the priest who came from San Diego, Rómulo gathered the men around a large mesquite fire.

"*Muchachos*," Rómulo had said, "we cannot let this stand. This *rinche* needs to be stopped or he will keep killing our loved ones. He does not care whether we are rustlers, smugglers, bandits, or innocent ranchers or shepherds. All he wants is to kill *Mexicanos*."

They all nodded their heads in agreement. They drank *mescal* and made plans for how they would respond. They listened as Rómulo told them what he had planned. Rómulo told them to get some rest and meet him at sunrise on the road to San Diego. The next morning, armed men came by the dozens, from Piedras Pintas, Mota de Olmos, Benavides, Concepción, Realitos, Peña, Palito Blanco and other ranches in southern Duval County. Some 60 men in all rode north, following Rómulo Arrieta.

As the group rode into San Diego, Rómulo directed five men to remain at the entrance on the road to Benavides. He ordered five other men to go on ahead and guard the entrance to town on the Collins Road. The men had orders not to allow Boyd to leave town. They were to detain him, and if he resisted, Rómulo told them to shoot him.

As the party entered town, they created a large cloud of dust from the dirt streets. Townspeople began to run hither and yonder in excited fashion, not sure what to make of the large outfit coming into town. The *Mexicano* residents quickly recognized many of the men who were friends, neighbors, and relatives. They knew they were not a gang of bandits. The white settlers were not sure what to think, but they definitely were threatened by such a big band of armed men riding through their town. Many ran to the courthouse to advise the authorities. As the group approached the courthouse, Sheriff Whitman came out with his two brothers, Dr. Whitman and Judge Whitman. The three formed the nucleus of an influential family in town. They were well liked by all elements.

"What do you want, *hombre*?" the sheriff asked Rómulo as he pulled up in front of the courthouse.

"My business is not with you. I want the *rinche* Boyd."

"He's not here," the sheriff responded. "You know that I am the law around here. If you cause any trouble I will have to arrest you."

"We have broken no law. There is no reason for you to arrest me, even if you could," Rómulo told the sheriff, who was fully aware he was considerably outnumbered.

"Where is Boyd?" Rómulo asked.

The sheriff told him he was not at the courthouse or anywhere in town. Rómulo signaled to several of his men, and they trained their rifles on the sheriff and his brothers as Rómulo rode his horse up on the steps of the courthouse and brushed past the sheriff. He entered the courthouse on horseback and peered into every office. Ten other men went upstairs to the second floor and searched the offices there. Rómulo exited the courthouse to the rear and directed some of his followers to enter the jail and look for Boyd there. Satisfied that the *rinche* was not in the courthouse, Rómulo ordered his men to release all the prisoners and then began a systematic search for Boyd in every house in town.

After an entire day of looking, Rómulo's company was unsuccessful in flushing out the *rinche*. Rómulo ordered his men to retreat to Piedras Pintas, where they disbanded to their own *ranchos*. They later heard rumors that Boyd had made his escape dressed as a woman. They would all have a good laugh about the thought of the brave *rinche* dressed as a *vieja*.

While they had been unsuccessful in finding the *rinche* and giving him a taste of his own medicine, for one day they had shown their immediate world that they were not going to take the abuse any longer, and that they had the courage and the unity to take charge of their lives.

It was a lesson that stayed with Balo for the rest of his life.

Chapter 8

Captain Hoffman had grown fatigued with America's railroads. As his latest train ride lumbered its way along the Texas Mexican Railway track to San Diego, he struggled to ease the pain in his posterior. The week's stay in Maryland had been a welcome break to the hectic schedule of the previous week. He had enjoyed his stay considerably. The only taint on the trip had been the community's obsession with the war in Europe.

Cumberland was settled by Germans, Swiss-Germans, and Scotch-Irish, so an interest in the German involvement was to be expected. But the overriding preoccupation surprised Hoffman. What he found particularly peculiar was the evenly divided attitudes. There were those who felt a sense of patriotic duty to the Fatherland. Hoffman could not determine to his satisfaction whether this loyalty was only temporarily given, since the United States was not involved, or whether it transcended loyalty even to their new country. The whole thing did nothing to alleviate his insecurities. There were many, on the other hand, who took the opposite view and felt that Germany was headed toward self-destruction and had nothing but disdain for its actions. His family was among this group. They judged German actions on a moral plane rather than submit to unreasoned and banal reactions. To them, Germany was embarked in an unprincipled, land-grabbing journey. They feared, as did Hoffman, that the United States would inevitably get involved, and it would most certainly not be on Germany's side.

This debate consumed the small community to the exclusion of much else. It was no surprise to Hoffman that his family was unaware of an obscure manifesto hatched in South Texas.

"How curious," he thought. "Here these people are overcome by the politics of another continent an ocean away, and know nothing, and cared less, about a potentially explosive situation in their own country."

The whole thing seemed only slightly ironic when Hoffman considered the possible connection of these two worlds. Nevertheless, he had been glad to visit with his family. Although his father talked nothing but politics, his mother provided a pleasant escape. The activities of recent days had been filled with intrigue, and the coming weeks or months promised more of the same. It was enjoyable for Hoffman to sit at the kitchen table of his childhood home and listen to his mother carry on about relatives he had long forgotten, all the while cooking his favorite meals. The innocence of his mother reassured him. This innocence after all had as its source self-assuredness. His mother's strength, derived from inner faith, had been something Hoffman had always admired and wished to possess. Yet his logical mind prevented him from accepting blind faith.

"God is not something you see or touch, Matthew," she would often tell him, as if to preempt his doubts. "He is what you are. If you believe in yourself, you believe in him. If you obey your laws, you obey his. But if you sell him short, you sell yourself short."

He dared not scrutinize too closely her reasoning. There was certain roundness to them, and more importantly, they offered him hope. It no doubt gave his mother the strength he so admired in her.

***

A screaming conductor suddenly snapped Hoffman out of his daze.

"Alice, next stop, Alice."

Hoffman slowly pieced together where he was. He had stayed in Washington a few days to do some research to supplement the information the president had provided him. He paid visits to his friend Brite at the State Department and Postmaster Burleson to see what else they could provide by way of information for his assignment. He had developed a good sense of the geography of South Texas. Alice was a relatively new community only recently founded, about 10 miles east of San Diego. He had switched trains in Corpus Christi where the Texas Mexican Railway began. The Texas Mexican had been built in the 1870s and was originally christened the Corpus Christi, San Diego, and Río Grande Railway, which gave an indication of San Diego's place in the development of the area. San Diego had been one of the original towns in the plains of South Texas. At the time of the first settlements, which consisted of *ranchos*, the area was still under Spanish rule. It quickly went from Spanish to Mexican to American in the short span of 30 years. Curiously enough, the people changed very little. Hoffman had been looking forward to his assignment. Somehow he could not take too seriously the "Plan" business, but he welcomed the opportunity to investigate an area of the United States with which he was unfamiliar. The opportunity for anthropological study was fantastic. The mere thought of the coming discovery excited him.

As the train pulled out of Alice, Hoffman decided to refresh his memory on some of the details contained in the folder the president provided him. He had been amazed at the thoroughness of the materials. So much so that he almost believed the possibility of the "Plan." He took out the report on the Reyna family. Baldomero Reyna's father, Servando, was still in Mexico, but not much else was known about him. He had sent his family to San Diego to get them out of the crossfire of the Mexican Revolution. The older son, Manuel, had moved to San Diego many years earlier and had become a printer's apprentice with a local Spanish weekly paper, *El Futuro*. Baldomero Reyna had been in San Diego only a few months before returning to Mexico and back to the United States and his arrest. The youngest was a sister named Monica Leticia. She, along with the mother, Genoveva, lived in San Diego with Manuel.

Hoffman was not sure what he was to find in San Diego, but he felt it was the logical place to start. The "Plan," after all, bore its name. According to Reyna, though, the Plan was written in Monterrey and was to be carried out through Matamoros and Brownsville. That scenario seemed as ridiculous as the "Plan" itself. Hoffman could not bring himself to accept the plausibility of such a wild scheme. He took out a copy of the translation of the Plan and began to read it again.

"We, who in turn sign our names, assembled in the revolutionary plot of San Diego, Texas, solemnly promise each other on our word of honor that we will fulfill and cause to be fulfilled and complied with, all the clauses and provisions stipulated in this document, and execute the orders and the wishes emanating from this provisional directorate of this movement and recognize as military chief of the same Mr. Agustín S. Garza,

guaranteeing with our lives the faithful accom-
plishment of what is here agreed upon."

As a student of history and politics, Hoffman was
very familiar with most affirmations of political independence. There was something peculiar about the
Plan of San Diego, beyond its incredulity. It did not
have much by the way of philosophical rationalization.
In fact, it was strikingly detailed. He could hardly imag-
ine the Declaration of Independence naming George
Washington as the general of the Continental Army.
Perhaps its author or authors were not Thomas Jef-
ferson or the signers of the American declaration for
independence, but it could not be denied that they
were intelligent men.

"On the 20th day of February, 1915, at 2 o'clock
in the morning, we will rise in arms against the
government and country of the United States of
North America. One as all and all as one pro-
claiming the liberty of the individuals of the black
race and its independence of Yankee tyranny,
which has held us in slavery since the remote times,
and at the same time and in the same manner we
will proclaim the independence and segregation
of the states bordering on the Mexican nation,
which are Texas, New Mexico, Arizona, Colorado,
and Upper California, of which the Republic of

Mexico was robbed in a most perfidious manner
by North American imperialism."

The more he read, the more Hoffman sensed the
tremendous contrast between this document and the
United States Declaration of Independence. The Plan
seemed more a blueprint to action, as opposed to the
Declaration's a litany of wrongs imposed on a people.
And yet there was a similarity. Interspersed with all
the attention to detail there was mention of some of
the alleged oppressor's evil doings. There were references after all to "Yankee tyranny," "iniquitous slavery"
and theft of one's land. He found particularly curious
the distinction references to "North America" and
"Upper California." Still, it did not have the rolling,
almost melodious, prose of the U.S. Declaration. It
was more strident. Perhaps some of its style was lost
in the translation.

"San Diego, next stop, San Diego," came the call from
the conductor.

Hoffman gathered all his notes and prepared himself for his final destination. As he looked outside his
window he saw a changing landscape. It was a flat
terrain with patches of soft rolling Bermuda grass
intermixed with rising young bushes of mesquite and
huisache. This area had always been cattle country,
but it had also been a thriving sheep-raising region.
Effects of the sheep culinary habits were still evident.

Whole areas of the landscape were almost barren of all vegetation, save the springing huisache and mesquite. An occasional small herd of sheep could still be seen here and yonder. Soon Hoffman saw some of San Diego come into view. The train moved slowly into town. Hoffman was sitting on the north side of the train, and his first sight was the town cemetery. It was a humble place, which Hoffman suspected reflected the town itself. The railroad entered San Diego on the northern fringes of town, so Hoffman's view was minimal, as most of the town lay opposite his windows. The train finally came to a hissing stop and Hoffman rose to make his exit.

As he stepped out onto the platform, he could see the white wooden depot in front of him. It was not a large or fancy depot; certainly, it did not compare to Union or Grand Central stations. Nonetheless, it had an air of sustenance to it. Crews were busily unloading all sorts of wares. Hoffman went inside the station hoping to ask someone for directions to the nearest hotel, but he found that all the personnel were quite busy. It was still an hour or two before dusk, so he decided to walk around town and ask one of the locals for directions. He crossed the street and headed south from where he could readily determine all the action was located. He saw a man getting ready to mount a horse, and he approached him with his inquiry.

"Excuse me, sir, can you direct me to the nearest hotel?"

The gentleman was dressed in a denim shirt with worn blue jeans and a somewhat tattered hat. He looked at Hoffman with a smile on his weather worn face.

"*Despense, señor, pero yo no hablo ingles*," the old man replied. "*Buena suerte y buenos dias.*"

He slowly but gracefully mounted his horse and rode away with no other explanation. Hoffman experienced his first taste of cultural shock. He had grown up in a German-speaking family and had never even considered that those around him were foreigners. German, like English, was part of his everyday life. Yet, he somehow felt strangely powerless by his ineptitude with the situation he had just encountered. Save for the quiet, dignified manner in which he was treated, he almost felt stripped of his self esteem. For the first time in ages he felt helpless.

"The best hotel in town, *señor*, is the Martinet," the directive that brought him back to reality came from a man in front of the building from where the old man had come. He wore what seemed to be a printer's apron over a khaki shirt and pants. He had a full head of brown hair combed straight back without even a part. His thin lips wore a smirk, when he spoke again.

"You asked the *vaquero* for the nearest hotel, which is the Miret only a few blocks down this street, but the best hotel, which I'm sure a gentleman of your means deserves, is the Martinet, which is only several blocks farther down on the next street in that direction."

The man, who was about Hoffman's age, pointed south from where the train had entered the city. Hoffman could easily tell that the fellow was Mexican both by his appearance as well as his heavy accent. Although he had an accent, he spoke English quite well, not unlike many men in his hometown.

"Thank you, sir, you are most kind," Hoffman answered.

"I don't want to mislead you," the man said as he turned to go back into the building. "I said it was the best hotel in town; I did not say it was any good."

Indeed, the Martinet had fallen from its early glory days after the assassination of Mrs. Martinet's son-in-law John Cleary, a leading politico in the county, several years before.

With that, the man in the printer's apron saluted Hoffman with his two forefingers and went back into the building where he apparently worked. As the man left Hoffman's view, he noticed the name of the business over the door, *Periódico EL FUTURO, Imprenta Esparza*. Although Hoffman did not understand Spanish, he could certainly make out that the name of that building compared closely to the name of the newspaper where Manuel Reyna worked. He could not help but wonder if his guide had not been the same Manuel Reyna. He temporarily entertained the idea of following the man into the building to query him along these lines but changed his mind. Soon it would be dark and he best find some lodging for the night. He would have time later to pursue his hypothesis. He walked away in the direction given him with one thought heavily on his mind.

"I have to learn some Spanish, and I have to learn it fast."

It was a Saturday afternoon, and as Hoffman strolled down Center Street, he observed that this was the town's business district, for much activity prevailed. After walking a few short blocks, he noticed a swinging sign reading "Hotel Martinet" on the second floor of a sprawling building two blocks ahead of him. As he came upon the hotel, he passed a saloon that was emitting the sounds of live music intermingled with an occasional whoop and holler. Just then, a man and woman bolted from the saloon. The man obviously was a cowman, for he was dressed in range garb and had the look of just having come into town. The woman dressed in a flowery and loose dress was apparently a prostitute. The pair loudly danced and laughed their way in front of Hoffman and went into the Martinet.

"*Un cuarto para mi y mi amor*," the man shouted at the clerk, who quickly handed him a key.

Hoffman stepped up to the counter but kept his eyes fixed on the couple as they rolled up the stairs. He hesitantly asked the clerk for a room. His recommendation of the Martinet had been somewhat reserved, but he had not quite envisioned sharing sleeping quarters with the town's degenerates. Hoffman maintained a liberal outlook regarding individual conduct, but nonetheless, his personal conduct was somewhat prudish. Allegany County was an established region, but this part of the country was still struggling to shed its frontier spirit. He resigned himself to the fact that he was in for a new experience, and it was not for him to judge, but to learn.

"Would you like a room, *señor?*" the clerk asked with a wide grin.

"Oh, yes," Hoffman responded as he slowly pulled his view away from the stairway. "Do you have a room for a few nights?"

"Sure, *señor*. If the gentleman likes, we can also arrange for some company during your stay," the clerk said, still grinning as he glanced up at the disappearing couple. Hoffman stared at him in stunned disbelief. He had traveled around in his adult life, but he had never been exposed to this type of encounter. He was aware, of course, that such places of ill repute existed, but he had never run into one. He certainly did not expect it in any place that had been presented to him as the best hotel in town. He thought for a moment about withdrawing his request but remembered his guide's admonition that it was the best but "not any good." Perhaps the other places in town had the same type of clientele. He resigned himself to this thought and replied to the desk clerk's inquiry.

"A room will be quite enough," he said in a tone above

a whisper. The clerk's grin was immediately replaced by an incredulous and troubled stare.

"Whatever the gentleman desires. You will be in room six above. It will be 10 bits."

Hoffman paid the clerk and started for the stairs. Once upstairs he quickly found his room and began unpacking. The walls were quite thin and he could clearly hear the shenanigans going on in the next room. He tried for a while to read but decided it was useless. The alternate purring and creaking in the next room was too distracting. He found the whole activity disgusting, and yet it struck an animal chord within him that he found disturbing. Finally, he decided he would go out and walk about the town and perhaps the situation would improve when he returned.

As he stepped out the hotel, he was greeted by the clamor from the *cantina*. It was already turning dark so Hoffman decided to walk back in the direction of the depot. It was familiar ground, and subconsciously he hoped to run into the man who had given him the guarded recommendation of the Martinet. He wasn't sure whether he wanted to see him to pursue his theory of him being Manuel Reyna, or merely to thank him for his choice of hotel. As he neared the depot, he heard the sound of some accordion and guitar music coming from the other side of the railroad tracks. He neared the place and saw it was a rather large building where people were gathering for what appeared to be a dance.

He decided to go in and see firsthand what was going on. As he approached the entrance, he heard several blasts, followed by screaming and general excitement. He recognized quickly that they were gunshots and ran inside to see what was happening. As he reached the entrance way to the building, he could see a body lying in a pool of blood, and amid the commotion there was still a struggle going on. As he took a step toward the area of activity, he was confronted by the guide of the afternoon, who grabbed him by both arms, and as they stood face to face warned him in clear English that he was in danger.

"Mister, this is no place for an *gringo* at this moment. Take my advice and get the hell out of here right now!"

Hoffman stared at the calm and firm face in front of him. This was the second time this man had offered him unsolicited advice. The first turned out to be short of disastrous, but somehow he felt that not heeding him now would result in a true calamity. Before Hoffman could say anything, however, he was spun around and shoved toward the exit.

Instead of fleeing from potential trouble, most people, as had he, were making their way to the center of the commotion.

"If you value your life, my friend, you better leave now for safer ground," the man whispered as he hustled Hoffman out of the hall. They marched off as people hurried and ran around them, making their escapes.

After sustained shoving, Hoffman and his rescuer finally got outside, where a crowd was gathering.

"Quick," the man with the brown hair and stern face said. "Let's head back toward the hotel."

They marched south and soon came upon a large cattle pen about the size of a city block. The stench of the manure was minimized only slightly by a steady north wind. After walking in silence for a while, the helpful Mexican pointed to a crude bench and instructed Hoffman to sit down.

"My friend, this is a violent place in violent times. If I had not pulled you out of that *salón*, you would have joined your *gringo* friend in that puddle of blood."

"Well," Hoffman said, "for my life I thank you, but I would be more appreciative if you could explain to me why my fate would have been so."

"For a Mexican to kill a *gringo* requires no more explanation than for a *gringo* to kill a Mexican," the Mexican said wryly. "I can tell you are not from these parts, *señor*, and you probably do not understand."

"You are right on both points. I am not from this section of the country, and I certainly do not understand."

"Because you are a white man," the man said, looking at him directly in the eyes.

"What does that have to do with anything?"

"It has to do with everything. Don't you understand?" the man replied in a testy mood.

"I'm afraid I don't understand," Hoffman said.

"Where are you from, anyway? How can anyone be so ignorant?"

"I'm from Maryland, and I am sorry to say that I am ignorant about what you speak of."

"Well that explains it," the man remarked as he bent over on the bench, resting his elbows on his knees and burying his face in his hands. He remained in this pose for a few minutes before sitting up again.

"In the north, my friend, you do not have many foreigners, and thus you avoid and are innocent of race hatreds," the man explained in a slow tone.

"Oh, but we do have foreigners. I myself am of German stock," Hoffman interjected.

"Please, don't be so damn naive. Sure, you have a variety of ethnic groups, but you are all white European. As German you should be keenly familiar with the Teutonic theory of white supremacy."

Hoffman was clearly taken aback by the last assertion. True, some people clung to that belief, but to attribute it to an entire race was absurd.

"Your reasoning is somewhat faulty, my friend," Hoffman said, trying not to reveal his anger or insecurity. "Your jumbling together of Anglo, white, Germans and Teutonic has many holes."

"What you, and others like you, fail to understand is that whether the logic is wrong does not matter. The reality is that to us, you are all the same. Furthermore, when you are trying to promote this idea as a political tool to arouse the poor and ignorant masses, it is smart to put it in the simplest terms. In any case, our logic is no weaker than the *gringo's*. You're new to these parts. Keep an open mind, and you will see what I mean."

Hoffman was intrigued by much of what this man had said. He was about to query him further when the man got up and started to bid him good night.

"It is late, and I need to get home and look after my mother and sister. Isn't it funny that no matter how old you get, mothers will still worry about you. Are you staying at the Martinet?"

"Yes."

"Well, it's over there. Just go down one block," the man said pointing to the west.

"Thank you," Hoffman said as he rose and extended his hand to the man.

"Thank you for your directions, your conversation, and most of all, for your actions at the shooting. My name is Matthew Hoffman, and I hope I'll see you again, for I would like to learn more from you about this part of the country."

"For your information, my friend, the shooting at the *baile* involved two *gringos* who had the same curiosity you have about this part of the country. They learned two things rather abruptly: First, that people around here don't much like each other, and second, they often express their dislike in very violent ways. Too bad they won't be around to tell what they learned. Hopefully, you will be more lucky."

The man started to walk away when he turned and spoke to Hoffman once again. "My name is Manuel Reyna. If I can be of further service to you, let me know. I work at the newspaper *El Futuro*," he told Hoffman as he walked away in the dark.

Hoffman went back to his room intrigued by the night's events. He was emotionally and mentally stimulated.

The long trip had been physically exhausting, but the comings and goings in the other rooms prevented Hoffman from getting a full night's sleep. He awoke about seven the following morning, only somewhat rested but eager to learn more about this provocative place. He made his way downstairs in search for a place to have breakfast before attending Sunday Mass. Although not a terribly religious man, Hoffman tried as often as not to comply with his mother's wishes that he remain close to her through observance of Sunday worship. He walked up to the clerk, who was asleep in his chair, and asked for directions to a cafe. Half startled and completely annoyed, the clerk pointed him to a *panadería* across the street.

As he approached the bakery, Hoffman was met with a delightful aroma. He could not make out all the fragrances, but it perked his taste buds no end. Hoffman had never before been in a Mexican bakery, or *panadería*, as the locals called it, but he had heard accounts from his friends in San Antonio of the fine pastries one could find in such a place. As he walked in, he encountered the cowman of the night before having some coffee and obviously enduring a sizable headache. He brushed by his neighbor at the hotel and took a table in the corner.

"What will you be having for breakfast this morning?" asked a young woman with a shy smile.

Hoffman looked up at her with a faint smile and blurted out that he was unable to make up his mind, thanks to the variety of enticing aromas.

"You see I am new to this part of the country, and I am unfamiliar with your cooking," Hoffman said. "Perhaps you can recommend something that I will enjoy."

"Very well, *señor*, but how hungry are you?" the waitress asked.

"Oh, not very hungry, but maybe a small breakfast and a piece of pastry will do."

The girl went off into the kitchen and returned a short while later with some hot coffee. It was stronger than what he was used to, but it provided the kick of energy he needed. Not long passed before the girl came back with a plate of what appeared to be eggs scrambled with some sort of red meat. Hoffman was unsure of what it was, but the girl answered his puzzled look.

"It's called *chorizo con huevo*, *señor*. It's Mexican sausage mixed with scrambled eggs. It is very good. You also have some refried beans, flour tortillas, and for your pastry, I brought you an *empanada*."

"What is an *empanada*?" Hoffman asked, looking at some sort of turnover.

"An *empanada*, señor, is a turnover made with unleavened dough and pumpkin filling."

Hoffman thanked the girl an embarked on his culinary adventure. To his delight, he found all items delicious, especially the *empanada*, which he thought was superb. After finishing his meal, Hoffman asked the young lady for directions to the Catholic Church. He had noticed it the night before, but was unsure of how to get to it. His experience that night had not only been hurried, but confusing as well. The girl pointed him in the right direction and told him that the Mass was to start in five minutes and that he should hurry if he hoped to make it on time.

Hoffman walked the short three blocks to the church in a quick march and was there with plenty of time. It was an attractive church. It appeared rather new and quite auspicious for such a poor community. It was made of yellow brick and had two towers from which rang the church bells. He walked inside and was equally impressed by the beautiful triple altars. There was a main altar directly in the center. It was adorned by a wonderful statue of Jesus in the center and was flanked by statues of the Virgin Mary and Joseph on either side. Off to each side of the main altar were two smaller altars with lesser but equally impressive statutes. The altar had a half-moon dome ceiling, and in front it had a beautiful baroque-looking rail where several worshipers were kneeling, consumed in prayer. They prayed in Spanish, so Hoffman was unsure of what prayer they were invoking, but the cadence sounded like the rosary. As he sat down in one of the wooden pews, the priest and his altar servers made their entrance from the sacristy and commenced Mass. As the Mass progressed, the priest gave his homily in Spanish, and Hoffman was in the dark to what he said. At Ss. Peter and Paul in Cumberland, the sermon was often given in German, but that he understood. Although Hoffman was slowly getting used to the Spanish influence in the area, he still found it hard to come to complete grasp with it.

"How strange," he thought. "These people would feel the same way I do if they were to walk into a church in my hometown." He wondered whether his fellow townsmen would be as tolerant of them as they seemed to be of him.

Not understanding what was going on, Hoffman decided to take a good look around at the congregation to get a feel for of the town itself. His introduction of the night before had been less than welcoming, but surely there were good and decent people in this town. Where better to observe them than in church? As he looked around, he noticed that most of the congregation was of Mexican extraction. There were a few Americans, as the local white people called themselves, but not many. The few who were there apparently understood the language, for they listened intently to the priest. How peculiar, Hoffman thought, that the white people would distinguish themselves as Americans when, including those of Mexican ancestry, they were all citizens. He guessed it was just a local custom of convenience, but still it seemed rather odd.

As Hoffman's eyes roamed the church, he suddenly came upon a most beautiful young lady. Indeed, Hoffman had never seen such beauty. She was thin, and although she was kneeling, she appeared to be tall. Her beautiful hazel eyes set above high and smoothly rounded cheekbones that dominated her face. She had a pug nose and near perfect lips. Her hair, long and black and abounded with natural curls at the ends, was covered by a beautiful black veil.

Hoffman could not pull his eyes from her, but he did not want to be seen staring, so he looked away. As he did, he saw a familiar face looking his way with a wide grin. It was Manuel Reyna. Hoffman smiled back and turned away. He noticed that Manuel Reyna was sitting next to the young lady and that on her other side was an elderly woman. Quickly, he surmised that it must be the Reyna family.

He could hardly believe the way things were happening since his arrival. In less than 24 hours, he had already had encounters with Manuel Reyna, and now he sat there mesmerized by Monica Reyna. He could not believe the cards fate was dealing to him. It was going to be a more interesting assignment than he had envisioned.

As Hoffman walked out the door of the church, Manuel, who had been waiting for him, met him.

"Good morning, my friend."

"Good morning to you, too, friend," Hoffman said.

"In conversation I mentioned to my mother" Manuel continued, "about your unfortunate welcome to this fine city. She feels obliged to make up for her fellow townspeople and has asked me to invite you to lunch at our humble house."

"I would be delighted," Hoffman said, relishing the thought of having some pleasant company, especially the thought of meeting the beautiful sister. The two walked over to the two ladies and Manuel introduced them.

"*Mamá*, I would like you to meet Mr. Matthew Hoffman, the gentleman I told you about. Mr. Hoffman, this is my mother, *señora* Servando Reyna."

Hoffman made a half bow and told the elderly woman how delighted he was to meet her. He looked up and glanced past the woman at the young woman.

"The pleasure is all mine, *señor* Hoffman," *señora* Reyna said in Spanish, which Manuel Reyna translated. Noticing Hoffman's interest in her daughter, who stood obediently behind her mother, she turned and took her by the elbow and introduced her to Hoffman.

"And this, *señor*, is my daughter, Monica Leticia."

"I hope you don't think me impudent, ma'am, but

I have never seen such beauty," Hoffman responded with unusual frankness. He caught himself, and at the same time noticed that the mother was taken aback by his forwardness.

"I am sorry if I was out of line, *señora*, but your daughter is truly very attractive," Hoffman said.

The woman merely nodded her head, indicating that she accepted his apology. Monica never said a word. She merely smiled and resumed her place behind her mother.

The four then proceeded to walk to the Reyna home, the men a few steps behind the women.

"It is only a short walk," Manuel said. "It is a good day for a walk."

"It is, indeed," Hoffman agreed as he took a deep breath of fresh air. A mild Texas norther was blowing, and it made for a very pleasant walk. It was Hoffman's first real opportunity to see the residential areas of the town.

He had only been exposed to the more seedy areas of the town. It was a rustic town, but pleasing to the eye. It still had much of the frontier look to it yet. But it also showed signs of becoming an established community. There were quite a few trees, mostly cottonwood around the church and park. The houses around the church were mostly made of caliche seal block with wooden roofs. They were good-sized homes that indicated the more affluent lived in this part of the town. After walking a few blocks, they came to a creek with a bountiful current and surrounded by many trees on both sides. There was a wooden bridge, which they used to cross over the creek.

"It's not too far away," Manuel said as he pointed to a house on the top of the bluff across from the creek. "That white house is our home."

"It looks like a fine home," Hoffman commented, noticing that it was a good-size home.

"It would make a fine fort," Manuel laughed. "Which is what it used to be. My father is accustomed to the high life, and he could not see his girls living in any other fashion. So when he brought them over from México, he looked for the finest house he could find. Finding none to his satisfaction, he bought this old fort and had it remodeled to suit his taste."

As they approached the house, Hoffman could tell that it did indeed look like a fortification. It was made of seal block, but it had some newly installed double doors. On close inspection, he noticed that there were five sets of these doors on the eastern side and three on the southern side. It was rustic, but clearly in good taste.

"Your father must be a refined gentleman, my friend," Hoffman said as they entered the home. "He has excellent taste, and has done an amazing job in converting an old fort into such a fine home."

After signaling Hoffman to sit down, Manuel served some wine for the both of them. The ladies excused themselves and went into the inner sanctums of the house.

"*Salud, amigo,*" Manuel said, toasting to Hoffman.

"I am truly grateful for your hospitality," Hoffman said.

"My father has always been proud of saying," Manuel said, "that to a Mexican the greatest virtue is hospitality. Of course, he always is quick to interject that every truism has a corollary."

"Very interesting," Hoffman said, "and what would the applicable corollary be in this case?"

"Simply stated," Manuel said, with a gleam in his eyes that Hoffman had not noticed before, "there is no greater vice than trespass."

"Very interesting," Hoffman repeated as he analyzed Manuel's smile.

For some reason, that exchange had brought home to Hoffman a reminder of why he was down here. It was as if Manuel was aware of his assignment and was teasingly reminding him of it. At the same time, he began to feel somewhat guilty enjoying the Reynas' hospitality and simultaneously investigating them and their actions. He was never good at secrets: They implied dishonesty, which he had never condoned.

"You see, my friend," Manuel said, interrupting Hoffman's brief lapse into guilt, "Mexicans have been extending hospitality to foreigners since the time of Montezuma and Cortez, to more recent times of Santa Anna and Austin. Always, the Mexicans opened their homes with a warm embrace, and every time, the guest became an intruder, and finally a thief."

"It seems to me," Hoffman responded, "that the ebb and flow of history is replete with much similar circumstances where the stronger nations make war on their weaker neighbors and conquer their lands. To quote an old but crude saying 'to the victor goes the spoils.' "

"Yes," Manuel whispered, "the question is whether the victory is complete or whether the war lingers on."

Hoffman was taken aback by this remark, and was about to pursue this line of conversation, but *señora* Reyna announced that lunch was ready. The two men walked in silence to the dining room.

The dining room was spacious, with a large hardwood table in the center with a setting for four. Hard but comfortable wooden chairs surrounded it, and the table was covered by fine woven linen. The china and silver appeared to be of the finer quality. Once they were all sitting, *señora* Reyna asked her daughter to say grace. As they all bowed their heads in silence, Monica began her prayer.

"Lord Jesus, make this humble meal as tasty as those prepared for you by your Virgin Mother, and as nourishing to our bodies as your words are to our souls. May our guest be pleased with our serving and enjoy his stay in this pleasant city to which we also are strangers. Amen."

Monica had recited the entire prayer in English, and Hoffman was more than a little surprised.

"That was a fine offering," Hoffman said as soon as they resumed with the serving of the meal. "Your commendation of my presence to the Lord is most kind, and I assure you that I will enjoy the meal as much as I will the fine company."

Monica only smiled and nodded acknowledgment.

"I must say," Hoffman said, "your English is superb for someone who only recently arrived in our country."

"My brother Baldomero," Monica said, in a sure but friendly voice, "would take exception to your assertion that this is your country. He would most likely suggest that you are a recent arrival to our country."

Hoffman's face reddened at the mention of Baldomero Reyna. Somehow he had feared Baldomero's name would come up and quickly thereafter he would have to reveal his mission. He was quite unprepared to have had the name brought up in such fashion and by his lovely and innocent-looking sister. He felt a rush of heat go up to his head as he shifted uncomfortably in his chair. Manuel was looking at him with an uncontrolled, almost proud grin. After what seemed several minutes, *señora* Reyna broke the embarrassing silence.

"Monica, your father and I have both told you time and again that politics is not a proper subject for the dinner table. You have been very ungracious to our guest, and I insist that you apologize."

Monica obeyed her mother with a compulsory apology, one without any real meaning.

"If my conversation has offended you, Mr. Hoffman," Monica said, "I apologize. I did not intend to cause you any discomfiture but merely to make conversation."

"No apology is necessary," Hoffman replied, as he regained his color. "I am indeed a stranger to this land and quite ignorant of its history. If I have overstepped my bounds, I offer my apology."

"No apology is needed," Manuel broke in. "You will soon learn much about us and our history, I'm sure."

His wily smile suggested to Hoffman that this man knew much more about him than what he was letting on.

"Surely," Hoffman thought, "he knows why I'm here."

"But my mother is right: Politics has no place at a table with such wonderful appetizers."

The group proceeded with their meal of *cabrito guisado*, which was a stewed kid goat with uncommonly good taste. It was a totally new experience to Hoffman, as had been just about everything about his short visit to this part of the country. While they ate whole pinto beans, Mexican style rice and delicious corn tortillas, they made small talk. Monica, he found out, had learned her English from the Catholic sisters at Incarnate Word School in Corpus Christi, where she had studied for several years. She was an extremely bright and confident young lady with no signs of the usual frivolous manners of most of the young women he had known in the East. He had met some interesting women before, but none quite like this one.

After the meal and pleasant conversation, they returned to the living room, and Hoffman bade his farewell.

"Your hospitality, *señora*, has been most generous. I assure you that it has more than made up for any unpleasantness I may have encountered before. Unfortunately, all good things come to an end, and I must leave such fine company. Again, I thank you for your hospitality."

"You are quite welcome, *señor* Hoffman," the mother said. "You be sure and feel free to pay us a visit again."

Hoffman wanted nothing better than to return and be able to get to know Monica better. His urge to ask for courting privileges was being held back by his natural shy tendency when it came to women, as well as his feelings of dishonesty for not revealing who he was and what he was doing. He finally overcame these crossed feelings and mustered just enough will to ask what was on his mind.

"Your invitation, madam," Hoffman said as he resorted to his Eastern manner, "is most kind and opportune. If I am too forward, please tell me outright, Mrs. Reyna, but I would like permission to come back and visit and get to know your daughter better."

Señora Reyna was not totally surprised. She had easily noticed that this man had taken an immediate interest in her daughter. Although he seemed a nice enough man, she was not sure of such an arrangement. After all, she knew very little about him, and what she did know was not too convincing that any real relationship could mature between him and her daughter. He was a *gringo*, after all.

"*Señor* Hoffman," *señora* Reyna said, "I appreciate your openness, and I am sure your intentions are honorable, but we hardly know you."

"That is true," Hoffman said. He felt obliged to tell them something about himself that would impress them sufficiently to allow him to return and see Monica on a more personal level. He toyed around with the idea of telling them that he was a personal emissary of the president of the United States but did not want to reveal any more than that. The president had assured him that his mission was not secretive, but that he should use discretion. It was quite unlike him to use his position to win favor with a lady, but he was so captivated by Monica that he decided to tell enough to impress them.

"While I cannot tell you all about myself, in a short while, hopefully with time you will know more about me if I am allowed to come back and visit. But you are right that my intentions are completely honorable."

Hoffman hesitated but then went on.

"What I can tell you now is that I am an emissary from President Wilson on a special assignment. I am not at liberty to discuss my mission at this time, but I hope that my association with the president is an indication to you that I am a serious and honorable man who would not easily abuse of your trust."

Monica had left the room as soon as this conversation had started, but Manuel stayed to interpret for his mother. Hoffman awkwardly stood at the door as *señora* Reyna thought over his supplication.

"I cannot give you an answer at this time *señor* Hoffman, but I will write to my husband and ask for his thoughts on the matter. You may come in two weeks for my reply."

"Thank you very much, *señora*," Hoffman said, somewhat excitedly, as he stepped backward out into the street, which was right at the door's edge.

The door closed behind him as he turned to walk away. He had been excited about his mission, but now he was exhilarated. Never had he felt this way. His whole life had been dedicated to scholarly pursuits, and romance had never been part of his life. It was a totally different feeling, one that he had never quite experienced, but he felt like whistling as he briskly walked down the hill toward the wooden bridge leading back to the hotel. He felt like a young boy and loved every minute of it.

Chapter 9

Servando Reyna sat in the hall of the temporary presidential palace in Veracruz, waiting to see First Chief Venustiano Carranza. As he waited he pulled out the *carta* he had received from his wife the previous day.

"*Mi querido, Servando,*

I hope that this letter reaches you in good health. The children and I pray daily for your well-being and for peace for our beloved México. Being away from you for so long has been very lonely for me. I miss you dearly. It is my fondest dream that this terrible nightmare will soon be over and we can all be back together as a family.

It is not easy trying to govern the family by myself in a far off and strange place. San Diego is a fine community with many good people, but it is still not home and you are not here. Manuel is no problem, as you know. He is a great source of comfort to me. But my poor Balo, how he gives me pain. He is still incarcerated in Brownsville and I do not know when I will see him again. Oh, how I pray to the good Lord for his safety. Please let me know soon if you are able to get *Presidente* Carranza to intervene with the American authorities on his behalf.

Your pet Monica is doing very well. She does share Balo's hard head, but she is not as bad. Thank God. We had an *Americano* over for lunch just the other day and she insulted him at the dinner table. Thank goodness that he was a very charming young man and he forgave her indiscretion. And why shouldn't he? He was quite taken by our *princesa*. He has asked to come call on her but I asked him to wait for an answer from you. He seems to me to be quite a gentleman. He is from the East and claims to be a representative of President Wilson on a special assignment. Please let me know how I should respond to his request.

I will close for now my dear husband. Remember that your family loves you very much and longs to be with you. Monica and Manuel send their love.

Con todo cariño, tu esposa, Genoveva."

News of Balo's escape had not reached San Diego, much less Veracruz. Servando Reyna put away his letter and let out a sigh of loneliness.

How the world had changed over the past ten years, he thought to himself. Ten short years before, he had been a successful rancher with a good *hacienda* near Linares. His children were young adults, innocent, and full of life.

Now war had torn his country apart. His beloved México, which had been a picture of order for more than 50 years, was now under a cloud of anarchy. His business had been ravaged by a series of rebel incursions. His family was forced to be far away from him. He was quite alone now, at least for the present.

He had never taken much interest in politics. His life had been that of rancher-businessman. He enjoyed making money. Not so much for money's sake, for he had little use for it. Money was only a means of keeping score of measuring his success.

Outside of his business and his family, he had noticed nothing. He had no awareness of the living conditions of his less fortunate fellow *Mexicanos*. He had no feeling about the system of government, so long as it did not interfere with his life.

When the revolution erupted, he hardly noticed it at first. But the waves of *revolucionarios* swept through the country and ravaged his herds and his *huertas* of fruit. They were no better than thieves, he thought. Their continued raids, however, had made him stop and listen to what was going on around him. He did not understand it. After all, his life was fine.

Nonetheless, the war was real, and it was pervasive. He had to choose a side or all that he owned would be lost. Political philosophy was not his concern, save as it related to his property. He was a pragmatist and that had dictated to him to choose the side of the particular faction that was strongest at the time. When it was all said and done, he figured, whoever won would reward his loyalty by letting him keep his land and resume his way of life.

He sat there now in the hall of the provisional presidential palace in Veracruz. It was a far cry from the *llanos* of northern México. It was as different a world as was the area north of the Río Grande to where he had taken his family for safety.

He had teamed up with the Carranza forces mainly because they seemed to be of the same economic and social class as he. Villa was no more than a bandit, and Zapata could hardly pass for anything but a peon. The money interests would prevail — they always did.

Señor Reyna, even though he was five years older than Carranza, had gone to school with the first chief. They both came from ranching families. The Carranzas operated a large cattle operation in Coahuila.

Though the two young men often talked about returning to their respective *haciendas* to raise cattle, Carranza often showed political interests. He was an astute student of Mexican history and often talked of the injustice México had suffered under Yankee influence.

The young Carranza would often gripe at the theft of *Tejas* from his native Coahuila. It was after all Coahuila-*Tejas* that had led the reforms against the central government. But the *gringos* had stripped *Tejas* from Coahuila.

The weakness of the central government on losing Texas was yet another grievance that Carranza would carry as a grudge. He pledged to himself through clenched teeth to restore México's dignity.

After school, both young men had gone home to work the *haciendas* for their fathers, but Carranza was soon pursuing political aims. He became mayor of Cuatro Ciénegas, which his great-grandfather founded during the push northward into the frontier. His family stock was steeped in the frontier tradition, having fought against the Comanche in expanding Spain's influence into the desert.

Carranza quickly rose in state politics.

Reyna had not been surprised that, ultimately, his good friend had gotten involved in national affairs. It was as if it were his destiny.

"*Señor* Reyna, the first chief will see you now," the clerk said.

As Reyna entered the inner office of the first chief, his old friend was sitting with his back to a window and was visible only as a dark silhouette. That was an old Carranza trick, Reyna remembered. Carranza would take his position in front of a window with the sun directly behind him. In this way he would be obscured but he could clearly see his visitor as the light came through the window. It was even harder to detect his moods because his eyes were hidden behind blue tinted glasses.

At age 55, Carranza was a large man, sinewy and strong. He customarily wore a gray hat, typical of those worn in the north by the *vaqueros*. He wore a gabardine jacket without military insignias but with the gold buttons of an army general. He had on mounting trousers and patent leather boots.

"Welcome, my good friend," the first chief said as Reyna walked over to shake Carranza's hand.

Unlike many of his fellow Mexicans, Carranza was not the demonstrative type. He was not inclined to hand out *abrazos*, as was the custom when reuniting with an old friend.

Carranza had a slow-paced quality, with a pause in his voice and demeanor. His personality was not pretentious, but rather calculative. It was nearly impossible to have a face-to-face conversation with Carranza.

"*Mi presidente!*" Reyna exclaimed with obvious pride in his old friend. "How good it is to see you again. God only knows I wish it were under more pleasant circumstances."

Carranza directed Reyna to a chair in front of him and stared at him pensively while he stroked his long gray beard with his fingers curled and his palm facing out from behind the beard.

"I was so sorry to hear about your brother Jesús," Reyna said in a sincere consoling voice. The first chief's enemies in the north of México had executed Jesús Carranza.

"Jesús knew that we are in a dangerous struggle," Carranza said without showing any expression of sorrow. "Our lives are not what is important. We live and die for the principles of our struggle. They are bigger than any of us and all of us."

Señor Reyna could not help but think that his old friend had grown too callous. Perhaps *señor* Reyna felt this way because to him, family was the most important thing in a man's life. His friend was willing to sacrifice everything for a struggle *señor* Reyna did not understand, much less one to which he would be willing to give his life or that of a member of his family.

The struggle to Carranza was a matter of principles, not personalities. He was adamant in fulfilling the aspirations of the struggle, namely the attainment of nationhood. He did not care who would govern or who would lead. What was important was that the goals of the struggle and the sovereignty for México be realized.

"A fight which vacillates is lost," Carranza added. "To waiver is suicidal. The struggle's grand social changes can only be achieved by a decisive victory over the powers of despots."

To the first chief, it was not enough to replace one dictator with another. All the sacrifice would be lost and the system would remain corrupt. As a young man he had believed in the rule of right, but the militarism of his age demanded the rule of might.

"But enough of such serious matters," Carranza said. "Tell me, Servando, how are your wonderful wife and family?"

"They have been better," *señor* Reyna sighed. "The times have changed for all of us. It seems that serious matters are all we have to talk about because that is the nature of our times."

Señor Reyna relayed to Carranza how he had moved his family to a small place in Texas called San Diego, where some of his wife's relatives had settled. It was a Mexican town, he told the first chief, and it was as close to home as he could find. Genoveva, his wife, and two of their children were doing fine in San Diego, but Balo, their "*rebelde*," provided enough worry for all his family combined.

"Venustiano, I need your help," *señor* Reyna said, referring to his old friend in the manner he had used in their youth, putting aside all the formalities of this new station in their lives. He spoke softly, in a depressed voice.

"My middle child, Balo, has gotten himself caught up in the spirit of revolution and has become involved in some movement in Texas that has landed him in jail."

"What sort of movement is he involved in?" the first chief asked.

"He has taken up arms against the United States under

something called *El Plan de San Diego, Tejas*," *señor* Reyna told the first chief. "Do you know of this movement?"

The first chief paused before he answered. He had been informed of it. In fact, there was little that affected México that he did not know about.

"My commander in Matamoros, General Nefarrate, has telegraphed me about some patriots who have taken up arms to try to return to México the lands the Yankees took during the great war," Carranza told *señor* Reyna. "It sounds a little absurd, but I can understand their passion, and in the end they may be of some help to us in our struggle."

"How so?" *señor* Reyna asked.

"The Americans have been meddling in our affairs for a long time. They think we do not know of their intrigue, but we have spies just like they do. They have played the various factions of the revolution against one another in order to sustain disorder. In this way they will have a pretext to intervene as our saviors. This *Plan de San Diego* could be a way for us to meddle in their affairs and keep them busy on their side of the river so that they can stay out of our affairs.

"The sanctimonious Mr. Wilson calls his spies emissaries, but they are spies just the same," Carranza said mocking piousness on the word "emissaries." "He has agents close to every revolutionary leader. They act as if they are our friends and counsels, but they are merely concocting trouble."

Señor Reyna wondered whether the young man wishing to court his daughter was a spy. He had said he was a representative of President Wilson. On the other hand, he was working on his side of the river, so how could he be spying on México?

"My wife wrote to me in her last letter of a young man visiting San Diego who claims to be a representative of Mr. Wilson," *señor* Reyna volunteered the information to see if it evoked a response. "Genoveva says he seems like a nice young man. They had him over for dinner and he asked permission to call on my daughter. Do you think he is a spy?"

"Probably," Carranza responded, "but who knows, he may be of some use to both of us."

Carranza asked his old friend if he would be willing to go to San Diego and meet the young man personally. *Señor* Reyna said he was planning a trip to go see his family already. Plus, he had to go by way of Brownsville to see what he could do for Balo.

"I will call General Nefarrate to see what he can find out on his case," the first chief told *señor* Reyna.

"The problem I have is that the Americans do not recognize me as the head of México. They continue to play their games with Villa in an effort to exert influence if he prevails. I will never abandon México's sovereignty, and the Americans know it.

"So you see, my friend, there may be little I can do for your son. But what I can do, I will do."

Carranza explained to *señor* Reyna that he, too, could help his son by taking a message to Wilson's agent in San Diego. He instructed *señor* Reyna to explain to the agent that in order for Carranza to be able to assist in putting down this *Plan de San Diego*, he needed to have official recognition, otherwise he could do nothing. How could he help if he had no authority?

"If we can get Wilson to do something, we can move to free your son from jail and free México from chaos," Carranza told *señor* Reyna as they bid each other farewell.

The thought crossed *señor* Reyna's mind that his friend had become quite the politician over the years. He seemed always to look at how he could "use" people. But then again, *señor* Reyna himself had come to see his old friend to ask him for help — to use him.

Chapter 10

Balo had a restless night. He had not been able to get his *tíos* out of his head. He even had nightmares about their hanging. No matter how much his mother had counseled him through the years that it was not his fault, Balo just could not bring himself to believe that. He was to blame, and now he had a chance to atone for his sin.

As he readied his mount to set out for Texas, his thoughts again drifted to his *tío* Rómulo. How brave he had been. He did not find the coward Boyd, but he had made a reputation for himself that he took to his grave. From the time he occupied San Diego forward, everyone in the county admired him. They came to him for advice and he was frequently asked to serve as *padrino* for the various sacraments of the *vecinos'* children. His network of *compadres* was truly amazing. Even the *gringos* respected him. Sheriff Whitman held no hard feelings over the incident. He had never been fond of Boyd, plus any man that commanded the loyalty of so many other men could be useful in the ever-shifting political tides of Duval County. The sheriff belonged to the *Huarache* faction that had control of the county at the time of the occupation. But the *Botas* were growing in numbers and were threatening the *Huarache* hold on the county. *Tío* Rómulo proved to be as wily a politician as he was brave. He played the two parties against each other and extracted what he could for his people. Rómulo never sought public office, but anyone who wished to hold office in the southern part of the county had to call on him if he expected to succeed.

Balo had never warmed to politics. It lacked intellectual honesty. It was devoid of true passion. To Balo, the only way to exact real change was through sheer power. He who controlled the weapons controlled the future. Balo's father had frequently chastised him for this way of thinking. The moneyed interests, he would tell Balo, always controlled people's lives and their destiny.

"You can buy guns with money," his father would say.

"But you can take money with guns," Balo would reply.

"Yes," his father would respond, "but you risk life and freedom."

"But guns is the only way to gain life and freedom from ruthless despots. Risking my life and freedom is a risk I am willing to take," was Balo's retort.

His father never understood. His father would mumble that he was "*cabezudo*" and walk away. If his father felt

Balo was hardheaded that was because Balo's heart had been hardened by the malignancy that was the *gringo*.

One of his men snapped Balo back to reality by calling to him that everyone was mounted and ready to head out. They were 25 men in all. Balo took the lead as they headed north to the Río Bravo and into Texas. He felt like his *tío* Rómulo leading his men into San Diego. But this army appeared much more ragtag. After two nights of drinking *mescal* and carousing with women, these poorly dressed and poorly armed men did not appear as disciplined and prepared as his *tío's* had 30 years before. Balo knew he had to do something to get them better prepared. He could control the drink and women but he was not in a position to improve their armament. That is why he was going to meet with General Nefarrate before crossing the river.

Cleto had left with his men to San Benito in Texas the day before, and the two men were to meet up there at the home of a mutual friend and supporter of the struggle. As they traveled north, they could see in the horizon that they were riding into some pretty bad weather. Soon it started to drizzle, and the drizzle turned into a strong April shower. Balo remembered his mother's old saying about the weather: "*marzo loco y abril otro poco.*" It was pouring and his men had no protection. They had no raincoats and there was nowhere to take cover in this desolate area south of the river. They just kept forging ahead until finally, after an hour, the rains began to subside. Balo pushed his men through the mud until they reached their destination.

As they pulled into *el rancho* they could see a sign dangling from an arch over the gate that read *"Los Borregos."* The *hacienda* belonged to General Felix Diaz, brother of the deposed President Porfirio Díaz. The *rancho* had seen better times. Now all that remained were some crudely constructed buildings made from lumber with roofs made from aluminum cans. Remains of the main house could be seen up the road a ways, a burnt heap. The revolution had certainly passed through this place. Balo told his men to dismount and get some rest, for in the morning they would continue their expedition.

"Jefe," one of the men said, "I don't think we will be able to cross the river. It is overflowing its banks."

"That is when we want to cross," Balo responded. "The *gringo* will not be expecting anybody to cross now. They will not see us come over and we will have the element of surprise."

"Bueno," the man said, as he shook his head and pulled his horse to a shed with the other men. He remained unconvinced of the wisdom of that strategy, but then who was he to question his leader.

As the morning sun came up, not even a rooster was around to wake them up. The rains had stopped but the day was still heavily overcast. More rain was sure to come before the end of the day. If they were going to cross that raging river, they needed to do it soon before it crested more. But Balo was waiting on someone, so the men milled around and rested their animals. Finally, at mid-morning, they saw an automobile slowly moving toward their location. It stopped suddenly and a man got off and waved for Balo to go to him.

As Balo approached the car, a second man who looked like a *gringo* stepped out of the car. He was blond and blue-eyed and wore a suit and tie. The man who had waved Balo over was dressed in plain gray military garb. Balo saluted him and the two shook hands.

"*Mi general*, I am glad you could make it with this terrible weather," Balo said.

"This is as far as I dared come in this contraption with all this mud," General Emilio Nefarrate responded as he waved his hand toward the car. "I want you to meet Herr von Mueller, who has offered to help out with our cause."

Nefarrate was the general who had control of the Matamoros district. He was loyal to First Chief Venustiano Carranza, but more important, he held a passionate devotion to México and anything or anybody Mexican. Like Carranza, his military dress was plain, without the markings customary to the head of an army.

As the general spoke, he walked to the back of the automobile with Balo following him and sneering at the German. The general noticed Balo's stare and explained to Balo that von Mueller was not a *gringo* but a German national who was providing the *sediciosos* with some real assistance.

"Such as this," Nefarrate said as he opened a long wooden box in the backseat of the German's Model T Roadster.

The box was full of German-made Mauser rifles. The Mauser was the best army rifle made, much better than the Winchester the *vaqueros* used on the range. In addition to the rifles, there were several boxes of ammunition and bandoleers. Balo's face turned from a sneer to a broad grin, and he turned to the German to express his appreciation.

"*Gracias*," Balo blurted out several times. The German smiled and walked over to him.

"Maybe your men can also use this," von Mueller said to Balo as he handed him an envelope. Balo opened it and saw that it contained several thousand dollars in cash.

"There is nothing like a little money in a man's pocket to lift his spirits," the German said with a grin.

Balo shook the German's hand and turned to Nefarrate and gave the general an *abrazo*. He knew this was not proper military etiquette, but he was overwhelmed with joy and relief that finally his men would have the means to launch a real war. After the three had unloaded the boxes with the ammunition and rifles, Nefarrate and von Mueller bid Balo farewell and drove off. As they did, Nefarrate told Balo to take care and not harm any

Germans in his campaign, for von Mueller had other compatriots throughout the Valley.

Balo signaled to his men to join him.

"*Miren, muchachos,*" Balo yelled as he pointed to the open box with the Mausers. "*Ora si podemos dar guerra.*"

They were ready to go to war. They had weapons and ammunition. They even had some money. They had always possessed the *ganas.*

Balo's men began whooping and hollering and jumping up and down with joy. Balo told them to line up and each get a Mauser, a box ammunition and a bandoleer. After each one of them was fully armed, he instructed them to get a second serving of each so that they could carry them to Cleto's, men who were already across the river. Balo knew the men would have no use for money for a while, but he gave each five American dollars to lift their spirits. He kept the rest for supplies and other things his Army would need as their campaign progressed.

After all the armament was secured, Balo led his men to the river. It had started raining hard again. The river was overflowing its banks and the *corriente* was quite menacing. They were all seasoned *vaqueros* and had crossed cattle over rushing water, but this situation was worse than any of them had encountered before. Adding to the challenge was the fact that they were loaded down with rifles and ammunition. They slowly began to nudge their horses into the river, and the horses swam with great strength against the currents. One by one they started to make it across. As they were almost all safely on the other side, a straggler lost control of his horse and fell off. The currents quickly carried him off, and it was hopeless to try to rescue him. He rapidly disappeared into the depths of the raging river. He would be recorded as the first casualty of war, Balo told his men, and his widow would be compensated when the victory was achieved.

Balo's assessment proved right. No one saw them cross the river in the rain. The company marched freely into San Benito several hours after crossing the river. They made their way to Zaragoza Serrata's house, where they were to meet up with Cleto and his men. The two militia leaders and Serrata, an old friend of Cleto's and a supporter of the movement, had planned a simple ruse to cover up why so many Mexicans were gathered in one place. They pretended that it was Serrata's birthday and he had invited all his *compadres* to the *fiesta*. Anytime a deputy or Ranger came by to take a look at what was going on, someone grabbed him, patted him heartily on the back and brought him to the yard and offered him a beer and some *carnitas*. In this manner they were able to hide from the authorities the planning that was going on inside the house.

Balo and Cleto were huddled in the kitchen going over strategy for their next move. Serrata came in and out. He had to keep up the sham of his birthday by going out to the courtyard to see visitors as they were hauled in. Balo told Cleto about his meeting with Nefarrate and von Mueller. Cleto simply shook his head in amazement as Balo told him about the cache of arms and the cash the German had provided. He also advised Cleto of Nefarrate's reminder to be on the watch out for other German sympathizers of the cause. Cleto assured him that he would instruct his men about this matter.

"We have to strike at the *rinches* first," Balo said, suddenly shifting the focus and tone of the conversation. His excitement over their new supplies to make war gave way to the seriousness of the realization of actually going to war.

"We must kill the *víboras* in order to cut off their venom," Balo went on. "That is the only way for an orchard to grow. You get rid of the weeds so that the good plants can flourish."

Balo clearly remembered his father's advice back in Linares, when, as a young man, Balo would help him in the *huertas*. Removing the bad weeds gave the fruit plants the ability to get the full nourishment of all the nutrients from the air, water, and soil, his father would tell him. "The same is true with people," his father would add. "The good people must live free of the bad, or the bad will harm or spoil the good."

After some more discussion, it was settled that they would hit the *rinches*' camp located at the outskirts of San Benito and they would do it before daylight. Everyone was anxious to strike the first blow and launch the revolution in earnest. This would settle their nerves somewhat. Cleto and his men already had seen some action but it was unintended. It had not been planned as a battle, and it was not against troops. What they did not know—and were not very confident of—was whether the fight could be sustained over time to its desired conclusion.

Cleto had received correspondence from Florencio García, who was organizing the Laredo district. He had indicated that recruits had been sent to Eagle Pass, San Antonio, and as far west as El Paso. Things would soon be on the move, Garcia had said. Balo wondered if they had the weapons and ammunition they needed. Even his group, which had received a generous allotment from the German, was not armed for a long campaign. Still, they must strike the first blow, and it must be good enough to stun their enemy.

At half past two in the morning, the last of the neighbors who had come over to celebrate Serrata's birthday had left. Cleto and Balo ordered his men to get some sleep. Little did the troops know that they would be awakened in a short three hours to engage in battle.

Balo and Cleto had planned their first attack well. They were confident of success. The selected target was a small Rangers camp at the outskirts of town. It would not require a long ride. They would make their way at night so the cool temperature would minimize the effect the night's merriment had on their men. The mud from the recent rains would help muffle their approach. They would attack at sunrise, with the sun at their backs and blinding to the enemy. The enemy would be asleep or still sleepy and would be at a disadvantage.

With the first cock's crow, the attacking party was already approaching the *rinches'* camp. Balo could see a lone guard sitting on a chair leaning against the wall of the camp house, half asleep. The rumble of 50 horses, even with the muddy ground, created enough of a noise to awaken the guard. He nearly fell off his chair as he saw the men rush into the front gate, past the mesquite fence. He fumbled for his rifle and yelled out a warning. As he did so, he was sent back with a fusillade of fire from Balo, Cleto and several others at the front of the oncoming army. In tribute to his *tío* Romulo, Balo rode his horse inside the house. The rest of the party encircled the house, alternating positions, with one man facing the house to pick off any *rinches* who tried to come out, and the next facing away from the house to face off and challenge any who came to the *rinches'* assistance.

Balo only found one *rinche* inside, trying to put on his trousers. He shot him before he had a chance to look up and see what had hit him. He was thrown back by Mauser fire and was dead as he landed on the bed.

The entire attack was over in minutes. They had expected more *rinches* at the camp, but the rest of the *rinche* contingent had been sent off to the river to patrol after they had received news that a well-armed *bandido* had been found floating in the river near Brownsville. Balo had his men take the dead *rinches*' weapons and any other weapons and ammunition they could find. Cleto had some of his men go to the *corral* and round up all the *rinches*' horses. They then rode off toward the west, where they would pick a good place to cross over the river back into México and plan their next attack.

Balo could not help but think that this first attack had been too easy. They had picked a weak target. He knew only too well that the killing of two *rinches* would both scare and infuriate the *gringos*, and they would be ready for them the next time. He also knew the *gringos*' pattern well. After an attack of this kind, they would take it out on any Mexican they would come across. Many innocent people would die because of this attack. Many innocent people had died already, giving rise to the attack, Balo reasoned, as he rode off with a heavy heart thinking of the blameless who would perish in the days to come.

Chapter 11

Major Arthur Woods walked briskly into the mess hall at Fort Brown and headed toward Hoffman's table. Hoffman stood and saluted, although he was in civilian clothes. Woods returned the salute, and the two men shook hands.

Hoffman had taken the St. Louis, Brownsville & Mexico Railroad from Robstown to Brownsville, after his stay in San Diego. He had wanted to get a first hand exposure to the activities in the Rio Grande Valley.

"Major, I'm Captain Matthew Hoffman from Fort Sam Houston," he said. "I am here on a special assignment for President Wilson to assess the situation regarding the Plan of San Diego and an insurrection of our citizens of Mexican extraction."

"Well, Captain, you are on a wild goose chase," Woods replied.

"How so?" Hoffman asked.

Woods went on to explain that it was his view that all the activity of a violent nature was a result of prejudice and banditry.

"The white settlers of this section are not like you and I who grew up with a different outlook," Woods said to Hoffman.

"How do you know where I grew up?" Hoffman asked curiously.

"From the sounds of your accent, I'd say you hail from the east," Woods said. "I'm from western Pennsylvania myself. After a few months down here you learn to appreciate a Yankee accent."

Woods briefed Hoffman on the white men who lived in the area. He told Hoffman they were cut from a different breed. They had come from the old Confederate states and from Europe, and some Yankees could also be found in the mix. What set them apart was that they were all speculators, adventurers, and fortune seekers; men who were just this side of the line from crooks, schemers, and thieves.

"They came to this place that had been settled and tamed by a hard breed of Mexican, and by hook or crook took their land," Woods told Hoffman. "It is no wonder, then, that the Mexicans reacted with violence."

Woods related to Hoffman how those responsible for the attacks that were commonplace in the area were descendants of these wronged Mexicans trying to set things right. Some unscrupulous Mexicans, like opportunists everywhere, had taken the opening that this environment created and used it to exercise some plain and simple banditry.

"They steal cattle, horses — whatever they can get their hands on," Woods went on. "They take them up North and sell them to other corrupt white folks who ask no questions. Then they do a little rustling in that area and return here to sell stolen stock to the same fellows they stole from in the first place."

"From time to time," Woods continued, "a deal goes sour and some stockmen want retribution, so they call in some special Ranger known for his brutality and they arrest some suspected rustlers. Before a trial is held, the rustlers supposedly try to escape and end up being shot or are caught by some unknown vigilante group and are strung up."

"It's all pretty nasty business," Woods said with a grimace, "but there is no humane way to wrest the land from the United States. It's all simple hatred acting itself out."

"What about the attack last night on the Ranger camp?" Hoffman asked.

Woods was surprised Hoffman had already gotten wind of that. But then again, it was all the talk in Brownsville. The entire countryside was up in arms and in a panic over the brazen murder of the venerable Rangers.

"You heard about that, have you?" Woods commented. "Well, that is all part of the quid pro quo. The Rangers, as I said, have a reputation of executing Mexicans, guilty or otherwise."

"I understand," Hoffman said, "but from what I was

told, this incident had the looks of some type of military operation."

"Oh, I don't know about that. We'll just have to wait and see," Woods said. "What we can certainly expect to come next will not be military."

"What is that?" Hoffman asked.

"The perpetrators are long gone, probably in Mexico, but you can be sure that some innocent, unsuspecting Mexicans will be rounded up and summarily executed without trial or witnesses."

Hoffman felt heavy-hearted at what Woods had told him. It did not sound at all like the America he had grown up in. Though Woods may be correct about the nature and source of the troubles, there were still some concerns Hoffman felt needed his attention. Perhaps the Plan of San Diego was not the issue, but the crossing of the border by those committing crimes in the United States, whether criminally or patriotically inspired, was an international problem that Washington needed to address.

Woods informed Hoffman that he was taking a small party out to the country to get a look at the scene of the attack on the Rangers and to see what had been the response thus far. He asked Hoffman if he would care to go along. Hoffman's answer was quick and in the affirmative. He just needed to change into some riding clothes. The two men agreed to meet in front of the officers' quarters in 30 minutes.

Hoffman caught up with Woods, who was waiting with a detachment of 10 men and a gray horse ready to be mounted. Woods gave a signal and the troop headed out the fort that hugged the Rio Grande across from the Mexican city of Matamoros. They went into Brownsville and headed north toward San Benito, which was an almost 20-mile ride away. As they rode through town they could see groups of men at street corners or outside mercantile stores animatedly discussing the latest episode in South Texas life. As common as violence was in this place, no one could really get used to it. Every occasion gave rise to cries for the government to send in more Rangers or more troops. As the cavalry unit rode by, people would turn and yell encouragement, but some were not so warm.

"Hey, Woods," a man coming out of a saloon yelled as the detachment slowed to allow a wagon to pass from an oncoming street, "can your boys handle it or do we need to get a couple of more Rangers down here to do your job?"

Woods simply ignored the comment and rode on. It surely grated him, Hoffman thought, for someone to suggest to him that a bunch of yahoos could do a better job than his trained and disciplined men. Men like the one who yelled at Woods were merely cowards who would run at the first of sign of trouble. His kind had been shooting off their mouths instead of their guns for years. When the real shooting started, it was not only their feet that ran. Woods was right to ignore him; there was no time to waste on his type.

After riding through town, the troop came upon some very wet resacas north of town. The resacas were usually dry but the recent rains had turned them into swamps. The men and horses got plenty wet as they muddled their way through these inland bayous of reed and other semi-tropical plants that had been flooded beyond their normal levels. As they came out of this area, with muddy hooves and wet trousers, the Army unit was blessed to see the sun appear. The clouds suddenly gave way to a burst of rays that warmed both men and beasts. They soon dried out and hopefully would avoid sickness. Indeed, by the time they reached San Benito they were dry.

As they pulled up to the Ranger camp, they saw only a few men mulling around. Woods asked, from atop his horse, who was in charge. Woods had been in Brownsville only a couple of weeks and still did not know the local constabulary. A scraggly-looking, unshaven man of about 40 came up to meet them.

"I'm Captain McWhorter of the Texas Rangers," the man said as he looked up at Woods and then spat a wad of tobacco on the ground.

"I'm Major Woods, commander at Fort Brown," Woods said as he dismounted. "Can you tell me what happened here, Mr. McWhorter?" Woods refused to address these vigilantes by the rank they professed.

The term "mister" even seemed stretching it to Woods. It seemed like everyone in this part of the country, even civilians, popped off some kind of military status. General so and so, Colonel what's his name, Captain me too. They had come by these formal titles from the Mexican War, Confederate service, or time with the Rangers. Some may have earned the honor, Woods thought, but for the most part they lifted it from their own imagination.

"Well, best as we can tell," the Ranger said, "a couple, maybe four, Meskins sneaked in here in the middle of the night while our guards were asleep and shot them where they lay."

"They were not much for guards if they were sleeping," Woods said with a hint of sarcasm.

"Well, they wus some of our older men," McWhorter said. "They've earned a little rest. That's why we left them behind while we went out searching for some bandits we heard had come in from Mexico the day before. Not much guarding being done on that border, either, I suppose."

Woods felt the stinger the Ranger sent his way. There was a constant argument between the state and federal officials over the watch on the border. The state felt it was an international border and the responsibility of the troops. Washington held back the troops for fear of creating and international incident when the real problem was local bandits.

"This un here," the Ranger said, pointing to one of two bodies laid out on the porch uncovered, "was shot inside while he was getting dressed. His name is Bob Boyd, an old-timer from up in the Nueces River country. He was a Ranger near 40 years but was getting on in age."

"How do you know the perpetrators were Mexicans?" Woods asked.

"Well, no white man would be so cowardly as to attack old men while they were asleep," McWhorter said. "They were Meskins all right."

Woods, irritated with the Ranger, mounted his horse.

Hoffman, meanwhile, had been scouting the camp and had easily noticed a furrow around the camp house that was caused by much more than four men on horseback. The trail leaving the camp westward also indicated a large number of horses involved. Hoffman thought about pointing this out but decided to let Woods handle the situation.

"Hope you catch those who did this, Mr. McWhorter. We are going to follow this trail to see where it leads us," Woods said as he motioned his horse to the tracks that Hoffman had observed.

"Oh, we already found them and strung them up," McWhorter said with a wide grin, as he spit out tobacco.

Hoffman could not believe these words. How could they have hanged any human being without a fair trial? They were officers of the law. They should know better.

As they rode toward the small town of Mercedes with the sun now burning their backs, Hoffman was oblivious to his surroundings, as he thought back to that morning's conversation and how elements of the unbelievable things he had heard about were unfolding so quickly.

***

Upon his arrival at Brownsville, an old friend of his father's met him. Frank Berlin's family had come to America together with the Hoffman family. Hoffman's dad and Berlin had grown up together in Cumberland, but Berlin's family had struck out to Texas as the young boy approached the age of maturity. They had landed on the Texas port of Indianola and continued on in a wagon train to New Braunfels and then to Fredericksburg, just west of San Antonio, where a German community had sprung up. The trip instilled in the young Berlin an adventurous spirit, and when he was old enough, he left home to find his own way in this new world. He had gone to San Antonio, old San Patricio, Corpus Christi, and eventually settled in Brownsville.

His father's friend knew this area well, Hoffman thought, and he would be a valuable resource. More important, he was someone Hoffman could trust. Berlin only had one nagging habit, that of reverting to German when he met someone who spoke the language. Like the Hoffmans in Maryland, most German settlers in Central Texas had been opposed to slavery and were Union supporters. The bitterness of the war led them to refuse to speak English, and they continued to conduct their business in German until the turn of the century. Although Berlin knew English well, he still carried a heavy German accent even these many years later.

"Gutenmorgen," Berlin said to Hoffman on their meeting. "Geben Sie mir Nachricht von Ihrer Familie."

Hoffman responded in kind and tried in the best German he could muster to tell Berlin that his family was fine. Hoffman had grown up speaking German, but through his years away from home, he rarely used it and had begun to lose proficiency. Berlin sensed Hoffman's discomfort with speaking German and broke into English.

"So, how do you find our valley?" Berlin asked Hoffman.

"It is a very lovely place from what I have seen," Hoffman said. "I only arrived yesterday, so I have not had an opportunity to see much, with the exception of Brownsville and what I glanced at from the train as we came in."

The two men continued with small talk. Berlin told Hoffman he had invited a couple of friends who could also be helpful in his mission. As he said that, two men walked up to their table at the The Texas Hotel on St. Charles and 9th Street. Berlin and Hoffman rose, and Berlin introduced Hoffman to Jeff Powell and Lawrence Mound. Powell was an attorney and Mound was a land speculator in the Mercedes section.

"Frank tells us you are doing some sort of investigation for Wilson regarding the Plan of San Diego,"

Powell said after the men had sat down and ordered their breakfast.

"What utter nonsense," Mound interjected. "The Mexicans wouldn't know how to recognize an insurrection if it bit them, much less organize one and create a new country."

"Even so," Berlin added, "there has been a lot more troubles since Reyna was apprehended, and worse even after he escaped. Look at what happened last night at San Benito."

All three locals had heard the news of the raid on the Ranger camp, and they filled Hoffman in on what they had heard. Mound remained the most skeptical and critical.

"They are just crazy bandits," Mound said. "What they are doing is scaring off a lot of good people wanting to come settle in this area."

"Perhaps they see that as a way to keep all these good settlers away from their good land," Berlin said to Mound with a smile.

"They weren't able to keep you away," Powell gently shot back. "The truth is that in the ebb and flow of civilization, peoples often come into conflict over land, and the strong always manage to prevail."

"How did you gentlemen come into your lands?" Hoffman asked.

"Old Powell here," Berlin said, "got his lands in payment for legal work he did for the original Mexican families who owned the land. He got the area around San Benito from the Fernandez heirs, who had received the Conception Grant from México. And I bought my land from Mr. Powell."

"I bought my land from a colleague of Mr. Powell who also did legal work for some Mexicans," Mound interjected.

"Some Mexican citizens feel that we stole their land," Powell said, "but they simply do not understand our legal system. They get behind on taxes, and the land is sold at the courthouse steps. They borrow money against the land and then cannot pay the money back and end up losing the land to the lien holder.

"They have large families and often get involved in complicated fights among the heirs over the ownership of the estate. Men like me step in to untangle the problem and naturally we charge for our services and all the Mexicans have of value for payment of my fees is their land," Powell concluded.

"I can see how someone could get sufficiently upset if they lost their inheritance, what they see as their birthright," Hoffman said.

***

Woods barked out orders for the troop to halt as they approached Mercedes. There, hanging on a telegraph wire post by the railroad before one entered the city, were the lifeless bodies of four men—two on each side of the center post. Several onlookers were milling around.

The men were drinking liquor and yelling obscenities at Mexicans in general. Children would throw rocks at the corpses while women sat on wagons casually observing the scene.

Hoffman's first reaction was a strong urge to puke. Other men in the unit were not able to hold back the urge and openly vomited. These were young men from the east whose innocence and decorum were molded by a more genteel lifestyle than the residents of South Texas, who seemed oblivious to the horror in front of them.

The major ordered his men to dismount, and he moved ahead to question the onlookers about what had taken place. Hoffman followed a sergeant who had signaled to him. The two men approached a group of Mexicans off to a side. Among them were mostly women and children. Most were openly crying. The sergeant, who had been stationed at Fort Brown and other Texas installations, had picked up the ability to speak some broken Spanish. He knew enough to understand what was said to him.

"*Buenos días*," the Sergeant said to the group. "My name is Sergeant Smith. I am with the United States Army at Fort Brown. This is Captain Hoffman."

The Mexicans only stared back without a response. Some exhibited faces of anger and disdain; others were simply scared. Smith explained that they were only trying to find out what had really happened.

"You want to know what happened?" an angry boy who was about 13 screamed. "The *rinches* killed my father and his friends for no reason! They did nothing wrong. They just went to a friend's *rancho* near San Benito to celebrate the birth of his first son."

The boy went on to tell Smith that the men had drunk *mescal* through the night, and when day was about to break they had started for home. The women and children had followed an hour later in a wagon. They had come upon the scene just after the *rinches* had strung them up. The *rinches* were firing their pistols into the hanging men as the other *gringos* who had gathered were cheering them on.

The Sergeant thanked the boy for the information and offered his condolences. As Smith and Hoffman rejoined the other soldiers, the major also returned to the squad. Smith reported to his superior what he had learned from the Mexican boy.

"This is unbelievable," Woods muttered. "This is nothing but a lynching. Those bodies reeked of liquor. They probably were so drunk they could not stand straight much less carry out a raid with the speed and execution we saw in San Benito."

Woods momentarily placed his hand on his horse and leaned into it in total dejection. He then ordered his men to remount and move south to circle back to Fort Brown. They rode on in silence for quite a while. As they approached the Rio Grande, they could see

several men on a ridge firing their Winchester across
the river. Woods rode ahead and stopped with a man
who was on horseback smoking a cigarette and holding
on to several horses.

"What is your name?" Major Woods angrily demanded
of the man.

"I'm Deputy Sheriff Smithwick," the man replied.
"And who are you?"

"My name is Major Arthur Woods, commander at
Fort Brown, and I order you to tell your men to seize
and desist their firing across an international border."

"They're just doing their duty," the deputy responded.
"We were following some Mexicans that had been involved
in the shooting of the Ranger camp and they ran across
the river."

"And just how do you know that they had been involved
in the San Benito incident?" Woods asked. "A group of
Rangers hanged four men just outside of Mercedes that
they claim were the perpetrators of the raid at the camp."

"Well, I'll be," the deputy said as he fanned himself
with his hat.

"What you should be doing is investigating that incident, for it was no more than a lynching," Woods said.
"Those men hanged were not given their due process
and were so drunk they would have been incapable of
the killings they were accused of. What that lynching
will do and what your shooting here will do is create
only more killings on both sides."

With that, Woods swirled his horse around and headed back to his men. The commander gave the order to proceed back to the fort. He was visibly furious at what he had seen over the past half day. Twilight was beginning to set in, and Woods did not want his men out in the dark. There was nothing they could do now. From the horse tracks they had been able to follow, the raiders were long gone across the border. There was not much he could do to control the vigilantes, since they were being led by sanctioned authority in the form of Texas Rangers and local deputies.

As the troop rode through the Brownsville commercial district toward the Rio Grande where Fort Brown stood, the town's activity was subdued, as it was past the dinner hour and people were getting ready to go to bed. They rode through town and approached the old fort that stood almost desolate by the edge of town. A few trees dotted the large expansive campgrounds. The fort faced the river, overlooking the Mexican city of Matamoros. It was, Hoffman thought, an appropriate symbol of the situation he had encountered since arriving in the valley, a strong and domineering and yet uncaring country on the watch for its poor, powerless neighbor.

It had been a long day and he had seen and learned much about his assignment, but he was left hollow. Hoffman simply wanted to go to bed and get some sleep. Perhaps in the morning he would see things in a new light.

Chapter 12

Cleto and Balo split into two groups as they returned to the American side. Their battle plan called for launching a series of attacks at both ends of the lower Valley to keep the *rinches* and the Army off balance.

Cleto was to lead assaults in Cameron County in the eastern section, where his family had owned land. He not only knew the land well, he also knew its people. He could draw reinforcements and cover from friends throughout the region. He also knew which *gringos* "deserved" the wrath he and his men would inflict.

Balo would lead his men in forays into Hidalgo County, in the western part of the Valley. It was in Hidalgo that he had been caught after a man he had been told would be receptive to the *Plan de San Diego* had betrayed him.

The country was alien to Balo, but the people were the same anywhere in South Texas. The *Mexicanos* were dirt poor and in a state of peonage. Balo knew he could find kindred spirits in such a population. The *gringos*, well, they were *gringos*; that was all Balo needed to know about them.

As they separated at the river, Cleto's men took the movement's flag with them. The standard bore the inscription *Igualdad y Independencia* in white letters over a red background. Balo grimaced, as he thought of the irony the flag evoked in him at that moment — the white *gringo* standing in a field of red Mexican blood.

The two insurgent leaders had planned to keep in touch on a daily basis, as much as possible. Each would send a courier to the other with news of their battles, casualties, enemy strength and movements, and any need for reinforcements of men and ammunition.

As Cleto and his men made their way north and east, they did not encounter any resistance. The troop numbered no more than 20 men. As they reached the outskirts of Raymondville, a *gringo* farmer surprised them. Cleto wasted no time in shooting the unarmed man as he stood by an irrigation ditch. Cleto rode up to where the man lay and spat on him.

"The only good *gringo*, *muchachos*, is a dead *gringo*," Cleto told his men, who broke out in laughter.

The next day, Cleto and his men rode into Lyford and robbed a store, killing the owner and taking ammunition and food. They continued their rampage, taking five prisoners near Harlingen, three *gringos* and two Mexican workers. After taking their money, Cleto had his men take the *gringos* into the brush and execute them. One *gringo* was spared when one of Cleto's men recognized the man as having helped him after a skirmish with

Villa forces attacking Matamoros. Cleto also ordered the buildings they owned be burned.

Cleto and his men rested at a ranch of a friend for a couple of days before resuming their strikes against the *gringos*. They left in search of a store where they could replenish their food and supplies. They found one in the new town of Moseville and proceeded to rob and burn it. As they left, in the early morning hours, they encountered the owner and his son rushing to the burning structure. Cleto personally shot both men and made sure they were dead by riddling their bodies with bullets.

It was not until the next evening, and a week after beginning their assaults, that Cleto and his men met up with any resistance. As they galloped away from a burning cotton gin they had set on fire, they were surprised to run into a patrol of regular Army troops from Fort Brown. A bullet that was stopped by a heavy leather pouch he carried under his shirt stunned Cleto. He pulled the pouch out to see if the bullet had penetrated his chest, and as he did so, the pouch flew out of his hand. The pouch contained letters to and from sympathizers to the cause, but Cleto could do nothing about it getting into the Army's hands. He and his men were making a quick turnaround to try to get away from a greater force coming after them. As they rode away at full gallop, Cleto saw the man carrying the movement's banner cut down, and the banner went with him.

That too had to stay behind in the rush to escape the approaching onslaught.

As if that were not enough, the Army had the backing of one of their newest weapons—an airplane. Cleto and his men were too preoccupied with their getaway to take much notice, but they did manage to get a few shots at the contraption. Cleto and his men managed to dodge into some thick overgrowth outside of Los Fresnos to successfully outrun the Army. After the dust cleared, Cleto counted his blessings with only his flag bearer killed and three other men wounded.

Cleto was enraged to have lost the incriminating papers contained in the pouch as well as the banner. He pledged revenge, and yelled at his men that they must exact payback. He told them they would rest for the night but they had a score to settle the next day.

Before dawn, Cleto and his men set out toward San Benito and soon came upon two men working on a railroad trestle. The men's rifles were off to a side of the bridge. Cleto directed two of his men to lasso the *gringos* and then two other rebels set fire to the bridge. As the bridge went up in flames, the two workers were dragged off over the railroad tracks, causing parts of their face and body flesh to tear off as they cried out in pain before they collapsed. Their bodies were left on the tracks so they could be run over by the next train.

During the 10 days of fighting, Cleto grew wilder with anger. They stopped at Agua Negra, a *Mexicano*'s ranch, and demanded that the ranch owner provide them with fresh horses and money. The rancher refused, so Cleto then summarily shot him where he stood.

"*Mexicanos* are either with us or against us," Cleto told his men. "If they are not with us, they are with the *gringos*, and they will meet the same fate."

The raiders took some money from the man's house and all the horses in his *corral*. Cleto gave orders to head toward the river. They needed to cross into México to recuperate and regroup. As the remaining 10 men approached the river, they came upon a small detachment of soldiers from Fort Brown. Cleto did not want to engage in another costly battle, so he directed his men to hide in the brush until it was clear for them to cross. One soldier strayed from the rest the American Army company to relieve himself. As he did, the rest of his company rode off unaware that he was still in the brush. Seeing an opening, Cleto ordered his men to make a furious rush over the river, and as they did, they grabbed the errant soldier and carried him off with them. They were across the river before the rest of the soldiers realized what had happened.

Once in México, Cleto ordered his men to make an example of the soldier so his comrades would learn a lesson. He commanded that the soldier's head, ears and fingers be severed and his dead body be tossed into the river so it could make its way downstream to Fort Brown.

Balo, meanwhile, had chosen different targets. Unlike Cleto, Balo did not like to assail civilians. That tactic, he often told Cleto, was no better than what the *gringos* did to innocent *Mexicanos*. Cleto, however, was driven more by a deep-rooted personal hatred of the *gringo* than by thoughts of a new country with liberty for all *Mexicanos*.

As his first target, Balo had chosen to blow up a water pump plant near Mercedes. He knew that the plant would be well guarded because of its importance to the area's economy. As Balo and his company, which had grown to 50, approached the plant, a contingent of Army regulars met them. In the ensuing battle, which lasted several hours, Balo lost two men and cut down at least two of the enemy, including the Army captain in charge. The pump station, however, had escaped ruin.

Balo and his men achieved success two nights later, when they burned three railroad bridges, cutting off rail service to that section of the country. They had not been challenged, and no casualties were recorded. The next day, they surprised an Army cavalry patrol west of Mercedes and killed one soldier, making their getaway without a loss.

Balo's luck changed for the worse the next day, when after attacking and killing one soldier and wounding another at the Saenz Store in Progreso, his men were confronted by a squad of infantry, which quickly opened fire on them. As the battle raged between Balo's men and the infantry, Army reinforcements arrived and the

Americans got the upper hand. Balo ordered his men to retreat, and they made a run for it, heading west. The Americans had sustained several casualties, and rather than pursue the raiders, stayed behind to tend to their wounded. Balo's company also sustained casualties: five dead and five wounded.

After resting in the brush country of northern Starr and southern Jim Hogg counties, Balo decided to return to action. He told his men that they would make a couple more assaults and then return to México. Balo wanted to make these last two attacks worthwhile. He sent several men into Mission to scout the town to see what they could learn about the Army troop locations and movements. He also instructed his men to let the word out in town that bandits were planning a raid on Mission itself.

Once Balo was ready to attack, he set his plan in motion by sending four men to the *banco de madera* at the edge of town to set the lumber yard on fire. Thanks to rags soaked with kerosene, the lumber in the buildings was soon a raging inferno. The town marshal fired his pistol to alert the community of the fire. Everyone misunderstood the shots as the signal that the bandits were attacking and quickly took their stations, awaiting an assault. They soon realized that the bandits were not coming but that the lumberyard was on fire and was threatening other nearby businesses. The entire community rushed to the fight the fire.

While the townsmen were preoccupied with the fire, Balo and his men rode to Ojo de Agua, eight miles to the southwest of Mission, and attacked U.S. soldiers camped at that place. Balo had his men shoot the telegraph operator first to keep him from calling for help. They then launched a full-fledged attack on the remaining 15 soldiers, most of whom were asleep at the start of the shooting. The soldiers responded quickly enough to hold off their attackers. A pitched battle ensued, lasting more than an hour. Balo counted at least three soldiers killed and a number wounded. As Balo and his men were getting the upper hand, Army reinforcements began to arrive from Mission and from Peñitas, to the west. Realizing that they would soon be outnumbered, Balo gave the order to flee toward the Río Grande, which was a mile away.

Balo and most of his men managed to make it across the river, taking with them a prisoner they captured at the soldiers' camp. Six of the raiders, however, were left behind with mortal wounds. Another six suffered less severe wounds and managed to cross over to México and get medical treatment at Reynosa. While resting in Reynosa, Balo learned that the *gringos* placed the men he had left behind on the battlefield on a pile of wood, drenched with gasoline and set them on fire. The macabre scene quickly became a curiosity for residents in the area. For some residents, it was too much to stomach. They returned to their homes and began packing. The exodus of both *Mexicanos* and *gringos* who had given up hope that peace would ever again come was emptying the Río Grande Valley.

Upon hearing what happened to their comrades, men under Balo's command took the American prisoner and beheaded him. They stuck the head on a pole and raised it high so that soldiers and *rinches* on the other side of the river could see.

This was done without Balo's knowledge, but once he found out, he could not blame his men for answering one act of barbarism with another. Still, Balo felt sick to his stomach at the open display of savagery. In the ensuing days, he would learn of many such acts, starting with the action of Cleto's men only a few miles downstream.

While he and his men recharged in Reynosa, Balo sent agents to the other side of the river to see what the mood was after four weeks of constant battles throughout the Valley. Balo was stunned with what he learned. Innocent *Mexicanos* were being killed at will. Vultures could be seen throughout the chaparral, as they feasted on dead bodies left by vigilantes. Eight men were reported killed in the San Benito area after Cleto had dragged the two railroad workers. The *rinches* and local deputies killed 14 more "suspects" in the Harlingen area, including a woman who was asleep in bed. Two of her children were also wounded. In Pharr, deputies had taken a waiter, a store clerk, and a *Mexicano* grocer out to the wooded area outside of town and shot them full of holes. Residents of

Donna one night heard four automobiles pass through town, and later shots rang out in the night. The automobiles returned through town. At daybreak, the residents found 11 *Mexicanos* dead in a nearby cornfield.

Balo had also received reports from his followers in the Valley that besides the many noncombatants the *rinches* had hanged or shot, many other *Mexicanos* were being arrested without cause. The *rinches* were on a rampage trying to atone for the death of their comrades. The number of dead innocent *Mexicanos*, men and women, was incalculable. No one was keeping count. No one cared; they were only *Mexicanos*.

Chapter 13

It had been three weeks since their last battle, and Balo was still exhausted—more emotionally than physically. The death of so many innocent people weighed heavily on his heart and his mind. He was in no mood to go back into battle, so it was welcome news to Balo when General Nefarrate sent word for the men to stay put for a while because the *Americano* army was patrolling extensively along the border.

In the meantime, Balo received word from his brother, Manuel, informing him that their father would be in San Diego and needed to talk with Balo about an important matter having to do with the *movimiento*. Balo knew his father had never taken an interest in the *movimiento*. In fact, he had always derided Balo for such foolishness, but Manuel was different. Aside from Balo, few people knew that it was Manuel who had helped draft the original language to the *Plan de San Diego*. It was because Manuel urged him to go that Balo had decided to make the trip to San Diego. The lull in the fighting presented him with the opportunity to travel. Besides, he missed his mother's loving embrace and her caring voice. Not to mention her delicious cooking. He also missed his younger sister, Monica, whom he delighted engaging with in philosophical conversations. Monica was not like most girls. She had studied and read extensively and could hold up her end of any conversation, no matter the topic.

The previous weeks at a *rancho* outside Reynosa, Balo and his men tended to their horses, cleaned their Mausers, practiced shooting, and played and drank to excess. As he prepared for the trip, he watched the men compete in *coleando* with the few steers at the ranch. Though Spain's tradition of the bullfights was celebrated in great *plazas*, the poor *vaqueros* made their own entertainment in the *corrals* where they worked. Many of these acts of entertainment would include the various elements of a *rodeo*. The *coleando* involved chasing a steer on horseback, grabbing it by the tail, and flipping it over. It was not as dangerous as facing a bull on foot, but it provided excitement. Occasionally, it proved fatal. Balo smiled as he recalled one of his father's stories about the *coleador* who was trampled by a steer and killed. His friends were hesitant to tell his wife of his demise. Finally, they chose a *menso*, or dim-witted man, to take the message to the new *viuda*.

"Are you the *viuda* García," the *menso* asked the lady who answered the door.

"No, I am the *señora* García, but I am not a *viuda*," the woman said. "My husband is at the *coleando*."

"Well that is why I'm here, *viuda*" the man said. "Your husband was just now killed by the steer, so you are now a *viuda*."

Balo's father would laugh hard and loud at this story. Balo did not think it particularly humorous, but it was one of the few fond memories he had of his father.

Balo mounted his horse and bid farewell to his comrades in arms. He told them he would return in a *quincena* to resume the fight. The fortnight would be long, Balo thought, but he needed to take care of family business. Manuel's plea sounded important. Balo rode off to the west to Reynosa where he stayed with a friend.

Whenever Balo traveled to San Diego, he used the same ruse to get by an especially mean-spirited immigration inspector at the checkpoint near Kingsville. Balo was *huero* with *ojos borrados*, or hazel eyes. He would always wear a suit when he traveled north on the train. His attire, coupled with his fair complexion, allowed him to pass off as an Anglo businessman or salesman. He topped off the ruse by covering his face with the *Brownsville Herald* and pretended to be asleep when they approached the checkpoint. Thus far he had never been questioned, much less caught.

That night he secured a suit and tie from a tailor who had a shop near his friend's house. Ordinarily, he kept a change of clothes at his friend's home, but since he had some cash on hand from the German, he felt the urge to buy a new set of clothing. It had been awhile since he had done that. He missed the nice clothes that his father had always provided and insisted they wear.

"Clothes define a gentleman," his father would say. Balo always thought that was somewhat shallow, but he still liked the feel and smell of a new suit.

Though he could sew you a suit from raw materials, the tailor also carried a good selection of pre-tailored suits. Balo did not have time to be measured, so he picked a black suit made of cheviot for $5. It was not a Kuppenheimer, but it was a nice fit for the price. He also purchased a new pair of shoes for $1 and a hat for $3.50.

Later in the evening, Balo made his way to the river, rode downstream and crossed over in a *lancha* in the dark of night. He made his way to San Juan, and from there he went to Harlingen on the back of a horse-drawn wagon. In Harlingen, Balo spent the night on a bench outside the train depot. In the morning, he bought his copy of the *Herald* and boarded the St. Louis, Brownsville, and Mexico Railway train heading north to Robstown. He looked around; few of his fellow travelers were *Mexicanos*. He saw two *gringos* take a seat opposite him and quickly thought about moving, but then it occurred to him that it would be good to be sitting among the white passengers; it would add to his subterfuge.

"Good morning. My name is Matthew Hoffman and this is Mr. Berlin," one of the men said to Balo, who merely nodded politely with a slight smirk and pretended to read the newspaper.

Berlin began talking to Hoffman in German. Balo was familiar with the language. There were several wealthy German families in San Diego who were active in the Catholic Church. The priest often said part of the Mass in German for their benefit. Father Bard was French, but he also spoke Spanish and German. Since arriving in San Diego, he had picked up English as well. In addition to the Germans, San Diego had a sprinkling of English, Scots, Irish, and a few French expatriates who had immigrated to Texas after Maximilian's failed conquest of Mexico. But San Diego was mostly inhabited by *Mexicanos*, most of whom had lived in the area since before the arrival of the boorish *Americanos*.

Listening to the two men in front of him speak a foreign language he did not understand reminded Balo of the many times he had heard *gringos* say to some poor Mexican, "Speak English, you are in America." They never stopped to think that the *Mexicanos* thought the same, and would whisper to themselves, "*aquí se habla español.*" They both surely experienced what he was feeling at the moment; he did not understand a thing the Germans were saying and was sure they were talking about him.

As the train approached Kingsville, it began to slow down. Balo knew this was his cue to begin his act. He stretched out his legs and slumped down on his seat. He yawned and covered his face with the *Herald*. When the train came to a hissing stop, a few passengers got off. An inspector with the Immigration Service came on board. It was his usual routine to inspect the train for *Mexicanos* that may be trying to get into the country illegally. On this occasion, one of Mifflin King's *rinches* from the King Ranch accompanied the inspector. They went into the car where Balo pretended to sleep.

"Where are you men from?" the inspector asked.

"I am Captain Hoffman on leave from Fort Sam Houston, and my friend is Mr. Berlin, a merchant from Brownsville."

"Who is this fellow," the ranger asked, pointing at Balo.

"I do not know the gentleman," Hoffman said. "He got on in Harlingen. He has been indulged in his newspaper and has kept to himself the entire trip."

"Must be a salesman," the inspector said. "I believe I have seen him on this route before."

The two officers moved on to the next car, where they hassled an old *Mexicano* traveling with his grandchildren. They embarrassed the old man in front of the children to teach the youngsters a lesson, Balo thought. The train began its slow acceleration and was back on its way. Soon it began to slow down again as it quickly reached its next stop in Robstown. At the announcement of "Robstown, next stop Robstown" by the porter, Balo rustled himself out of his slouched position. He stretched his arms over his head and sat up, going through all the motions of a man who had just awakened.

At Robstown, Hoffman and Balo would board the westbound Tex-Mex, as the railway was commonly known, headed for San Diego. Berlin would get on the eastbound train to Corpus Christi. Hoffman and Berlin bid each other farewell, and Hoffman went off looking for a restaurant to get a bite to eat before the train for San Diego arrived. They had been on the tracks all morning and he was hungry.

With the help of a local, Hoffman found a restaurant down the street from the train depot. As he entered, he saw Balo at a table ordering. He thought about joining him, but believed it would be impolite since he had not been asked. He sat at the next table.

"Did you take a good, restful nap?" Hoffman asked Balo as the waiter pulled away.

"*Yo no hablo ingles*," Balo responded.

Hoffman was taken aback. He, like the immigration inspector, had taken him for an Anglo.

Balo did speak English, but, like the Germans of Fredericksburg, had refused to use the language of "brutes".

The two men ate their respective servings in silence and then returned to the depot to board the train to San Diego. It was not a long ride, but both men continued to observe their silence and they both actually took a short nap. As the train pulled into San Diego, Balo first saw the Martinez gin that had been a bustle of activity during the town's cotton growing era that had mostly passed. After the cotton gin he saw the freight depot that also had seen better days. During the sheep-raising period, it had thrived as a shipping point for tons of wool. Finally, they pulled up to the passenger depot and Balo saw Manuel waiting for him in the small crowd milling around.

As the two brothers exchanged an *abrazo*, Manuel noticed Hoffman looking at them with an incredulous gaze. Manuel knew instantly that the "investigator" had figured out who he was embracing. Manuel knew from their first encounter that Hoffman was a clever man. He also sensed that he was a fair and compassionate man and hoped that he would not turn Balo into the authorities. Manuel gave Hoffman a simple facial acknowledgement and turned with his brother to leave the station. As they walked away, Manuel turned again to see if Hoffman was still there. Indeed, Hoffman continued to stare at the two as the brothers walked away. Noticing that Manuel was looking back, Hoffman stole away his stare and started his march to the Martinet.

Balo noticed his brother's concern over the man in the train and asked Manuel if he knew the man.

"Yes. He arrived here several weeks ago claiming to be an emissary of the American president on a special mission," Manuel responded as he continued to glance over his shoulder. "My suspicion is that he is looking into the affairs of our revolution."

"He was in the train when I got on at Harlingen," Balo

said. "He was with a German until Robstown where they split up. He spoke to me in Robstown."

"What did you tell him," Manuel asked.

"That I did not speak his language," Balo responded. "I did not wish to speak with a *gringo*."

"Why do you think he is looking into our business," Balo asked Manuel.

"It's just a hunch," Manuel said. "I met him when he first arrived and we struck up a conversation. He seemed quite friendly and open, unlike the *gringo* ruffians of this area."

Manuel went on to relay to Balo about the night he and Hoffman had gone to the *baile* and how they had met again the following day in the church. Balo was not pleased to learn that a *gringo* had been invited to their house for lunch and said so to Manuel.

"*Cálmate, hermano,*" Manuel said to his brother. "Remember the wise *dicho* of our grandfather. 'You can catch more flies with honey than with vinegar'."

"There is no more honey in me when it comes to *gringos*," Balo told Manuel. "Their actions and conduct have soured me to their kind more than the strongest vinegar."

Manuel then told Balo about Hoffman's request for permission to call on Monica.

"And our mother said no, of course," Balo said in the form of a command.

"She left it up to father," Manuel said. "That is why, ostensibly, he came up from Linares."

"He is not really contemplating approval," Balo asked, knowing that with his father, anything was possible. His father had a blind spot where it came to *gringos*. He thought they were very successful in business, ranching, and trade. They had to be *inteligente* for them to achieve their kind of success. He would not buy into Balo's argument that what the *gringos* had, they got through means of deceit, thievery, and murder.

"The old man has something else up his sleeve," Manuel said. "He has not confided everything with me, but he met with his old friend Venustiano, and the first chief asked him to come up and meet with the president's man."

"And I thought he had come up to see me," Balo said with a tone of sarcasm.

"Stop complaining," Manuel told him firmly. "You are all he has been talking about. You should have seen his reaction when we told him you had escaped from jail. He nearly wrestled *mamá* to the ground. He hugged her tight and twirled her around."

"I would have loved to have seen that," said Balo with a loud laugh. "I can already see *mamá* tapping him on the arm and whispering to him, 'Servando, the children'!"

"Oh, yes. You know her well," Manuel responded with a laugh.

The two brothers walked quietly over the Victoria Street bridge. They had become reflexive. Balo was taking in the sights of his old stomping grounds. It was not really his home, but he had spent so much time in San Diego he felt like it was home. He knew every street and hiding place and many of its people, especially the older residents. He felt a special warmness every time he returned to San Diego. It had its terrifying memories, but it also held much love and friendship.

Manuel's thoughts were on Hoffman. Manuel needed to confirm what Hoffman's full mission was, and more importantly, Manuel needed to appease the disquietude Hoffman exhibited when he saw Manuel greet Balo at the train station. Manuel sensed, even more so after that encounter, that Hoffman was looking into the Plan's activities. From the look in Hoffman's face, he must already know of Balo's involvement and his relationship to them. Manuel felt strongly that Hoffman might have guessed correctly, after Balo and Manuel's embrace at the depot, that his traveling companion from the Valley was Balo. As they walked, Manuel decided on a plan. He would go see Hoffman later in the evening and explain that Balo was a cousin visiting from the Valley. He would also try to elicit from Hoffman his true mission.

As the two brothers walked off the bridge that crossed over the San Diego Creek, their sister, Monica, came out running from the back door of the house and ran through an open fence gate to greet them. She almost jumped on Balo as she gave him a strong embrace. Balo lifted her of her feet and twirled her around. They were overjoyed at seeing each other. They embraced for a while longer holding each other tightly.

"I suppose I'm considered no more than an old shoe?" Manuel said smiling as he looked at his siblings embrace.

"*Hay, hermanito,* you I see every day, but it's not everyday that I get to see such a fine specimen of a man," Monica teased Manuel as she caressed Balo on the cheeks.

They broke out into a laugh and continued through the backyard and into the old house.

As they walked into the back door of the kitchen, their parents were sitting at the table with coffee cups and a plate full of *pan dulce* in front of them. They had the *merienda* ready for his arrival.

Balo's mother got up first and gave him a quick and strong embrace and then stood back to look him over from head to feet.

"It is me, *mamácita,*" Balo said to her.

"I just want to make sure you are still in one piece," his mother responded as her eyes welled up with tears.

"*No llores, mamá,*" Balo said as he grabbed his mother into his arms. "I am all right; nothing will happen to me."

"Nothing would happen to you if you stayed here with your mother and take care of her and your sister like your brother," the voice came from behind Balo's mother from his father.

"I can take care of them fine, *papá.* Balo has important work to do," Manuel responded.

The mother stepped aside to allow her husband and estranged son to face each other. They both stood, staring at each other. The stares were not of acrimony, but of what seemed as a suspended joy at seeing each other after so much time had passed and so many things had happened.

Finally, the two stepped forward and embraced.

"It's good to see you, my son," *señor* Reyna said softly as they held the embrace for a while.

"It is good to see you, too, *papá*," Balo said as the emotion finally got to him, and he became teary-eyed. He was a man, and it was said that *machos* did not cry, but his tears were of an overpowering joy, not of pain or fear.

As *señor* Reyna released his son and turned around with his left arm still around Balo's shoulder, father and son saw mother and daughter holding each other at the waist with tears running down their cheeks.

"*Vamos*, let's have our *merienda*," *señor* Reyna said in a loud voice, in an attempt to gain his manly command over the family.

They all sat around the family table and had some delicious *pan dulce* from one of the local *panaderías*. They dunked their *molletes* in the coffee and sampled a little of all the other pieces. There were *empanadas de calabaza*; *cuernos*, a crescent-shaped bread covered with sugar; *marranitos*, a molasses-based bread cut in the shape of a pig; and *semita de anise*, an unleavened bread flavored with aniseed. The bread was the uniting part of the ritual of the *merienda*, a mid-afternoon snack, but the underpinning of such a gathering was an opportunity for family, and sometimes neighbors, to come together and talk about their day. On occasions such as this, when someone had been absent for some time, it gave the family an opportunity to catch up with their lives.

After they ate, Genoveva and Monica gathered the saucers and plates, and the men went out to the yard to continue their talk. Balo and his father walked toward the *arroyo* in the rear of their house, and Manuel slipped off and started walking over across the bridge toward town. He decided to let his father speak alone to Balo while he went to seek Hoffman. He had some talking to do of his own and needed to do it before it got late and things got out of hand.

Señor Reyna lit a cigarette as he walked alone with Balo. They found a large rock protruding from the ground, inviting them to sit, and they did.

"*Hijo*," *señor* Reyna said to Balo, "your mother pretends to be strong, but she has suffered a lot with your jailing. She is in constant fear for your safety. She cries herself to sleep most nights."

"I know," Balo said, with his head down ashamed of the pain he was causing his mother.

Chapter 14

Manuel had left his father and brother alone and sneaked away in search of Hoffman. It was a small town, and finding a newcomer was not hard. Hoffman was having supper at the restaurant near the Martinet Hotel. He was alone as Manuel approached him.

"Good evening, friend," Manuel said.

Hoffman looked up and appeared surprised to see Manuel standing in front of him. Hoffman finished chewing his food and then stuttered out a greeting.

"May I join you?" Manuel asked.

"Please," Hoffman said as he motioned his hand to the chair across from him.

"I saw you come in on the train when I met my cousin Alberto," Manuel told Hoffman in hopes of allaying his obvious suspicions.

Manuel had entertained the idea of confessing to Hoffman who the man on the train really was, but he decided against it. Hoffman, was not only a stranger, but a *gringo*. Manuel was not sure how far he could trust him.

"Your cousin," Hoffman noted, in disbelief. "For a moment I thought he was your brother, Baldomero."

Manuel was truly taken aback by Hoffman's revelation. Not only that he knew, but that he would reveal his knowledge in such a casual manner. On the other hand, Hoffman's method certainly had an affect on him, Manuel thought.

"You know my brother, Balo?" Manuel asked, trying to remain nonchalant.

"I know about him," Hoffman said. "I have not actually had the pleasure of making his acquaintance."

"Well, to be honest, I have yet to know of a *gringo* who has expressed pleasure at meeting Balo," Manuel said with a wide grin.

"Tell me," Manuel said, "how and what do you know about Balo?"

Hoffman sat back, pushing away his still full plate of enchiladas and beans. He proceeded to tell Manuel about his travels of the past two weeks. He told Manuel that he had known about Balo all along. He had been briefed in Washington about everyone known, at that time, to be involved in the Plan of San Diego. It was the Plan that he was investigating for the president, Hoffman told Manuel. Balo, having been apprehended with a copy of the Plan, was naturally a part of his briefing, Hoffman said.

"What I did not know, and could not have known, was that he was a member of your family," Hoffman said, without a trace of his deception. "I learned that the day after I was a guest at your home."

Hoffman had known of the relation all along and had it confirmed the first night he was in town when Manuel introduced himself to him. Still, he did not want to let on to Manuel that he knew while he was a guest at his home. He told Manuel that he had made a courtesy call to the Duval County sheriff before heading to the Rio Grande Valley, and it was from him that he had learned that Balo's family was living in San Diego.

"I'm glad to hear that," Manuel told Hoffman. "It would have been disappointing if you had taken advantage of my family's hospitality to spy on us."

"Oh, no," Hoffman exclaimed. "I would not have done that. I am not a spy. My assignment is not a secret. The more people I tell about what I am investigating, the more information I am able to gather, more quickly."

Hoffman appeared to be sincerely contrite when he apologized to Manuel for any appearance that he may have given to the Reyna family that suggested he was spying on them. He told Manuel he had been very happy to meet such fine folks upon arriving in a place where he was a stranger.

Hoffman went on to tell Manuel all he had seen and heard in the two weeks since they had last talked. He told him about the raid on the Ranger camp and his experiences on the trail afterward. Hoffman's voice broke when he told Manuel of finding four Mexicans hanged without as much as an examining trial.

"I have learned there is a lot of hate between the Anglos, as your people call the non-Spanish speaking citizens, and the Mexicans, as they call the Spanish-speaking citizens," Hoffman said.

Hoffman, who suffered acute paranoia about his Teutonic blood and heritage, had been surprised at how all white men who were not Mexican were called Anglos, be they German, French, Slav, Irish, Swede, or whatever.

"As you point out, many of the so-called *Mexicanos* are citizens as well," Manuel said. "But setting them aside and distinguishing them as foreigners is only a symptom of the greater problem.

"This hate you speak of did not just fall from the sky with a spring rain," Manuel continued. "It has been blowing in the wind for many years. Every few years or so, the winds of resentment grow to a tornado of hate spinning out of control and destroying lives as it rumbles across the land."

Manuel began to relay to Hoffman the history of hate, as he and his *Mexicano* brothers knew it.

"It all started with your country's aspirations of 'manifest destiny'," Manuel told Hoffman. "It was the American people's destiny to settle the land from the Atlantic to the Pacific oceans. No matter that other people were already claiming most of the land in the West. That is what brought Stephen Austin, Sam

Houston, and the rabble from Tennessee. They stole *Tejas* from México."

"But Austin was a settler who complied with Mexican law," Hoffman said. "Many of your own people joined in the struggle against Santa Anna."

"Their hope was for the Constitution of 1824 to live and be obeyed," Manuel responded. "They did not fight for a new *gringo* republic, which was no more than a pretense for annexation to the United States."

What happened next, Manuel said, was more directly tied to the current troubles that he was investigating.

"This land, with cactus and mesquite thorns and brush so thick you cannot walk through it, was settled over 100 years ago by our people," Manuel told Hoffman.

Manuel went on to tell the Yankee of his own great-grandfather, who had received a grant from King Carlos VII of Spain for five sitios of land in southern Duval County. His great-grandfather, Don Alfredo Cadena Molina, had been a captain in his majesty's frontier guard under Col. José de Escandón when they had moved families and clergy to northern New Spain to settle the lands of Nuevo Santander. Later, Don Alfredo had been one of the founders of Agualeguas. In his old age, the king rewarded Don Alfredo with land in an area no one wanted to settle. As a young soldier under Blas María de la Garza Falcón, captain of Camargo, Don Alfredo had made forays into this forsaken area and found little to attract settlers.

"The old timers called this section '*El Desierto Muerto*,' or the desert of death," Manuel went on. "The area was infested with bobcats, coyotes, rattlesnakes, tarantulas, and, worst of all, the Coahuiltec and the savage Carancahua Indians.

"Into this unwelcome environment," Manuel continued, "my great-grandfather and many of his *compadres* brought their families. They surveyed the land, paid their subscriptions to the royal treasury, and received titles to the land and the right to eke out a living as best they could. They usually found a spot near water, a running *arroyo* or a *tinaja* fed by an underground spring. They cleared the area and built their *ranchos*. The main house on the ranch was customarily built of *sillares*, a large block quarried from caliche pits in the area. The home always had *troneras* from where the ranchers could fight off the Indian attacks. Small thatched huts near the *casa mayor* lodged shepherds, *vaqueros*, and other ranch hands. A fence made of mesquite and huisache branches encircled the homes. A *corral* and *canoga* for the animals was near the houses.

"Many enterprising souls dared to venture into this wasteland to make an inheritance for their children. Before long, *ranchos* dotted the entire countryside between the Nueces River and the Río Bravo. *Ranchos* with names such as San Diego, Amargosa, Concepción, Los Indios, Randado, Agua Poquita, San Leandro, and many others. The Spanish-speaking, Catholic-worshiping population grew gradually. They raised cattle, sheep, goats, pigs, and chickens. They planted corn, *calabaza*, beans, sugar cane, and other staples needed to subsist for long periods.

"The families visited each other in the *ranchos* during special occasions such as birthdays, weddings, and religious feast days. From time to time, a *padre* made a visit to the *ranchos*, but for most of the time life in the brush country was desolate. The *rancheros'* only contact with outsiders was when ox-cart driven trains passed by on their way to trading locations up north to Goliad and later at Kinney's Rancho on Corpus Christi Bay. The road from Camargo to mission Espíritu Santo at Goliad traversed through many of the *ranchos*. Later, a road was opened from Laredo to Corpus Christi, and another from Corpus Christi to Eagle Pass.

"When the *gringos* initiated the war against México in 1835, things changed for the worst," Manuel told Hoffman. "The *ranchos* had been thriving with growing herds of sheep and cattle. The trade in hides and tallow was brisk. But, when the war began, General Santa Anna sent orders to the *rancheros* that every Mexican was needed to fight off the *gringo* land grab."

Manuel explained that many *rancheros* naturally felt duty-bound to respond to the call from their country's leaders. Some acted out of national pride, and others were more practical and feared losing their land—land that they had toiled hard to get in order to pass on to their children. If the *gringo* won the war, they would surely take the land. If the *gringos* lost, the Mexican generals would take the land from those they viewed as traitors for not joining the fight or for taking the side of the *gringos*.

The *rancheros* had no choice, Manuel explained. Most fought under Santa Anna's command. Others abandoned their claims temporarily and returned to the communities along the south side of the Río Bravo. After the cessation of hostilities, word came that it would be treason to stay in the land north of the Bravo. Many more *ranchos* were deserted.

"This allowed the bandit element among your people to come into the area and plunder," Manuel told Hoffman. "They came to the abandoned *ranchos* and took what they wanted. But what they wanted most was the land itself, and they took that especially, if they could."

Manuel told Hoffman of the Mexicans' age-old grievances against the American system of injustice. How the *gringo* land speculators used the American laws, judges, sheriffs, and the hated *rinches* to steal thousands of leagues, totaling millions of acres.

"The *gringo* officials would charge that we did not pay our taxes," Manuel said. "Between our efforts to simply stay alive, fighting the elements, the Indians, the bandits among our own people, and the *gringo* outlaws, it was hard for many to hold on to their records.

"Add to this the poor record-keeping and outright fraud of the *gringo* tax collectors, and it was no wonder that the claim could often be made to stick," Manuel said, as his usually composed demeanor began to break.

"Those of our ancestors who had the required documents were made to prove their land titles in court," Manuel continued. "They had to hire *gringo* lawyers who, by the time the case was finally won, ran up legal bills that people could not pay except with land itself.

"The people who managed to get through the legal morass usually ended up ruined financially and had no means of working their land. They borrowed from Anglo-controlled banks, and more often than not, ended up losing the land to *gringo* creditors. Others who managed to make a living from the land would often run afoul with unscrupulous local sheriffs or the *rinches*.

"They would trump up some charge of stolen horses and make the landowner a bandit," Manuel said, anger increasing in his voice.

"How else could these dirty greasers get wealth, if not by illegal means?" Manuel mocked. "That is how they killed two of my *tíos*. They charged them with horse theft and executed them in their jail cell without a trial and then strung them up in the *plaza* for all to see.

"And that is why my brother Balo fights with such anger and passion," Manuel added as he sat back, his body seeming to let go of the emotion that had engulfed it as he told his story.

Hoffman sat numbed by the history lesson he had just heard.

"I guess we don't learn about that in our history books," Hoffman finally said after sitting in silence for a few moments.

"That is because it is not your history. It is our history," Manuel responded. "We settled this section. We tamed it. We cultivated it. We brought culture and civilization here. You merely stole it. And that, my friend, you will not find in your history books, either," Manuel added. "It will not be found in your newspapers, your songs, or your folk tales. History, after all, does not record what happened. It only records what we did to glorify our existence."

"And what does history omit about your people that fails to glorify the Mexican story?" Hoffman asked.

"I see I'm not dealing here with an uneducated, ignorant *gringo*," Manuel said with a smile.

Manuel was glad that his listener was bright enough to ask such a question that suggested Manuel was bright enough to have understood the reason for the question.

"Indeed, my people are not candidates for sainthood," Manuel said. "The greatest blot on our history is our treatment of the indigenous people of the Americas. Through the centuries, we wiped out the entire Aztec culture that was, in many ways, far more advanced than our own, and at the same time was far less brutal.

"Just as the *gringo* stole our land, we stole it from the Coahuiltec, Tejones, Carancahua and the many other tribes that were here even before us. We not only stole their land, we exterminated their languages and cultures and forced upon them an alien religion.

"But that is the story of mankind," Manuel said. "It repeats itself in every part of the world. It is interesting but not really helpful in your current assignment."

Manuel returned to his story of the antagonisms between Anglos and Mexicans in the South Texas frontier. He told Hoffman that Balo's war was not new to the region. Others had launched insurgencies in the past. Juan Nepomuceno Cortina had sustained a rebellion for years in the Río Grande region prior to the American Civil War. Don Catarino Garza had launched an insurrection in the brush country of South Texas some 25 years before the present conflict. Don Catarino had published a newspaper in Corpus Christi and had a firsthand acquaintance with the injustices committed against his people. He had experienced first hand Anglo bigotry and Anglo injustice.

Though historians and faraway politicians did not know the full history of this section, Manuel told Hoffman, the people who lived it certainly did. That is why men like Cortina, Garza and his own brother, Balo, were able to secure strong followings. They were only expressing outwardly and aggressively what the masses felt and yearned for.

"Striking back at injustice is deeply imbedded characteristic of all freedom-loving men," Manuel said to Hoffman. "That is why only as recently as a few years back, our people cheered and rallied behind Gregorio Cortez when he struck back and killed two *gringo* sheriffs who were unjustly implicating him in horse theft. As I have told you, that is an old tactic. It will not work in today's world, as men like Cortez and Balo have shown."

The days when thieves charged the innocent with bogus crimes to cover up their own misdeeds were over, Manuel told his listener. *Mexicanos* were no longer predisposed to accept injustice simply because it was administered by the *gringo* justice system. The *rinches*, the courts, the newspapers, the banks, even the Army, were all controlled by the *gringo*, Manuel went on, and they all have one purpose: to subjugate the Mexican and exculpate the *gringo*.

"But we still have a long way to go," Manuel continued. "Only three years ago, three *Mexicanos* were ambushed and killed by *gringos* in the public square of this very town and the perpetrators were set free by your courts.

"I'm sorry, my friend, for having gone so long about this," Manuel told Hoffman. "But I get very emotional when I think of the injustices my people have endured."

"Oh, no," Hoffman responded. "I needed to hear this. It explains a lot I could not make sense of."

"In any case, it has gotten late," Manuel said. "I ruined your supper, the least I can do is let you get a good night's sleep."

"To the contrary, my supper was very fulfilling, in more ways than you know," Hoffman said. "It is my sleep that I fear may suffer as I try to digest all I have learned."

"In any case," Manuel said again, "I wanted to give you some good news. My father is in town and would like to meet you to see what his decision will be regarding your interest in his *princesa*, Monica. Will you join us for lunch after Mass tomorrow?"

"I would be delighted to," Hoffman eagerly responded. He had thought about Monica often while he traveled in the Valley the past few weeks.

"Then my business here is done. Good night," Manuel said as he rose from the table and walked off.

Hoffman remained sitting at the table for quite a while. He had thought that the tiring trip on the train was going to allow him to get a good night's rest. Now, he could not sleep. He felt both exhilarated and saddened at what he had learned.

Chapter 15

Balo and his father were already seated at the breakfast table drinking *café prieto* when Manuel walked in. He had woken up later than usual after a restless night following his long conversation with Hoffman of the night before.

"*Buenos días, mamá*," Manuel said as he kissed his mother on the cheek while she stood over the stove preparing breakfast. "*Hola hermanita*," Manuel said to Monica as he poured himself a cup of coffee and joined his brother and father at the table.

"You were out late, *hermano*," Balo told Manuel, with a devilish smile. "Was she pretty?"

Manuel forced a smile at his brother's lame joke. Their father frowned at the mention of a man's possible indiscretion in front of the women.

"*Mas respeto para tu mamá y hermana*," *señor* Reyna snapped at Balo. As the elder in the family, it was his duty to enforce respect.

"It's OK, *papá*," Manuel said. "Actually, I met with the Army officer who wants to court Monica."

"What business do you have with that *pendejo*," Balo growled. "The gall of that *gringo* thinking of my sister is available for his pleasures."

"Be quiet, Balo," Monica snapped at her brother, as she helped her mother prepare breakfast. "I can take care of myself. I don't need you thinking and mouthing your *cochineras*."

"All right," *señor* Reyna interrupted. "I will take care of Mr. Hoffman, and I will take care of this family."

Señor Reyna turned to Manuel and asked what had transpired at his meeting with Hoffman. Manuel told his father his concerns over having seen Hoffman at the train depot when he had met Balo upon his arrival. Manuel explained that he had been worried that Hoffman might have made a connection between him and Balo and would report Balo to the authorities.

"How would he know you two were related, or even jump to the conclusion that the man you met at the train was Balo?" his father asked.

"Oh, but he does know and he indeed make the assumption," Manuel told his father. As Manuel continued with his explanation, he could see Balo growing more and more agitated.

"You forget, father, that he is an officer in the Army and an investigator," Manuel said.

They did not have to worry, Manuel told his father and brother, because he had told Hoffman that Balo was a cousin from the Valley.

"You do not have to deny your own brother to some *gringo* to protect me," Balo shouted in anger.

Manuel just shrugged off the comment and went on to tell his father about his meeting with Hoffman. Manuel told of how he had filled the *Americano's* head with the tragic history of the *Mexicano rancheros* losing the lands left to them by their fathers.

"I believe he understands better our struggle," Manuel said, turning to Balo.

"He is a *gringo*. He will never understand," Balo said. "He is the problem, and the only thing he understands is that eliminating us is the solution. We understand that game well, and we will eliminate them before long."

"That is enough talk about all this intrigue," *señora* Reyna interrupted. "We must get ready for Mass."

"I am dressed and ready, *mamácita*," Manuel said playfully to his mother, hugging her at the waist as she walked by his chair.

"You must get ready in your mind and in your heart, not just in your garments," *señora* Reyna said incisively, to no one in particular but to everyone.

After breakfast, they all walked across the *arroyo* to St. Francis de Paula. Even Balo made it to the service, although he had long ago made it known to his mother that a God that kept his people in misery was no God of his. Still, Balo loved his mother dearly and would do what he could to make her happy. He knew that in the past few months he had caused her much grief.

But, for Balo to be seen in church was risky. People in this town knew him well, and they also knew he was wanted by the law. Most worshipers, though, were his fellow *paisanos* and would not turn him in.

The Mass was short and to the point. The priest had little to say in his homily other than complain, as always, about the meager offerings of the congregation. Even his mother, Balo thought, could not have been spiritually enriched by the service. *Señora* Reyna remained in her pew after Mass to pray a rosary. It was her way to feel close to God and his divine mercy. "From one mother to another," was the way *señora* Reyna described her prayers to the Virgin Mary.

It was not yet noon, but the *cantina* next to the Martinet was already open and several men were drinking their bottles of Schlitz and Budweiser. *Señor* Reyna and Balo stepped in to refresh themselves and were greeted as heroes. Every man in the bar came over and shook Balo's hand and patted *señor* Reyna on the shoulders for siring such a man of the people.

"Drinks are on the house," Ismael, the bartender told the two men. "No one has brought this kind of pride to San Diego since your *tío* Rómulo chased the *rinche* out of town dressed like a *vieja*."

Everyone in the bar broke out in laughter and shouted *gritos* of "*Viva Balo*," "*Viva San Diego*," and "*Viva la Raza*."

Señor Reyna felt proud and at the same time was embarrassed by the display of affection for his son.

He did not see Balo as a hero. To *señor* Reyna, Balo was only his *rebelde* who was always getting himself into trouble.

Balo, on the other hand, was soaking in the adulation. He felt especially moved to be compared to his *tío* Rómulo by the people who had known him best. He was getting accustomed to the hero treatment and felt an obligation to live up to the reputation that was building around him.

"*Para la libertad y el respeto,*" Balo said as he raised his beer in brindis. "*Para nuestro destino.*"

After relishing a cold beer and warm hospitality, *señor* Reyna and Balo went on to the *panaderia*, where Balo was again given the hero treatment and was not allowed to pay for his *pan dulce*.

As father and son walked back home, *señor* Reyna could not help but feel a newfound respect for his Balo. Without giving it a second thought, *señor* Reyna began to discuss the war in México and in Texas with Balo as if he were talking with an equal. He had often done that with Manuel, but he was older and had for many years exhibited intelligence and maturity. Balo, up to now, had been a hot head.

Señor Reyna told Balo of his meeting with his old friend Venustiano, *El Primer Jefe*. He had asked Carranza to help gain Balo's release but that was no longer necessary.

"*El presidente* has helped us a lot in our struggle," Balo told his father. "He has lent us the support of General

Nefarrate and has even helped us secure money and arms from the Germans."

"Venustiano cannot be trusted, son," *señor* Reyna told Balo. "I know him well. I've known him since we were young. Don't get me wrong, he means well, but his concerns are with México and not with a bunch of *pochos* in Texas."

Carranza, he told Balo, had asked him to talk to the *gringo* officer interested in Monica. He wanted to work out a deal with the American president.

"What kind of deal?" Balo asked his father.

"If President Wilson recognizes the first chief as the legitimate government in México, he will put a stop to the raids in Texas," *señor* Reyna said matter of fact.

"But that is preposterous," Balo shot back. "He cannot turn against us just as we are beginning the war."

"Venustiano knows what you should know and accept," *señor* Reyna continued. "The Yankee Army is too strong and too well supplied to defeat. Carranza, Villa, Zapata, all three together, could not defeat the American war machine. What makes you think a few men, devoted as they may be to their cause, can even begin to make a difference?"

Señor Reyna told his son that he truly admired his courage and dedication to his cause. He respected him taking up for his mother's brothers and their people. But his people and his home, *señor* Reyna told him, were in México. And México was being torn asunder and left in ruins. Everything needed to be done to bring peace to México so that the family could return home and their *hacienda* could once again flourish.

"I cannot abandon my men," Balo said, more in resignation than in anger. "They believe in me. They believe in the cause I have promoted and rallied them to."

"And you should not abandon them," *señor* Reyna said, to Balo's surprise. "Continue your struggle until you realize and they realize that it is hopeless. And then do not risk another single life."

Señor Reyna told Balo he would know when the cause was lost in the battlefield. It would be foolish and cruel to wager the life of one single man more after they knew the struggle would not succeed.

"But, my son, not all battles end when the blood stops flowing and soldiers stop dying," *señor* Reyna told Balo. "The battle you have started will continue, for the cause is real and just, and it is deeply ingrained in the hearts and souls of the people you have inspired.

"They will carry on the fight. It may take years; it may take generations. But change will come to this part of the world, and despite your doubts at the moment, God will play a hand in the final outcome. Your mother may seem like a lamenting old woman, but she is right to rely on God, for he will see to it that the meek and the just will indeed inherit the earth."

"You may be right father, and mother may be right, but I still have too much anger in me to stop now," Balo told his father. "But I will stop, as you say, when I see it hopeless. I cannot send men to die if I do not believe there can be a victory."

"Sometimes to assure the victory, one must inflict pain and destruction," *señor* Reyna went on. "It is the only thing those who inflict pain and suffering understand. So, as I said, do not stop now. Do some more damage so that when you do stop, they will remember that the snake can be awakened again and the sting can be deadly. I assure you, they will think twice about changing their ways."

Señor Reyna put his arm around Balo as the two men approached the house.

"Let's see what this *gringo* wants, and, more importantly, what he can do for us," *señor* Reyna said.

"You will forgive me father if your *sobrino* does not stick around for this part of the game," Balo said to his father with a smile.

Manuel had waited for Hoffman and invited him to dine with them again. His father would be at home and Hoffman could ask for courting privileges, Manuel told him. Monica had waited for her mother and they followed at a distance from Manuel and Hoffman.

When *señor* Reyna and Balo arrived back at their home, Manuel and Hoffman were sitting outside on some stools underneath a large mesquite tree. The two men got up as *señor* Reyna and Balo approached. Balo glared at Hoffman and continued walking into the house without stopping to offer a greeting. *Señor* Reyna stopped in front of Manuel and Hoffman.

"*Papá*, this is Captain Hoffman," Manuel said in Spanish. *Señor* Reyna had made sure his three children had learned English, but he did not speak the language, although he understood much of what was spoken. Hoffman put his hand toward *señor* Reyna and expressed his pleasure in making his acquaintance.

"I am very grateful for you and your family's hospitality," Hoffman told *señor* Reyna as the older man took a stool to sit on. Manuel took on the role of interpreter.

"*Dile que si gusta una cerveza,*" *señor* Reyna told Manuel.

"*Si, gracias,*" Hoffman responded, in his limited Spanish.

Manuel went inside to fetch the beer as Hoffman and *señor* Reyna fidgeted in their stools trying their hand at small talk about the weather. While inside, Manuel exchanged words with Balo over his rudeness. Balo shot back that he did not have to play their game with the *gringo*.

"Go on outside to your father. I will talk to Balo," *señora* Reyna told Manuel.

"I must apologize about my cousin's impudence," Manuel told Hoffman as he handed him a beer. "He is from a remote village in México and is very awkward in his social graces, especially with foreigners."

Hoffman found it curious to be referred to as a foreigner in his country. He did not respond verbally, he only nodded his head in acknowledgment.

Señor Reyna wasted no time getting down to business. It was difficult, and useless after all, to engage in chitchat when neither one understood the other.

"I understand you wish permission to call on my daughter, Monica," *señor* Reyna said through Manuel.

Hoffman was somewhat surprised at *señor* Reyna's directness. He had thought a lot about this moment the night before and had reached the conclusion that it would be best to put off his request until his investigation was complete.

"Thank you for your candor, sir," using Manuel as his interpreter, Hoffman told *señor* Reyna. "But after some extended thinking on this matter, I have decided that perhaps it would be best if my interest in courting your daughter be postponed. As I am sure your son Manuel has informed you, I am in the middle of an investigation for President Wilson that, well, frankly, involves your other son, Baldomero."

Señor Reyna sat quietly and listened to the officer explain his predicament. He had to admire a man who would put off matters of the heart for the exigencies of business.

"Please understand," Hoffman went on, "that I am not conducting a criminal investigation. Baldomero's involvement in the alleged revolt is only secondary to learning the underlying reasons for the insurrection. Still, I am concerned that some may view any involvement with your daughter as somehow compromising to my work. I must not let anything color my mission on behalf of the president.

"Please know that I do indeed have a great deal of admiration for your daughter and your family as well, but I am an officer in the Army of the United States, and I must remain loyal to my oath of office."

Señor Reyna instructed Manuel to tell Hoffman that he understood him perfectly. It was admirable — *señor* Reyna told Manuel to translate to Hoffman — that he was able to separate his two interests. As a businessman, he appreciated a man who put business first.

"And as a father of a beautiful and attractive young daughter," *señor* Reyna said with a smile, "I appreciate even more that she would have someone as honorable interested in her."

"But," *señor* Reyna said, "that does not mean we cannot do business."

"What do you mean?" Hoffman asked.

Señor Reyna told Hoffman that he too was on a mission for his president. Perhaps the two of them could be helpful to each other, to their presidents, and to their countries.

"My old friend President Carranza wants you to take a message to your President Wilson," Carranza told Hoffman. "It is a very simple message. You see, Venustiano cannot help your president with his problems along the border if he is not recognized as the legitimate head of México. How can he exercise any authority over the use of México as a sanctuary by the raiding bandits if he has no authority to exercise?"

"That sounds somewhat like of a circular argument," Hoffman said. "What came first, the chicken or the egg?"

"Indeed," *señor* Reyna said with a loud laugh. He then turned quite serious.

"Well the truth is, México came first," *señor* Reyna said. "México and *Mexicanos* were in this country long before the *Americanos* ever heard of the longhorn cattle that once roamed these parts. It is not easy to tell your countrymen, much less a fervent son, that to fight for one's land is wrong.

"But, the first chief is not interested in fighting old battles. The Río Bravo is the border between our two countries. He is prepared to respect the sovereignty of the border if your country is prepared to accept his rule over México."

"The situation in Mexico is hardly settled," Hoffman said. "How does Mr. Carranza expect President Wilson to recognize him over Generals Villa and Zapata?"

"The situation in México is for *Mexicanos* to decide," *señor* Reyna said with raised voice, which Manuel tried to soften in his interpretation knowing his father would regret appearing disrespectful to his guest. "It is that air of intellectual and moral superiority on behalf of your president, in particular, and *Americanos*, in general, that have kept our two countries from moving forward from old grievances. We do not presume to tell your government how to run its affairs. Why does your government feel the need to tell us how to run our business?"

Señor Reyna did not wait for an answer to his rhetorical question. He rose from his stool and took a few steps down a slope to the *arroyo*. He turned and continued his conversation.

"The fact of the matter is, that neither the bandit Villa nor the poor excuse for a farmer Zapata can do anything about your problem here in Texas," *señor* Reyna went on. "If your government wants peace in Texas and the border, Carranza is the only man who can guarantee it. This is the message I would like you to take to Mr. Wilson."

"If the president agrees to recognize Carranza, what can the United States expect in return?" Hoffman asked.

"First, the raiders will be deprived of a sanctuary in México. Any zealot who engages in acts of war or banditry will be treated as an enemy of México and peaceful relations between our countries," *señor* Reyna told Hoffman. "They will be apprehended in México and extradited to the United States.

"Second, the Mexican government will take every step to stop the flow of arms and ammunition to the *revoltosos*. Illegal arms dealers will be dealt in the severest way by our government."

"One final thing," *señor* Reyna said. "Charges against my son Baldomero will be dropped by your government and he will be free to return to his home in Linares."

"Is that a request of Carranza?" Hoffman asked.

"That is a condition of mine," *señor* Reyna shot back. "Without that condition being met, I will insist that my good friend Carranza, not accept any overtures from Mr. Wilson. If the first chief does not honor our long-standing friendship, then I will provide my son and his followers the money and arms they need to continue to cause havoc to your fellow countrymen and your economy. I hope I make myself clear on that point."

"Very clear," Hoffman responded.

"Good," *señor* Reyna said. "Now that we have cleared up that, I want to be completely honest with you. The man inside that Manuel has told you is his cousin, is actually my son Balo. He is not here on any mission. He is here to visit his family at my invitation."

Manuel asked Hoffman forgiveness for deceiving him and said he had only wanted to protect his brother. He was sure Hoffman would have done the same under similar circumstances.

"I have encouraged Balo to seize operations against your people. He will do so when we get a positive response from your government," *señor* Reyna said.

Señor Reyna told Hoffman that as a man of honor he expected the captain to report to the authorities that Balo was in San Diego. He asked him, however, to put that off until the morning.

"Besides," *señor* Reyna said, "I have it on good authority that the sheriff takes the train to Corpus every Sunday.

He does not go there for church services, you understand. He has a young girlfriend of his liking."

Señor Reyna told Hoffman, the sheriff's deputies were all *Mexicanos* and they already knew Balo was in town.

"We had a beer with some of them in town before coming here," *señor* Reyna said.

Manuel always marveled at his father's tactics. He was a superb poker player. He instinctively knew what hand to play and to bluff when it was unlikely to be called. That is the way he was in business. It did not surprise Manuel to see him use the same tactics now. His father did not know whether the sheriff had a girlfriend or not but he knew the deputies knew Balo and would not make any effort to apprehend him.

Monica came out and informed her father that the meal was ready and the table was set. *Señor* Reyna told Manuel and Hoffman to join him as he rose and walked into the house. As they entered the house through the kitchen, they came face-to-face with Balo, who was making his way to the dining room.

"*Balo, saluda a nuestro invitado,*" *señor* Reyna instructed his son. He told Balo he had already told Hoffman who he really was.

"Captain Hoffman, this is my brother, Balo," Manuel made the formal introductions.

Hoffman extended his hand, and after a hesitation, Balo took it, all the while glaring at Hoffman, whom he viewed as the enemy. Neither man said a word.

When everyone was seated at the dinner table, *señor* Reyna asked Monica to say grace.

"Most Heavenly Father, we thank you for this meal that we have taken from your bounty," Monica prayed in Spanish, and then switched to English. "Thank you also, Lord, for bringing our family together and for keeping us all in good health. During this time of trouble throughout our lands, we pray, Lord, that you give us wisdom and understanding. Allow us, Lord, to be hospitable to our guest. We ask that he, too, may be blessed with wisdom and understanding. Amen."

"Thank you, Miss Reyna, for including me in your prayer. I do indeed need wisdom and understanding," Hoffman said to Monica. She merely nodded and proceeded to attend to her meal.

After a few moments of silence, punctuated by the clatter of silver utensils and china, Balo surprised them all, especially Hoffman, by addressing a question at the captain—in cogent English, no less.

"So, what have you found from your snooping around our country?" Balo asked, looking straight at Hoffman.

Before Hoffman answered, *señora* Reyna rebuffed Balo. Although she did not speak English she understood some and she knew Balo had been disrespectful.

"But, *mamá*," Monica mockingly interjected in Spanish, "then I will not be able to listen and learn from the learned men at the table."

"Nor will we be able to share the bright jewels of wisdom my little sister is known to inject to such conversations," Manuel teased Monica.

"*Basta*," *señor* Reyna told his children.

Señora Reyna steered the conversation to less touchy areas and asked Manuel to inquire of their guest about his family.

"My mother, the diplomat of the family," Manuel translated with editorial comment, "wishes to know of your family and upbringing."

"Well, *Señora*," Hoffman responded, "I come from a family very much like your family. I have a wonderful mother who, like you, is deeply religious and the bedrock of our home. My father, like your husband, is a stern but gentle man who sees as his main task in life to protect his family. And like Manuel, he is a printer and a newspaperman by trade. Alas, I have no brothers or sisters."

"Our ancestors came from Spain," Monica pointed out. "Where did your people come from?"

"My grandparents came to this country from Germany," Hoffman's said. To his own surprise, Hoffman was not troubled by the question that usually haunted him.

Balo's anger and apprehension toward Hoffman dissipated somewhat with the knowledge that he was a German, the same as his latest benefactors.

"There are some Hoffman families here in town. Perhaps they are your relatives," Manuel commented.

"No, I do not believe so," Hoffman said.

Señora Reyna seemed happy that the dinner conversation had wandered off the politics of the day. The rest of the meal was peppered with benign conversation. After the meal, the men went outside again to enjoy a beer and *señor* Reyna could light a cigar. *Señora* Reyna prohibited both inside her house.

"Well, *señor* Hoffman, perhaps now you can tell us what you have discovered in your investigation," Balo said, returning to his question at the dinner table.

"What I have found," Hoffman answered, "is not as simple as most people believe. No, it is quite complicated."

Hoffman explained that Gov. Ferguson was attributing all the trouble to Mexican revolutionaries. Others were telling President Wilson that the difficulties in Texas were the cause of bandits and outlaws.

"And what do you think is the source of the so-called troubles?" Balo asked Hoffman.

"I have seen and heard so much hate and discrimination that I am convinced the problem is a genuine desire of the Mexican population of Texas to enjoy the same rights and benefits we all enjoy as Americans," Hoffman told Balo.

Balo paused for a while. He was surprised by the answer. He had not expected a *gringo* to give him such a response. Hoffman was German, but he had still been raised in America and had surely been imbued with the *gringo* thought process.

"That is a strange observation for a *gringo* to make," Balo told Hoffman.

"Not all *gringos*, like not all Mexicans, are the same," Hoffman responded. "If you treat us all with the same contempt, you end up being no more than a Mexican *gringo* yourself."

Balo, who had been staring at a *liebre* near the *arroyo*, took his eye off the jackrabbit and turned abruptly toward Hoffman. He had never heard the term 'Mexican *gringo*' before, but he was sure he did not like it. He was unsure, however, how to react. Manuel broke Balo's confusion when he busted into laughter.

"No one has ever called my brother a *gringo*," Manuel said. "He has at times been confused for a *gringo* because of his light complexion and hazel eyes, but I can assure you Captain Hoffman, he is no *gringo*.

"He may have the passions for liberty and freedom of the American revolutionaries, but that passion has never and will never manifest itself in wanton and discriminatory killings," Manuel said.

Manuel's impassioned defense of his brother calmed Balo down. He had always been close to his older brother. Balo could always count on Manuel to come to his defense. Manuel had always been the sensible brother, but Balo knew that though Manuel was not a violent man, he could do battle with anyone in the arena of ideas.

"That is precisely what I meant," Hoffman said. "A defender of the rights of the downtrodden must conserve his passion, but must keep his actions in check. He must always strive to correct a wrong but must never become like the oppressor and perpetuate wrong against others."

"That is the ideal, but the ideal too often borders on the naive," Balo interrupted. "What the corrupter of power understands most clearly is power itself. The brutality of power calls for an equal response."

"I'm not unsympathetic to your concerns and point of view," Hoffman told Balo. "But the way to resolve them is to have them taken to those who can make a difference, like President Wilson. He is a caring man and would listen if I took him your message of hopelessness for your people.

"Your way, too many innocent people will get killed, especially your fellow countrymen. I have seen some of that already in the Valley."

"You try it your way, and I'll do it my way," Balo said.

"Perhaps a combination is the only way," Manuel said.

"Indeed, that is the way it will have to be," *señor* Reyna added. "It is time we all get some rest. It is getting late."

Hoffman said his good nights and returned alone to the Hotel Martinet. Balo gave his father and brother an *abrazo* and went inside. They all knew that before the rooster crowed in the morning, Balo would be gone.

Chapter 16

Balo had left his parents' temporary home before dawn and headed south. He traveled on foot, at first, over familiar trails until he reached the *rancho* called El Guajillo some six miles south of San Diego. The owners of Guajillo were old friends of his *tío* Rómulo and they gladly let Balo borrow a horse, which he would drop off at a mutual friend's *rancho* in Palito Blanco, which was on his way to the Norias Ranch south of Kingsville where he was to meet up with Cleto and his men.

After having breakfast and coffee at Guajillo, and regaling his friends with stories of "their" revolution, Balo headed out. He rode nine miles east southeast through Tienditas and on to Palito Blanco. He arrived a little after noon and found his friends at home for the *siesta*, a welcome respite from the midday sun. The *vaqueros* got up before dawn to take advantage of the coolness of the morning and worked hard before they sought shelter and relief from the heat. They would eat and rest, and often take a nap, until the sun relaxed its grip, and then they would return to the range to work another four to six hours. It was a long day with many hours of demanding work, so a midday *siesta* made perfect sense.

Balo pulled up to the main ranch house, and old *Don* Gustavo García came out, grinning from ear to ear. He was very happy to see his friend who had become so well-known in recent months.

"*Hola, mijo,*" the old man said as he held on to the mane of Balo's horse.

Don Gustavo called Balo "*mijo,*" a contraction of the words *mi* and *hijo*, or "my son." It was customary for older men to call young friends their sons. Young men often referred to each other as *hermanos*, or brothers. The range culture made family of all men. In Balo's case, the terms had taken on new meaning. Everyone in the *ranchos* wanted to be his father and brother.

"*Que tal, viejo,*" Balo responded with the endearing term of "old man." *Don* Gustavo invited Balo in for lunch. After lunch, Balo found a spot on the kitchen floor to take a nap. He rested a couple of hours and then asked his host if he could borrow a horse for the next leg of his trip. *Don* Gustavo quickly assented. Balo told the old man he was going to try to reach a friend's house on the Rancho Santa Gertrudis, 20 miles further southeast, in the middle of the night and would leave the horse there.

Santa Gertrudis was part of the large landholdings that Richard King had amassed through the years. His ranch hands referred to the various *ranchos* King owned as La Kineña, or the "land of king." The *vaqueros* on King's ranches had all come from a village in México close to *señor* Reyna's *hacienda*. Balo knew well some of the young *vaqueros*, having grown up with them in the *llanos* of northern México.

After five hours on the trail, Balo approached a *vaquero's* house lighted up with kerosene lamps. He called out as he neared so the owner, whom he knew, would not mistake him for an intruder. Balo told his friend that it was late and he did not want to bother his family. Balo asked if the owner would permit him to sleep just inside the entrance, so that he would be protected from the elements. The owner of the *jacal* told Balo that he could stay but needed to leave before sun-up, for word had been spreading that the *rinches* were looking for him.

Balo immediately thought of Hoffman, who must have reported him to the sheriff. "It does not matter," Balo thought. He soon would be joining his men. Before he left the Valley, he and Cleto had made plans to join up south of Kingsville and launch an attack on La Kineña itself at a ranch called Norias. But Balo was hungry and tired, so he put off thoughts of everything else and sat down on the dirt floor to have a late meal. *Don* Gustavo had put some *pan de campo* and *carne seca* in a *morral* for his trip.

Balo ate and then lay himself down. As he did, he felt a moist texture on the floor. He touched it with his hand

and brought up to his nose; he smelled chicken excrement. Balo got up quickly and left his guest's accommodations sooner than they both had expected. Balo made his way down the trail and found the railroad track that went to the Valley. He found shelter under a railroad bridge and got some badly needed sleep.

The rumble of a train passing above awoke Balo. It was still dark, the time just before dawn. Balo got up and stretched and wasted no time in continuing on his trek. He was still on schedule to meet Cleto and his men by mid afternoon. He had to walk the rest of the way.

***

As he started walking along the railroad tracks, Balo was taken back in his thoughts to when he was 13 and he had run away from home, following the railroad line from Linares to Monterrey. His paternal grandmother had lived with them in the *hacienda*. Balo always sensed that *mamá grande* had always favored his uncle Norberto's kids. From a very young age Balo had developed an innate aversion toward injustice. On several occasions he had challenged his grandmother's acts of favoritism until his father decided to send him to live with his maternal grandmother, who had moved to Linares to be close to her daughter Genoveva.

Huelita Simona was a kind old lady, but she had living with her a matronly daughter, *tía* Lucinda, who had grown bitter without a husband and children. She would take out her frustrations on Balo, who soon tired of his new situation. One day he decided he had enough and made up his mind to run way to San Diego to *tío* Rómulo's ranch. Balo had always loved going there. He was treated with respect and was given the responsibilities of a young man not of a child.

Balo knew that if he followed the railroad he would ultimately make it to San Diego. In the old days, the ox cart trails had made their way to San Diego through Camargo and Mier. The iron train went through Monterrey and the two Laredos.

After three days of walking on and along the tracks Balo reached Monterrey. He needed to rest up and nourish his body. He soon found a job as an apprentice at a *panadería*. The *panadero* gave him a spot to sleep in the back of the shop and generally welcomed him as part of his family. Balo stayed on longer than he had planned, until one day his father showed up at the *panaderia*. The kindly *panadero* had, over time, extracted enough information from the young boy to determine he was a runaway from an old family in the Linares area. He had gotten word to *señor* Reyna about his son's whereabouts.

Balo had returned home in silence as his father lectured him about what a foolish thing he had done. He told Balo that life was not perfect and one had to deal with the imperfections. Only cowards ran away from their problems, *señor* Reyna admonished him.

***

A cloud of dust from a company of some 50 men coming toward him shook Balo out of his daydream. They were still several miles away, but Balo believed it was Cleto and his men. They were in the right place at the right time. Still, Balo remembered one of the lessons taught to him by his *tío* Rómulo. The old man, wise to the ways of the brush country, would always tell Balo not to trust anything he could not see, hear, smell, or feel. No matter how well developed one's instincts were, they never took the place of what was certain.

Balo went behind some large *cenizo* and watched for the band of men and horses to get close enough for him to see them before he would allow for them to see him. Within minutes they came into full view, and Balo immediately recognized Cleto at the head of the small army. Balo stepped out from behind the bush and began waving his arms. Cleto raised his Mauser high in the air with his right hand and waved at Balo.

As the men reached Balo, Cleto pulled to a stop and jumped off his mount. He rushed to Balo and the two men embraced as brothers. The other men circled their two *jefes* and shouted "*viva Balo, viva la revolución.*"

Cleto ordered his men to dismount and rest. It was after the *siesta* hour and they had been riding hard since before dawn. Cleto pulled Balo aside and asked him about his trip.

"There is nothing like the love of family to renew your spirits," Balo told Cleto.

Balo also shared with Cleto his encounter with the *Americano* Army officer. He told Cleto about his father's advice about not sacrificing innocent men in a hopeless cause.

"Your father is a wise and good man," Cleto told Balo. "But our cause is not hopeless. We have plenty of arms and ammunition. Men are coming into our camps every day.

"The *gringos* cannot keep themselves from acting like animals. Every time they commit an atrocity against our people, we gain more followers and sympathizers."

Plus, Cleto told Balo, a lull in the fighting in México had developed, and many of Nefarrate's soldiers were joining the fight in *Tejas*. Balo looked at the men who came with Cleto and could see that about half wore uniform pieces of Carranza's forces.

"We should attack quickly," Cleto said, "so we can have enough time to reach the *río* in darkness and not be seen."

"I don't know," Balo said. "When I passed Norias, I sensed some commotion. It seemed as if they were on some kind of alert. We should send some scouts to reconnoiter the area."

Balo did not want to unduly concern Cleto by telling him of the warning he had received from the *vaquero* at his last rest stop. Besides, Balo always tried to live by *tío* Rómulo's advice. He preferred to know what he was going up against before engaging in a fight. The more he knew about his enemy, the better the results of the encounter would be.

When Balo walked past the Norias headquarters, a two-story wood frame house, he saw several men ride off to the south. The ranch's Mexican help that had stayed behind set about to secure animals and seal off the house by closing shutters and doors. As Balo watched the commotion, hidden in the brush on the other side of the railroad track, he got the feeling that they were preparing for an attack.

What Balo did not know was that Cleto and his men had been spotted riding north as they passed through the Yturria pasture. A telephone call had been placed to Brownsville authorities that in turn telegraphed a warning to the law officers in Kingsville and Corpus Christi. Maj. Henry Hutchins, the Texas adjutant general in charge of the Rangers, was in Harlingen at the time and quickly rounded up a posse of Rangers and local deputies and headed north. Richard Kleberg at the King Ranch was also notified, and he put together a force of his own private rangers. At Fort Brown, a unit of U.S. Army soldiers were put on board a special train and headed north in search of the bandits, as the Anglo population of Texas called the *revoltosos*.

As the sun began to set, Cleto ordered his men to mount. Balo mounted a horse Cleto had brought for him. Cleto insisted on a quick attack and told Balo he worried too much. The outfit galloped toward the Norias headquarters house. They rode under a red flag emblazoned with the words *"Libertad y Independencia."*

As they approached the ranch house, the soldiers who had arrived at the ranch hours before spotted them. Cleto noticed that men were taking up positions behind the railroad embankment and gave the order to commence firing.

Bullets began to fly some 250 yards from the ranch house. Balo yelled at his men to hold fire until they were closer. The return fire came quick and furious. The Army troops and Rangers had come well armed. A couple of Cleto's men were hit and fell off their horses. Balo and Cleto rushed the men behind the embankment, jumping over them with their horses. Balo shot a Ranger, who fell to the ground. Cleto shot a *kineño*, killing him instantly. Balo saw Cleto turn his horse around and head back, and he too pulled his horse around; as he did, Balo shot and cut down a soldier.

As Cleto and Balo rode away from the house, they saw that their men were in disarray. The *Mexicano* recruits, who had no stake in the cause of liberating *Tejas* for *Tejanos* who had long ago abandoned México, had run off. The local *Mexicanos* were simple ranch hands unaccustomed to the fierceness of the fighting they encountered. They had retreated into the brush at a safe distance.

Cleto and Balo reached their *vaqueros* and dismounted. Cleto began shouting at them to fight.

"*Cobardes*," Cleto screamed. "We fight for you and your liberty, why do you run away?"

The *vaqueros* were no longer moved by Cleto's words. They knew Cleto was fighting to reclaim his land. When it was all said and done, the life of the *vaqueros* and the other *pobres* would change little. The *patrones* would speak Spanish, but the poor would remain poor, no matter who owned the land.

Balo knew that the *vaqueros* were not cowards. They were trained, like his *tío* Rómulo, to face danger only after the elements were in their favor. Attacking a well-fortified target with no cover was not the odds they preferred.

"*Miren, muchachos,*" Balo said in a calm voice, "We need to put on a fight. We do not want it said that we ran with our tails between our legs like dogs."

Balo directed the men to dismount, tie their horses to a fence on the ranch house's perimeter, and follow him back to the house on foot. They moved to the enemy guerilla style, hiding behind bushes and doing whatever was necessary to gain an advantage. Within minutes, the firing resumed from a distance. As the men advanced closer to the enemy, they stumbled over bodies of their comrades. They found five of their own dead.

The fighting continued for two hours, but neither side gained an advantage. Fearing that the *gringos* would have called for more help, Balo passed the word to his men to return to their horses. Their ammunition was beginning to deplete.

"We are running out of bullets," Balo told Cleto. "And the *gringo* Army is probably sending in more troops. If we stay here, we will be trapped and killed."

"*Sí*," Cleto agreed. "Let's head back to the *río* to rest, reload, and reassess."

"*Vámonos, muchachos*," Balo gave the order to mount up and ride out.

They rode all night. At dawn, they crossed the *río*, 20 miles west of Brownsville. They were tired and appeared soundly beaten. Balo looked at his remaining troops and could not help to think back at what his father had said. The truth was that his ragtag army was no army at all. Despite the infusion of ammunition and some money, the powers they faced were simply too much for a small band of *vaqueros*.

Reality was swiftly sinking in, and Balo could not feel anything but despair and hopelessness. Men had died because he had filled their minds and hearts with hope. But their cause was hopeless.

Chapter 17

After Hoffman left the Reyna home at the end of his last visit he had been unable to sleep. His conversations with Manuel kept coming back to him, shedding light on the root of the problem of his investigation. *Señor* Reyna's offer to mediate with President Carranza also intruded his sleep. Whether to report Balo's whereabouts also nagged at Hoffman. He finally fell asleep when his thoughts turned to Monica.

Even though Hoffman had decided he could not at this time get too involved with Monica, he could not help but be entranced by her. He could remember every strand of black hair on her head; her soft tanned face; her beautiful lips; her perfectly shaped stature; her engaging conversation.

When Hoffman awoke the following morning, he still had dreamy images of Monica on his mind. He decided to do something about it. He would write her a letter expressing his feelings and explaining to her why at the present time he could not act on those feelings. After writing the letter, Hoffman left for the train depot. On the way, he stopped by the print shop where Manuel worked and gave him the letter to deliver to Monica. He also told Manuel that he was leaving for Washington and had not had time to visit with the sheriff before his train departed. Manuel smiled and waved Hoffman goodbye.

As Hoffman settled in for yet another long train ride, he unfolded the copy of the *Corpus Christi Caller & Daily Herald* he had picked up from a boy hawking newspapers at the train depot. Hoffman was flabbergasted by the headline:

Ropes and Guns Are Fast Ridding Border Country of Mexican Outlaw Bands

The article went on to say that at least a dozen "marauders" had been captured or hanged. There was no mention of courts, trials, or the law. Hoffman shook his head in exasperation. He could not comprehend how a civilized people justified killing by lawmen in the name of maintaining order. The justification may have rested with the Biblical admonition of "an eye for an eye." That, among many of the passages of the Old Testament, had always given Hoffman pause. He believed in a loving God to be worshipped, not a vengeful God to be feared.

Even under the Old Testament, an eye for an eye provided for some form of judicial procedure. In the case of the Rangers and some local deputies, who worshipped the Rangers more than God, they saw themselves as not the only law, but judge, jury, and executioner rolled into one. Hoffman saw no distinction between the so-called bandits and the Rangers. They were both thugs who had no appreciation for the law, much less for justice.

Hoffman decided that this newspaper would bolster the presentation he had planned to make to President Wilson. But the long train ride to Washington was only now rolling out of the South Texas bay city, and Hoffman did not want to have such heavy matters dominate his thoughts. He wanted to rest and be fresh for his meeting with the president.

Hoffman again turned his thoughts to Monica. Despite having forgone the opportunity to call on her, Hoffman could not get her out of his mind. He had never met a girl with her qualities. She had as much physical beauty as any girl he had ever known. What made her even more attractive was her ability to carry on an intelligent conversation about things that mattered. But perhaps most enticing was her inner beauty. Her conversations were not only lucid; they expressed thinking with feeling and passion almost with a spiritual zeal.

As Hoffman sat back on his train seat with his legs stretched out, he closed his eyes and thought about every word Monica had spoken in his presence. He could hear her strong and confident yet feminine voice.

He could see the words come out her shapely lips. He could see the depth of her feelings in her rich hazel eyes. All these things and more thoughts of Monica lulled Hoffman to sleep.

Hoffman woke up as the train pulled into Houston, where he would change trains. At the depot, all the talk was about the troubles on the border and the country's likely involvement in the conflagration in Europe. One topic of conversation especially caught Hoffman's attention. William Jennings Bryan had resigned his position as secretary of state. The populists' voice had become frustrated with the delicacies of diplomacy and the president's penchant for being his own spokesman on relations with other powers. Hoffman found relaxing the prospect of not having to deal with Bryan. The captain did not know Bryan's replacement, but reasoned he could not be any worse.

***

While Hoffman's train rolled toward Washington, D.C., back in San Diego, Monica was opening his letter. Manuel had waited until his father left for his return trip to México before he gave the letter to his sister. Old men, Manuel believed, did not understand matters of the heart. The young—women, in particular—could be counted on more often to listen to the heart. There was a lot to be said about the *macho* stereotype that was often attributed to *Mexicano* men, Manuel thought.

Monica had found a quiet time and place in the house where she could relish what she hoped was her first love letter. She sat on a mahogany bench in the living room late at night, after her mother had gone to sleep. Manuel was in his room writing poetry, as he always did at that time of the night.

The letter began:

"My dearest Monica,

I hope you do not think me too forward in my greeting or for writing. I felt a strong desire to explain to you why I did not go forward with my intentions of asking your father's permission to call on you. Since our first meeting I have felt a strong attraction to you.

Monica laid down the letter on her lap as she thought back to that first meeting. She had thought the captain was a handsome man, but his position had tempered any warmth she may have felt toward him. At that time, Monica had been very concerned over her brother Balo and his fight against *gringos* in general. She could not honestly say that she had been attracted to Hoffman during their first meeting. She continued reading:

I would be less than honest if I did not say that your physical beauty did not catch my eye.

But, frankly, I have seen and met many beautiful women throughout my travels. Your attraction to me goes much beyond good looks. I was most impressed by your intelligence and your willing-ness to express your views with such passion. That is not a trait that is too common in women in this day and age.

Monica paused from reading again to contemplate what she thought was quite an extraordinary admission by a man. Most men she knew, including her father and brothers, did not think much of women with brains, much less one with the tendency to speak her mind. Perhaps, Monica mused, there was more to Captain Hoffman than met the eye.

As you know by now, I am conducting a special investigation for President Wilson on this affair referred to as the Plan of San Diego. Since your brother Baldomero is involved in this matter, I thought it best for all concerned if I kept my relationship with your family at arms length. I do not wish for my reports to the president to be prejudiced by the warmth I have developed for your family, nor do I wish for you and your family to think that I am only interested in fos-tering this relationship with the intent of getting information from you.

To be sure, the discussions I have had with Manuel and your father have been quite helpful in my understanding of the environment that gave rise to the Plan of San Diego and what can be done to improve the situation. Still, I believe it would be best for me and for everyone if I did not encourage a more personal relationship that would allow emotions to tamper with reasoned judgment.

I have no doubt that this matter can be rectified soon, and at that time, it is my sincere hope that you and I will have the opportunity to get to know each other."

With kindest regards,
Matthew Hoffman"

Monica sat quietly for a long time, thinking about her letter from "Matthew." She felt conflicted by the openness, honesty, and ethical tone of his letter and her own feelings of loyalty to her brother and his cause. Matthew, despite all his good attributes, was still a *gringo*. His kind was the cause for much of the suffering her people had experienced over the years.

It was not right, Monica reasoned, for her to treat Matthew with the same prejudice she detested when used against her people. Was it not as much bigotry to stereotype Matthew with all *gringos* as when *gringos* treated all *Mexicanos* the same without getting to know them as individual human beings? Prejudice,

Monica thought, can go either way, and it was right
neither way.

***

As Monica finished reading her letter from Hoffman,
the captain was several thousand miles away, saying
good night to his friend Jim Brite in a Washington
hotel. Unlike his previous meeting with the president,
Hoffman had decided to come a day early and be
rested for the meeting. He had telephoned Brite from
Houston and asked him for a meeting. Brite was still
working at the State Department, and Hoffman wanted
some background information on the new secretary
of State. All Hoffman knew was that his name was
Robert Lansing.

Brite had filled him in on his new boss. He was a lawyer
educated at Amherst. His specialty was international law,
and he had been involved in several arbitration cases of
minor significance. He was a loyal Democrat and had
received an inconsequential appointment at State. When
the counselor at the State Department resigned, Lansing
was promoted to the No. 2 position at the agency. Several
months later, when Bryan himself quit, Lansing was given
the nod to move up to the head of the line.

"He considers himself a gentleman," Brite had said
facetiously. "If you ask me, he is quite an indolent man.
It does not really matter because President Wilson is
bent on being his own secretary of State. Lansing is
only there to fill in a formality."

The following day, Hoffman made his way to the
White House for his 9 a.m. meeting with the president.
He wondered whether Lansing would even be at the
meeting. Upon arrival, he was immediately ushered into
the Oval Office, where he found the president behind his
desk and the secretary of State sitting across from him.

"Good morning, Matthew," the president greeted
Hoffman without standing up.

"Good morning, professor," Hoffman responded in
a confident, relaxed tone.

The president signaled toward Lansing and introduced him to Hoffman.

"Matthew, shake hands with Secretary Lansing, who
took over for your friend, Mr. Bryan," Wilson said with a
smile. "Mr. Bryan is off extolling the virtues of grapefruit
juice. Mr. Lansing is new to the job, so you will have to
bring him up to date as you brief me."

Brite had told Hoffman of Bryan's penchant of boring
foreign diplomats with his nonstop babbling about the
fruit from his Rio Grande orchard. Lansing stood and
shook Hoffman's hand and extended a greeting that
was almost inaudible.

"Good morning, Mr. Secretary, I am honored to meet
you," Hoffman said in a firm voice. "Captain Matthew
Hoffman at your service."

"Matthew was a student of mine at Princeton," President Wilson informed Lansing. "He did a tour at State
with the previous administration and now is on a special

assignment for me. He is looking into the so-called Plan of San Diego and the increasing disorder on our Mexican border with Texas."

The president went on to say that Hoffman had been in South Texas for several months surveying the problem firsthand. The president also gave Lansing a brief account of the exposure of the Plan and subsequent confrontations between South Texas authorities and what appeared to be organized paramilitary bands. Lansing sat silently, only occasionally nodding acknowledging as the president spoke.

"Until we know different, we are assuming these encounters are a result of banditry and lawlessness and that it is the responsibility of local authorities," the president said as he turned to Hoffman, giving him an opening to began his briefing.

"I'm afraid, Mr. President, that these raids or attacks are more than local outlaws," Hoffman said. "They do have a basis in local grievances, but they are driven more by a desire for redress than by the baseless greed that moves common criminals."

The president leaned back on his chair and smiled. He was reassured he had picked the right man for the job.

"Go ahead," Wilson said.

"Well, Mr. President," Hoffman continued solemnly, changing his salutation from "professor" to fit the seriousness of what he was about to say. "What we have on our hands is a genuine homegrown rebellion. Some Americans of Mexican extraction feel that they have been unjustly treated, deprived of their rightful inheritance and disenfranchised. In true American fashion, they are seeking to right wrongs with words and bullets. They have set out their manifesto in the Plan of San Diego, and now they are going about carrying out their rebellion.

"Agents of the American government—whether it be local, state, or federal, law enforcement, judicial, administrative, or legislative—have deprived these citizens of their rights, their land, and, in many instances, their lives."

"What you describe, Captain Hoffman, hardly befits the American democratic system. It is more fitting of a rogue country inhabited by ruffians and swindlers," Secretary Lansing said to Hoffman, with an air of civility and disbelief.

"That is correct, Mr. Secretary. The frontier border region lacks the restraint we see here in Washington or that which you have been exposed to in European capitals," Hoffman responded. "The reality is that those who feel afflicted and wronged by the system have lost hope in that system and now see violence as their only recourse."

Hoffman relayed to the two highest-ranking officials in the American government the story that Manuel Reyna had told him. He recounted the early history of South Texas when Spanish citizens of Mexico took up the challenge of the "Desert of Death" in hopes of owning a parcel of land they could leave to their children. These fearsome souls went from being Spanish to Mexican to American to Confederate and back to American citizens in a short span of 50 years. Throughout all the wars that brought about these convulsions of the body politic, these humble workers of the soil had tried to hold onto their land. Some had succeeded, but many had not. Despite state commissions and laws, they had lost everything to land speculators and land grabbers who used legal and extralegal means against a people who were unfamiliar with practices that were foreign to them. If all else failed, the unscrupulous Anglo types used bloodshed to achieve their ends.

Hoffman then made them aware of his own experiences during his brief stay in the Río Grande Valley. He told the president and the secretary of State of his firsthand account of seeing innocent men hanged by Texas Rangers without the benefit of trial by jury before an impartial judge. He told them of many other secondhand stories told to him by others or reported by the press, which served as apologists for those committing the atrocities.

"These are horrible stories that demand the attention of fair-thinking men everywhere," President Wilson said. "But it still remains a problem of local origin that cries out for a local solution."

Hoffman could not help but stare at the president in disbelief. The protégé could not fathom how his mentor, the leader of the progressive movement in America, could be so callous and unfeeling toward the degree of human misery and civil rights violations that had been discussed.

Sensing Hoffman's disappointment, President Wilson told the captain to proceed.

"I am sure there is more," Wilson said.

"Yes, Mr. President, there is," Hoffman responded in a restrained voice. "The facts are that, though many of the participants in the insurrection are American citizens with legitimate claims against their government, many others—including some of the leaders—are Mexican citizens. Some Mexicans, such as Baldomero Reyna, have a sincere empathy with the Tejanos' cause. Others are in it only to foment trouble for our authorities so that they can gain advantage in their dealings with us.

"It is common knowledge in the Rio Grande Valley that the Carranza general at Matamoros is sympathetic to the cause. He has been known to look the other way when rebels cross the Rio Grande into Mexico to seek a safe haven. He has even allowed his own men to join the revolt in Texas when their own revolution is at an impasse."

Hoffman paused for a moment while he recalled a conversation he had with Frank Berlin, the German friend of his father.

"Finally, though I do not have firsthand knowledge, I have learned from a reliable source that German operatives in Northern Mexico and in the Rio Grande Valley are providing financial assistance, arms and munitions to the revolution in Texas."

President Wilson remained calm, leaning back on his chair without changing expression upon hearing Hoffman's last point. Secretary Lansing, on the other hand, was visibly taken aback.

"We cannot rely on hearsay, Captain, on matters of such an explosive and diplomatically sensitive nature," Lansing said to Hoffman, in a manner that could pass for anger for a man of the utmost civility.

"We cannot dismiss it, either," Wilson interjected.

"Tell me, Matthew," Wilson said as he leaned forward with hands intertwined, placing his elbows on his desk, "how do you know Mr. Reyna is concerned with the plight of the Mexicans that reside on our side of the border? I must say, I sense a note of sympathy from you for these fellows."

The meeting had reached a point when it would get interesting, Hoffman thought. He not only would reveal his association with the Reyna family, but would also relay the proposals from Carranza, made though *señor* Reyna.

"Incredulous as it may sound, Mr. President, I had the opportunity to meet Mr. Reyna and his immediate family during my stay in San Diego."

Hoffman went on to explain the extraordinary coincidence that had led him to the Reynas. Hoffman told the president of his initial meeting with Manuel Reyna and the subsequent encounter with *señor* Reyna and Baldomero Reyna himself. With a twinge of guilt, as his thoughts turned to Monica, Hoffman pointed out that he had kept these meetings at arms' length, but that he had pursued the liaison in order to gather information important to his investigation. He did not mention the Reyna women at all.

"Baldomero Reyna's sympathies are very personal and run very deep," Hoffman continued. "As a young boy of 10 years, he witnessed two of his uncles strung up by Texas Rangers. The experience left an indelible mark on him. Ever since and to this day, he has been driven to avenge his uncles' execution and the tragic hangings of countless others of his people."

Hoffman explained that his meeting with Baldomero Reyna had been without notice and without an opportunity to report him to the authorities. Hoffman added that at the meeting with the leader of the rebels he had also met Servando Reyna, Baldomero's father.

"*Señor* Reyna is a wealthy rancher and grower from Mexico who wants the fighting to stop so he can take his family back to their hacienda and resume a normal life," Hoffman explained. "*Señor* Reyna is apolitical; his allegiance is to his family and his ranch."

Hoffman went on to tell the president and the secretary of State that *señor* Reyna was a childhood friend of Venustiano Carranza. S*eñor* Reyna had gone to his old friend with the idea of getting his son released from jail. Before he learned of Baldomero's escape, *señor* Reyna had met with Carranza, and the two men had devised a plan to help *señor* Reyna's family and Carranza's objectives for Mexico.

"The proposal from Mr. Carranza, professor, is this," Hoffman said, looking directly into President Wilson. "He will cut off the rebels' Mexican sanctuary and put a stop to General Nefarrate's aid in return for your recognition of his faction as the legitimate government of Mexico."

For a moment no one spoke. Finally, Secretary Lansing broke the silence.

"What guarantee do we have he will live up to his end of the bargain?" Lansing asked.

To Hoffman's surprise, the answer came quickly and forcefully from the president.

"You will tell *señor* Reyna," the president told Hoffman, "that if his so-called president fails to put a stop to the raids, I will send an expeditionary force of 50,000 men to stop this wanton violence and we will occupy northern Mexico until order is restored throughout Mexico."

Hoffman waited to see if this was a genuine offer or whether the president was only letting out steam. Secretary Lansing, too, seemed to be waiting for what would come next. The president leaned back on his chair again, appearing to be decompressing from a build up of anger. Finally, the president spoke again.

"I'm sorry, Matthew. But this hooligan who sees himself as leader of a country gets under my skin," the president said. "The gall of this man to dictate terms to the president of the United States. Damnably, I have very little choice in the matter. The whole mess in Mexico just seems to be getting worse. There is not one real leader in any of the warring factions. It will certainly be the ruination of Mexico that in the hour of its greatest need, all it could raise were rascals.

"If we do not do something to settle the matter on our border, we will be spread too thin if we are dragged into the war in Europe. God knows, I will do my best to stay out of that fray, but my prayers may not be enough. We cannot afford to tie up our entire military establishment watching over the border. We must bring a resolution to that matter."

The president looked away, over Hoffman's shoulder, as if he were looking for a magical solution somewhere in the distance. Hoffman suddenly noticed how much the office of the presidency and all the pressures of world events had aged his mentor. On top of all that, the president had suffered the loss of his wife the previous year. The strain was clearly visible on his face.

"Okay, Matthew," the President resumed, "you go back to Texas and meet with your *señor* Reyna and tell him we will recognize Mr. Carranza, but the raids must be stopped immediately. Peace must reign over the entire border between the United States and Mexico. The first sign of a break in this peace, American troops will march into Mexico and restore the peace."

"There is one more thing, Mr. President," Hoffman said. "*Señor* Reyna also has a request. He will relay your response to Mr. Carranza and he assures me that Carranza will indeed close off the sanctuaries in Mexico, but *señor* Reyna wants an assurance that his son Baldomero will not be prosecuted."

"That is preposterous," Secretary Lansing interjected. "We cannot let lawbreakers dictate terms to the president of the United States."

"Baldomero Reyna is committed to his cause," Hoffman said. "He will not stop his activities even if he can no longer find refuge in Mexico. *Señor* Reyna believes he can get his son to stop his campaign but will not do so unless he is assured that his son will no longer be prosecuted."

"Baldomero Reyna is a Mexican citizen, is he not?" the president asked.

"Yes, sir," Hoffman answered.

"You can tell *señor* Reyna that we will not dismiss the charges against his son, but if he returns to Mexico and stays there, we will not ask Mr. Carranza for his extradition," the president said. "And that goes to *señor* Reyna and the rest of his family. They will return to Mexico and stay there."

Hoffman's thoughts immediately turned to Monica and he felt a pain in his gut. He had not even had an opportunity to get to know her and now the president was proposing to ban her from the country.

"But, Mr. President," Hoffman pleaded, "I do not believe that in our system of justice we can assign guilt and punish people merely on association or relation. To punish people for being related to someone who may have committed a crime strikes me as inconsistent with our ideals, if not with our laws."

"That is my proposal," the president said wryly. "*Señor* Reyna can take it or leave it. I can assure you that if his son insists on pursuing his fight strictly on our grounds, he will not long survive. I have directed General Funston to move several thousand men into the Valley to nip this so-called revolution in the bud. I cannot see how the Reynas have a choice in the matter."

The meeting drew to a close, and President Wilson bid farewell to Hoffman in uncharacteristic haste. It was obvious to Hoffman that the president was under ever-increasing stress. World events had overtaken his domestic progressive agenda, and personal tragedy had compounded the president's life.

President Wilson ordered Hoffman to return immediately to the border to convey his terms to Carranza and Reyna. It was urgent that this thorn on the border be removed so that the country could prepare for the bigger problem in Europe.

Hoffman moaned to himself that he would not be able to make a quick trip to Maryland to visit his family. He longed for his father's counsel and his mother's cooking. Still, Hoffman was excited about his prompt return. His thoughts turned to the prospect of seeing Monica again soon.

Chapter 18

Captain Hoffman had written to Manuel Reyna, letting him know that he was returning to Texas and would need to meet with Manuel's father again. He asked the son if he could set up a meeting for them.

Upon his arrival in San Diego, Hoffman met with Manuel at his usual eatery. The captain had resisted the urge to see Monica on such a short stay. He had thought of her constantly, but he knew this visit to San Diego would be brief. He wanted more time for their next encounter, in hopes that they could have some time to themselves so that a meaningful relationship could blossom.

"*Buenas noches, amigo,*" Manuel Reyna said to Hoffman as he approached the captain's table.

"Hello, Manuel, how are you?" Hoffman responded as he rose to extend his hand in friendship.

"Please, sit down and join me for dinner," Hoffman said to Manuel.

"How was your trip?" Manuel asked as the waiter

came by with a couple of Schlitz beers that Manuel had ordered when he walked in.

"Long and tiring, as always," Hoffman responded as he tipped his beer to Manuel.

"*Salud*," Manuel said. "Otherwise, did the trip go well."

"That all depends on one's point of view," Hoffman said with a note of sadness. "I think your father will be pleased. I do not know about you and the rest of your family."

"In our family, Captain, what pleases my father is usually what pleases the family," Manuel said with a grin. "My father has the weight of centuries of a patrimonial tradition on his side."

"I suppose that at times when we reach a juncture in the road, it is good to have someone with a map to follow," Hoffman replied.

Hoffman explained President Wilson's decision to Manuel. His voice was low and heavy, as that of a man reporting bad news.

"You know that you are really under no legal obligation to leave the country?" Hoffman told Manuel after explaining to him the aspect of President Wilson's proposal that the entire Reyna family would be expelled from the United States as part of the deal to seize and desist from prosecuting Balo further.

Hoffman felt angry. On the one hand, he felt he was betraying President Wilson's trust by suggesting to Manuel that his family was not legally bound to honor the president's orders. On the other had, Hoffman felt the president's proposal was counter to every provision of United States jurisprudence that assured individual liberties. Balo's family, after all, had committed no crime. They were not even suspected of any crime.

"Do not worry, my friend," Manuel said to Hoffman in an attempt to reassure him. "It is a good proposal. My father will indeed like it. My mother will as well. As for us children, we are young, and time is on our side. We will honor our father's wishes.

"And do not concern yourself about our legal rights. We are aware of what the divine law is regarding freedom. Sometimes your countrymen forget the words of your own Declaration of Independence, that all men are created equal," Manuel told Hoffman.

"More often than I care to admit," Hoffman responded instinctively. An instinct developed after several months of hearing and witnessing firsthand the atrocities committed by his fellow citizens against human rights and human beings.

"Besides," Manuel said, in a cheerful tone, "I will be back. I have met the woman of my dreams in this small town. I intend to marry her, and she intends to stay here. So you see, I have no choice but to come back. Her name is Aurora, and she is as beautiful as the phenomenon that bears her name."

Hoffman's feelings again resumed distress. He was happy for Manuel, but at the same time he was overcome with the realization that the object of his affections would be gone. She might as well be a star in the heavens. That way, Hoffman imagined, he could at least see her. Manuel sensed Hoffman's misery and offered him some hope.

"You know, Monica has grown quite fond of this little town, as well," Manuel said. "I would not doubt if she, too, would return when I do."

"I hope there is not a northern light in her life as well," Hoffman said, hoping for the right response from Manuel.

"Oh no, my friend," Manuel said with a laugh as he leaned back on his chair, swiveling on its rear legs. "Believe me, your last letter is what consumes her thoughts these days."

Hoffman smiled widely. He felt the anxiety within him flow out in a torrent, as a rush of joy pushed it out. He was overjoyed Monica had thought about him occasionally, but the thought of her carrying his letter close to her heart was much more than what Hoffman had dreamed.

"My sister was hoping to have seen you on this visit to town," Manuel told a grinning Hoffman.

"Please tell her that was my wish as well, but I must leave first thing in the morning to meet with your father. There simply was not sufficient time to give her the attention she deserves," Hoffman told Manuel, who had arranged for Hoffman to meet *señor* Reyna in Matamoros. "And tell her that I, too, think of her often and am looking forward to my return so that we can have some time together. That is, with your mother as chaperone."

Manuel laughed and assured Hoffman he would deliver the message. Manuel then changed the conversation back to the business at hand. He told Hoffman he was to meet *señor* Reyna at the Café Principal on the Main Square in Matamoros. He should be alone and dressed in South Texas garb. No Army uniform and no business suit. After going over a few more details, the two men said good night. Manuel walked away whistling, no doubt off to see his Aurora. Hoffman went up to his room to think about Monica and write her another letter.

The following morning, Hoffman went to the Gueydan Brothers mercantile and bought some denim jeans, a hemp shirt, and a pair of boots. He topped off his new style with a Stetson hat. With purchase in hand he headed to the Texas Mexican Railway depot just north of the town center. On the way to the depot he stopped at *Imprenta Esparza* where Manuel Reyna worked. Manuel was standing at a 4-foot-tall work table looking over an iron form used to set type in place, when he noticed Hoffman walk in.

"Good morning, Captain Hoffman," Manuel yelled out over the din of a letterpress churning out letterhead for the Duval County judge. "What a surprise to see you here. I was getting ready to go look for you myself."

"Good morning, Manuel," Hoffman responded as he handed Manuel a sealed envelope. "I was hoping you would do me the favor and deliver this letter to your sister."

"That is a coincidence," Manuel said as he took the envelope and reached for his back trouser pocket and took out another letter.

"My sister asked that I deliver this letter to you," Manuel said, handing Hoffman an envelope.

Hoffman smiled as he took the letter. He noticed the feminine handwriting on the envelope and caught a scent of a very pleasant perfume as he tucked the letter in his suit's inside chest pocket.

"Hopefully that will make for a more enjoyable train ride then what you are accustomed to," Manuel told his sister's suitor.

"Indeed, it will," Hoffman responded still grinning from ear to ear.

"I better be off," Hoffman said as he shook Manuel's hand and walked off on his way to the train.

"Where are you off to today, captain," asked the agent who sat behind the telegraph machine.

"Back to Corpus Christi for now," Hoffman responded, not wanting to give the agent too much information. Hoffman did not trust the agent, despite or perhaps because of his extraordinary friendliness.

The first words Hoffman read as he opened his letter from Monica were:

"My Dear Matthew,

For the last few weeks I have thought long and often about your letter. My first thought, I must admit, was to ignore it. After all, what could the two of us have in common? Upon deep reflection, however, I have come to the realization that we have a lot that we share. In particularly, in the things that really matter.

I am sure that on the surface many would say I was wrong. We have different skin color, but what does that really add to a person's character? We have different native tongues, but cannot languages be easily learned? We come from different parts of the world, but are they not still in the same world?

What we have in common, I believe, is much more important. We both worship the same God and are members of his universal church. We both have a deep appreciation for the importance of family. It is my sense that we both have a profound and abiding faith that all God's people are equal and must be treated in a just and moral way. I believe Jesus said it all when he said that we must treat the least of his children as we treat him.

Still, I must confess that our present personal situation makes a relationship between us most difficult. Stripped to its barest form, your mission is to undermine all that my brother Balo is risking his life to do. On the other hand, for all his passion and for what I believe is the rightness of his cause, if followed to its logical conclusion, Balo's aim is to eradicate you and all your kin who he sees as evil.

While I believe my brother's cause is just, I no longer believe that his way is right. I have come around to my father's side, for completely different reasons. My father is a pragmatist who believes in the value of personal possessions. I am an idealist who cherishes individual freedoms. I recently read about an Indian barrister in South Africa who has taken on his oppressors by using the law and demanding moral certitude. He has said that he is willing to die for his cause but he is not willing to kill for it. That is what I have come to believe is what we need to do to our tormentors in South Texas. It is, after all, what Christ believed and taught us.

I do not know where our current circumstances will lead us. I do know that violence is not the answer. Equally important to me is that you believe as I do. I am given hope for the future when I talk to my mother whose simple judgments are based on pure intentions. She, by the way, thinks you are a good man. I have never known her to be wrong.

Perhaps on your next trip to San Diego, things will have changed for the better and we can talk about less serious matters.

Until then, I remain your friend and admirer."

Hoffman put the letter down on his lap and took a deep breath. He was flushed with joy. He knew he had been right all along in his assessment. This was indeed a unique and strong-willed woman. Her intelligence and insight matched her beauty. What else could a man desire? Monica's letter reenergized Hoffman. His mission to stop the killing on both sides was ever more imperative.

After savoring Monica's letter and all its implications for half an hour or more, Hoffman turned his attention to what was ahead of him. The imperative to succeed was now more pressing. He had to fulfill Monica's prophetic views.

Hoffman was headed to Matamoros to meet with *señor* Reyna to present the president's proposal. Hoffman had never been to Matamoros; the closest he had gotten was Fort Brown across the Rio Grande from the border town. Hoffman thought for a moment about the name "Matamoros." He realized the significance of the name, which celebrated the triumph of Spain over the Moors who had held reign over Spain for seven centuries. The United States had been a country for just over a century. The Mexicans whom Americans in the Valley ridiculed

and belittled were heirs to a culture, language, and history that stretched over a millennium. These so-called
Meskins or greasers were the descendants of the people
who sent Columbus on a trip that resulted in the discovery of the new world called America. These people
were offspring and successors of the same explorers that
charted the new world from Florida to California and
from California to the Straits of Magellan. Yet, the so-
called Anglos, who had less than a century in this land,
professed to be of a superior ilk. Hoffman thought it
a curious irony that the high and mighty Americans
took their very name from an Italian whose travels were
sponsored by the Spanish from whom the Mexicans
descended. The whole idea of Anglo superiority seemed
preposterous to Hoffman.

After switching trains in Robstown, Hoffman
headed south toward the Valley and into what had
become—since he had last been there—and active
battlefield. On the stop at Kingsville's depot, all the talk
was about the daily assaults on civilians, towns, troops,
and trains. The Norias raid, which occurred just south of
Kingsville, had started the campaign and was the center
of talk at local coffee shops.

Hoffman picked up a copy of the *Corpus Christi Caller
and Daily Herald* at the depot and read reprinted accounts
from the *Brownsville Herald* of the "atrocities" in the Valley.
One story that caught Hoffman's eye involved two Cameron County deputies that left San Benito late one night

with a prisoner suspected of being a revolutionary. They were taking him to Brownsville for a hearing before federal immigration agents when a group of masked men in another automobile stopped the deputies and kidnapped their prisoner. The masked brigands had sped away with their prisoner, and after traveling a safe distance took him out by the side of the road and riddled him with bullets. Wishing to make an example of the man, who had not been convicted of or even tried for any crime, they hung the corpse on the limb of a nearby tree for all to see. The incident reminded Hoffman of stories Manuel had told him. It was the same method, but instead of horses, the "law" was now traveling in automobiles. That provided little comfort for the victims of vigilantes.

After another raid by Mexican insurgents in which two Anglos were killed, a posse was formed by local residents and conducted a manhunt for anyone with brown skin. After no time they had rounded up 15 local Texans of Mexican ancestry and summarily executed them. The newspaper gleefully reported that this kind of retaliation was what Texans in this section believed to be their right, and the only way to stamp out the banditry on the border.

Hoffman put the newspaper down on his lap and leaned his head back. "If my efforts do nothing else but stop this madness, they will be worthwhile," Hoffman said to himself in silence.

A gunshot suddenly broke Hoffman's peace as well as the glass window two seats in front of where he was sitting. The squealing of several ladies was heard, and someone yelled for everyone to crouch down below the windows. Hoffman could see a band of men rushing the train on horseback all the while aiming their Mausers toward the train and firing at will. As Hoffman dodged down below the window he heard a loud explosion ahead of the engine. The engineer hit the brakes and they screeched for a few moments before the train cars slid off the tracks. Some toppled over but the car Hoffman was in remained upright in the middle of some cenizo.

It was not long before several of the assailants boarded the train car. Hoffman had no doubt that they were Mexican insurrectionists. One of the intruders shot an Anglo businessman in the front of the car and then quickly made his way through the car, pushing women and children aside. Others were behind the aggressor, but Hoffman could not get a good look to see how many were on board.

As the rebel came upon Hoffman he raised his rifle and pointed it with the intent to fire, but the man behind him pushed his barrel up and yelled at him *"no dispares, es alemán."* Hoffman knew enough Spanish to know that he had been spared because he was German.

As Hoffman got a good look at his savior, he was astounded to see that it was none other than Balo. Their eyes locked, but Balo made no motion to outwardly acknowledge Hoffman. He walked past him to the rear of the car, where a Mexican passenger was pointing at the bathroom door, giving away the hiding place of two cattlemen who had sought refuge in that most unlikely place. Balo and the other man opened fire through the restroom door and heard yelps inside as they hit their mark. Without bothering to check on their prey behind the door, they turned and began to leave.

"*Vámonos*," Balo told the *Mexicano* who had given up the location of the cattlemen, "you are one of us now."

The man picked up his *sombrero* from the car floor and followed; as he passed he looked away, hoping not to be recognized in the future.

"*Viva la independencia, viva la libertad*," shouted the *vaquero* in front of Balo as they disembarked and both mounted Balo's horse and rode off into the brush.

Hoffman rose to his feet and immediately went to the restroom to check on the men who had been trapped inside. As he opened the door he saw one man slumped over the other, who was sitting on the toilet.

"Are you OK?" Hoffman asked the man on the seat who was facing Hoffman as he opened the door.

"I was just nicked on the shoulder, but this fellow on top of me took some serious hits. He is still breathing, though."

Hoffman took the seriously wounded cowman off his cabin companion, and the two carried him to a bench at the rear of the car. He had been shot on his buttocks, but a graver wound was to an area near the spine, which exited the front of his torso just right of his heart. The man was clearly in distress, and Hoffman called out to see if a doctor was on board. A middle-aged woman came forward and said her father had been a doctor and she could at least try to stop the bleeding and make the man comfortable until help arrived.

Hoffman left her to tend to the wounded cattlemen and moved down the car to see who else needed help. There were a couple of women scared and shaking but otherwise all right. At the front of the car he reached another man who was no longer breathing.

Hoffman jumped off the car, and after a few minutes, he realized he was the only male passenger whose life had been spared. Several others had not been killed but were suffering from gunshot wounds. After getting off the train, he continued to help the wounded and comfort the women. Soon Hoffman heard the rumble of an approaching pack of horses. As Hoffman looked up, he saw the stars and stripes at the front of a troop of U.S. soldiers. When they arrived at the scene, Hoffman learned they were a detachment of the 28th U.S. Infantry headquartered at Fort Brown. Hoffman showed the commander of the troop his credentials and provided him a report of what had occurred.

"Did you offer any resistance, Captain?" the commander asked Hoffman.

"No, I was unarmed and events unfolded quite suddenly and rapidly," Hoffman answered.

"Why are you out of uniform?" the commander queried. He appeared troubled that Hoffman had escaped without a scratch while civilians the Army was supposed to protect had been killed.

"I am on a special assignment for President Wilson on my way to Mexico," Hoffman said. "My mission is of a diplomatic nature that is best carried out in less forceful means."

The cowman who suffered only a minor wound in the restroom onslaught came forward to Hoffman's aide.

"He helped the wounded and calmed the women after the bandits made their escape," the man told the Army commander. "I heard the one bandit tell another not to shoot him because he was German."

"I guess some of us cannot get away from our looks," the six-foot-three, blond, blue-eyed Hoffman told the Army commander. "For some of us, our looks work out for the better, for others they do not work out as well."

Hoffman asked the commander for a mount so he could travel back with the troop to Fort Brown, where he had planned to spend the night. The commander ordered a corporal to give Hoffman his horse and for the soldier to double up with someone else.

On the way to the border fort, Hoffman went over the events of the past few hours. He thought to himself how after that train ride he came closer than ever to understanding the fight in men like Balo. Their struggle was for far more than land and liberty; it was for the simple respect that men deserve for inhabiting God's earth and toiling to make it a better place. After arriving at Fort Brown, late that night, Hoffman was too tired to eat or bathe. He took his boots off and went to bed. He fell asleep reading Monica's letter again.

Chapter 19

Balo was getting woozy from the pain on his arm, and the bleeding was taking its toll. The rising sun indicated another scorcher was in store, so Balo determined that he needed to find shelter and treatment for his wound. He spotted a *jacal* in the distance in western Hidalgo County and told his men to go home and rest up with their families while he sought help. He told them he would meet them in two weeks in Reynosa. Balo did not want to bring attention to or scare the people who might be living in the *ranchito*.

As his men headed off in several directions, Balo approached the *jacal* on his horse, which was also showing signs of fatigue. They had ridden half the night at full gallop to get away from pursuing cavalry. They had dodged into some thick brush to make their escape. Both Balo and his steed showed the impact of such a hard ride.

A *campesino* in white garb and a *sombrero* walked out of his poor abode. He had a stern look on his face and held a *machete* in his hand, ready to defend his family.

"*Buenos días*," Balo said. "I mean you no harm. I have been shot and need your help."

"Who shot you and why should I help you?" came back a brusque reply.

"A *rinche* shot me and you should help me because I am fighting for you and your family so that you can have your land back," Balo responded.

"We have no land. We have never owned land, and if your kind keeps on with your *guerra cochina*, we never will," the man said.

"Then maybe we should help him because he's one of God's children and you have taught us to be good Christians, *papá*." The words came from a young woman about 25 years-old standing at the door of the *jacal*. She was a natural beauty, but standing next to a thatched wall of dried *mesquite*, she appeared almost saintly to a weary Balo, who was on the verge of losing consciousness from the loss of blood. The scene before Balo suddenly went blank as he slid off his horse to a thump on the ground.

The next thing Balo saw was the young woman applying some cool water to his face, and her father and other family members standing behind her looking on. They had all carried him into the shack and laid him on the dirt floor. The water had snapped him back to consciousness.

"You will be all right," she said to Balo. "It is only a small wound. The bullet did not lodge in your arm."

Balo merely acknowledged her with a nod. He did not have the strength to speak.

"Arnoldo, go to the *cochera* and bring some *telaraña*," she told a boy of about 12 standing behind her.

"I've sent for some spider web," the young woman told Balo. "That will stop the bleeding."

Balo was in no condition to argue about what was obviously some kind of folk remedy. He closed his eyes and tried to relax.

***

His mind kept wandering to the events of the night before when he had been shot after the attack on the Frisco train, a local rail service which served Cameron and Hidalgo counties. Balo and his men had run into a troop of U.S. cavalry and several *rinches* scouting for raiders. They were taken by surprise as they had crossed the Arroyo Colorado, south of McAllen. Balo was shot on his left arm with a 30-30 rifle. The bullet entered and exited his arm above the elbow. The initial sting quickly turned into a throbbing pain, and his arm felt 20 pounds heavier. Blood flowed freely, drenching his shirt.

Balo instinctively shot back, holding his rifle with his right arm pressed against his body. He then turned his mount and shouted to his men to make a run across the *arroyo* to the dense brush they had passed through minutes earlier. The ploy was successful, and they lost their pursuers, but they lost one man in the encounter. Balo had one of his men remove a string of leather from his holster and apply a tourniquet. The bleeding was controlled.

While hiding in the brush, Balo sent one of his men to reconnoiter the area and see if any more troops were still around. The scout came back with astonishing news. He had met up with a *vaquero* who had just returned from Harlingen and the *vaquero* told Balo's scout that four trainloads of soldiers were heading south toward Fort Brown. The train was also hauling four Howitzers. During the next day, while they lay low, Balo's scouts became aware of 20 carloads of soldiers heading south. It was clear that the Army was getting sizable reinforcements. Balo had already been having second thoughts about the war, and the news of an ever-increasing Army presence was even more troubling. His men could handle a couple of hundred *rinches* and their local vigilantes, but taking on the U.S. Army with their heavy artillery was something else. Balo had even heard from Cleto that the Army had an airplane in use around Brownsville.

***

Balo was jerked out of his daze when he felt a burning sensation on his arm. The young woman had cleaned his wound, and then for good measure, had doused it with *tequila*.

"It will sterilize the wound so you will not get an infection," she said as she held him down. She then applied the spider web to the wound. Balo did not know much about the ways of folk healers, but this young *curandera* seemed to know what she was doing, and she was pretty to boot.

"You need to rest to regain your strength," she told Balo. "My mother has prepared some lentil soup for you. You must sleep after eating some soup."

The girl's mother, a pleasantly plump woman, no more than 5 feet tall, brought the soup and a *tortilla de maíz*. Balo ate the warm and tasty meal and was ready to follow his attendant's orders and take a nap. He looked at the young woman who had an innocent and caring face. She had light brown eyes with black hair. She was true to many of the area's women who were called *morenas* for their tan complexion.

"What is your name?" Balo asked her.

"Christina," she replied with a smile that endeared her even more to Balo. "Now you must rest."

***

While Balo slept on a dirt floor in the *jacal*, Hoffman had entered the San Carlos Hotel restaurant in Brownsville to await his contact to take him to *señor* Reyna in Matamoros. Hoffman was surprised when he saw none other than Manuel Reyna approaching his table.

"Good morning, *amigo*," Manuel said to Hoffman. "I'm sure you are surprised to see me in these parts."

"I must say that I am surprised," Hoffman responded.

"Well you might as well learn something about my father," Manuel said as he pulled out a chair across from Hoffman. "He trusts only his family in matters that affect its well-being."

"That is understandable," Hoffman said. "How are your mother and sister?"

"They are fine," Manuel responded. "They are preparing to return to México as soon as they hear from my father."

Hoffman was not pleased to hear that. He felt he was finally getting closer to Monica, and now she was readying to leave for parts unknown to him. He wondered and worried whether he would ever see her again.

Manuel told Hoffman that they needed to get started, for they had a long ride. His father, Manuel told Hoffman, was actually waiting for them at *señora Reyna's* ancestral home of Agualeguas and not in Matamoros as he had told Hoffman. Agualeguas was a short distance across the river from Río Grande City. Manuel had a taxi waiting for them outside the San Carlos. As the two men stepped out into the streets of Brownsville, many white men looked at them suspiciously. Manuel was used to having leering blue eyes focused on him, but Hoffman found it unnerving. The two quickly boarded their waiting car and headed out, stopping first at Fort Brown to pick up some traveling items Hoffman had brought for the trip.

The men had not traveled 10 miles out of Brownsville when a posse on horseback stopped them.

"Where you Meskins heading," a stocky mustachioed man asked Manuel and his driver, who occupied the front seats.

"We are taking *señor* Hoffman to McAllen, meester," Manuel said, in a half mocking tone. At that point, Hoffman opened his door and stepped out to confront the posse's leader.

"Are you men officers of the law?" Hoffman asked the leader, who had a dozen vigilantes behind him.

"In these parts, we make the law as we go," the man with the mustache answered Hoffman.

"Well, we are still on the American side of the river are we not?" Hoffman asked. "The sheriff, Rangers, and Army provide plenty of law to go around. So, if you gentlemen don't mind, we need to get on to McAllen for important government business."

With that, Hoffman got back into the car and told the driver to move on. The roar of the car's engine startled the horses, and their riders made way for the car.

"What you did was pretty dangerous," Manuel said to Hoffman. "Just because you are a *gringo* doesn't insulate you from hate. You just painted yourself as a Mexican lover."

"So be it," Hoffman said tersely. He did not know that love was the word he would use, but he respected all people. He certainly did not hate anyone.

After driving nearly all day through small towns and *rancherías*, the three pulled into Río Grande City. The drive had been long and grueling. South Texas, Hoffman thought, had no recognition of the seasons. Despite it being well into autumn, the temperature and humidity continued as if it were the height of summer. Hoffman had merely sat in the back seat engaging in casual conversation with Manuel, but by the time they reached the river crossing he was spent. The driver, who in keeping with *señor* Reyna's rule of trusting only family was Manuel's cousin, had no trouble crossing into Mexico. The inspectors on both sides of the river knew him well and just waved him on.

They quickly drove through Mier and headed southwest toward Agualeguas, which they reached in less than an hour. The sun was beginning to set, and Hoffman asked Manuel if they could stop at a place where he could freshen up and reinvigorate himself.

"We will soon be at my grandfather's house," Manuel told Hoffman. "We will freshen up there and have a good supper. My father is not expected until late, so we will have some time to unwind."

"Good," Hoffman responded quickly. He truly needed to rest or he would not be able to rely on his mind being at its peak. The issues to be discussed with *señor* Reyna were not very complicated but they were sensitive, and Hoffman wanted to be in good form during their discussions.

The men pulled up in front of a white adobe-looking house across from the town *plaza*. It was a very clean and spacious house. Clearly, Hoffman thought,

Manuel's grandfather was a man of means. Manuel hugged and kissed an elderly, slightly hunchbacked woman who opened the door for them. Manuel told Hoffman that the old lady was his great aunt who took care of the house for his family. Manuel's maternal grandparents had lived in the house that had been handed down to them by her grandfather's family. It had been their home since the founding of the town in 1772. Both of Manuel's maternal grandparents had passed away, and the home now belonged to his mother. It was used primarily as a retreat for when the family wished to get away from the pressures of running the *hacienda* near Linares. Manuel's great aunt, who lived next door, watched over the place when the family was away.

A solitary servant was busy in the kitchen preparing supper; otherwise the house was vacant. Manuel showed Hoffman to his room and where he could bathe if he desired. Hoffman wasted no time taking him up on that offer. After a sumptuous supper of *carne guisada* and *sopa de arroz* with *tortillas de maíz*, Manuel invited Hoffman for a stroll in the town. Agualeguas was a small, quiet town whose inhabitants seemed a universe away from the battles that were being waged around them.

"Does the war ever come to this town?" Hoffman asked as he enjoyed the peacefulness of the place.

"Oh, indeed it does," Manuel said. "Not often, but often enough to force my family to move farther north."

"Actually," Hoffman commented, "this place seems very similar to San Diego, but life moves at a slightly slower pace."

"That is true," Manuel said. "You see, San Diego was settled by people from these parts. They merely picked up and moved with their customs and way of life.

"My mother and Monica love this place," Manuel continued. "They wanted to stay here, but my father insisted it was not safe so he sent them up to San Diego, the next best thing to Agualeguas."

Hoffman was glad that *señor* Reyna was a cautious man; otherwise he may not have met Monica. He could envision Monica strolling around the *plaza* as he was doing now, although she would be going in the opposite direction. Hoffman remembered that Manuel had explained to him, while in San Diego, that the custom was for the single girls to walk around the plaza in a counterclockwise direction and the boys or men in the opposite, or clockwise, direction. For a moment he imagined the two of them walking together arm in arm, engaged in deep conversation about their future together. Hoffman quickly realized that they might not have a future together. Events were moving in a direction that troubled Hoffman regarding his chances with Monica, even though they could result in peace for the area. Hoffman returned home with Manuel to get some sleep before talking with *señor* Reyna the following day.

***

Balo awoke from a long sleep and opened his eyes to see Christina asleep on the floor next to his bed, while her father sat on a chair nearby. He felt well rested. It had been quite a while since Balo had slept that long and sound. The sight of Christina only soothed him further. Even in his groggy state, Balo knew he was feeling something very different toward this angel of mercy who had tended to his wounds. The attraction was strong. It tugged at his heart not his male lust.

As Balo laid staring and admiring Christina's beauty she awoke. She blushed when she noticed Balo's obvious admiring gaze. She smiled and looked away.

"Good morning," she said. "Are you feeling better?"

"Thanks to you, I feel great," Balo responded. "I would like to get some fresh air and sunshine," Balo added, hoping she would get his meaning about his need for natural relief.

Christina rose and helped Balo stand up. She gave him a shirt she said had belonged to her brother. Balo feigned dizziness and placed his arm around Christina's shoulders to steady himself. She grabbed him around the waist and led him out to the back of the house, with her father always maintaining vigilance close by. At the far end of their *solar* was an outhouse. Balo showed discretion and let go of Christina halfway to the outhouse and asked her to wait for him. On his return, Christina led him back to the house, where her mother had prepared some *atole de avena* and some *pan de campo.* Christina's father gruffly walked away with a scowl on his face.

"Why does your father hate me so much? He doesn't even know me," Balo asked Christina as he sat to have his breakfast.

"It's not you he hates, its what you represent," Christina told Balo. "He is still grieving over my brother."

Christina told Balo about her brother Miguel, whose shirt Balo was wearing. No doubt that added to his unwilling host's anger. Miguel had gone to see his girlfriend at a neighboring *rancho*. It had gotten late before he started back to his home, and on the way back, Miguel had decided to sleep under the stars. He found a place in the brush and drifted off to sleep. At dusk, a posse looking for marauders nearly trampled him. As he arose, frightening the horses, he was shot down by one of the *rinches*. He died instantly. He was left for the *coyotes* and vultures. The incident occurred close enough to their house that Christina's father heard the shot and hurried to the place, knowing that Miguel had not returned. On the way to the *brazada*, he met up with the *rinches* who callously told him they had just killed a bandit in the brush.

"My brother was no bandit, but the *rinches* believed he was one of your men. So, you see, my father blames you and your followers for Miguel's death," Christina said.

"Why do you say me and my followers?" Balo asked her.

"Everyone around here knows who you are, *señor* Reyna," was Christina's response.

Balo did not know whether to feel pride or shame. It was somewhat exhilarating to have acquired such prominence, but the price people were paying for his notoriety was too high.

"My brother believed in your cause," Christina told Balo. "So do I and most young people. Our elders believe in God, a good education, and patience. They are convinced that with these three beliefs, our lives will be better. They tell us constantly that our lives are better than what they had in México, and that our children's lives will be better still."

"Don't they realize," Balo asked, "that the *gringo patrón* took the land their fathers had owned? That had been given to them from the Spanish crown."

"As he told you yesterday, our family did not own land, never has. Neither have any of the families we know around here," Christina told Balo. "Only a privileged few *Mexicanos* had owned land, and they were as bad as the *gringo* in their treatment of the poor.

"I have told my father he is misplacing the blame," Christina continued. "It is, after all, the *rinches* who killed Miguel and all the other innocent people. Still, my father is convinced that none of it would have happened if you and your followers had not killed the *gringos*."

"I am truly sorry for your loss," Balo said in a voice Christina knew was sincere. "I, too, have lost loved ones. I understand."

A melancholy expression fell over Balo's face as he thought about his *tíos*. Christina at once recognized the deep emotional pain.

"It is not your fault," Christina said as she gently placed her hand over Balo's hand. "It is the times we live in."

Her words were comforting to Balo. He noticed Christina's father and younger brother were loading up a wagon with all the family belongings.

"Why is your father loading up the *carreta*?" Balo asked.

"He feels it is best we return to México," Christina said. "At least there they won't shoot us down simply because we are *Mexicanos*."

Christina explained that they would join a caravan of other families who were also going to leave. Many people had decided to return to México and were traveling in groups to assure some degree of protection. Others, like those at the neighboring *ranchería* of Azadón had taken another course. They were asking the soldiers for protection. They believed they needed protection more so than did the *gringos*.

"It is their way to show loyalty to this country," Christina told Balo.

"As you can see, the choices we have are few, and all are bad," Christina said. "We can stay and fight alongside you and face certain death. We can side with the *gringo* and face certain servitude. Or, we can abandon all we have worked for and return to México and face certain uncertainty."

Balo sighed at the prospects these poor people faced. When it was all said and done, if he survived, he had a comfortable life to return to. His father was a successful *hacendado*. His family owned property in Linares, Aguale-guas, and San Diego. Balo had choices, and they all had promise. Christina's family only had one another. Though that meant a lot, it did not always put food on their table, clothes on their backs, or a roof over their heads.

Balo left Christina without saying a word, and walked toward her father, who was still trying to arrange as much as he could of his family's belongings on the wagon.

"I just wanted to tell you how sorry I am about what happened to your son," Balo told Christina's father, who did not stop what he was doing or look at Balo. "I know how you feel."

"How could you possibly know how I feel? You live to kill and bring pain to others," the older man snapped at Balo.

"You are right, but it has not always been like that," Balo said, as his earlier melancholy grew into a deeper sadness. "When I was a boy of 10, the *rinches* killed two of my *tíos* and hung them in the town square so my *tías* and my *familia* could see their brutality."

Christina's father stopped what he was doing and for the first time looked at Balo face to face. He could see tears swelling up in Balo's eyes. The heartbreaking pain he could see in the hardened, battle-scarred war-rior took the older man aback.

"Like your son, my *tíos* had done nothing wrong," Balo continued. "I told the *rinches* that a horse in one of my *tío*'s pasture belonged to my *tío* when he was only holding it for someone else. It turned out the horse was stolen, and based on my words, the *rinches* believed my *tíos* were horse thieves. They arrested them and later that night they executed them while they slept in the *cárcel*. In the morning we found them hanging in the *plaza*, in front of the church."

Balo began to feel weak and sat on the ground, leaning against the wagon's wheel. Christina, who had been following behind him listening to his story, sat next to him as his chest heaved from the pain he was trying to hold in. Christina told Balo to rest, but he continued with his tale.

"Ever since that time," Balo told Christina's father who was now squatted in front of him, "I swore I would avenge my *tíos*' death. That is why I fight and kill *rinches*.

"But with every passing day I come to realize that my anger and need for revenge is only resulting in more innocent men dying. Like your son Miguel."

"No, son," the older man said in a voice calmed and sobered by Balo's account about his *tíos*. "You are not responsible for my son's death. My grief needed someone to blame, and you just happened to come along at the wrong time. My daughter is right. It was the *rinches* who killed my son. And like your *tíos*, he had done nothing wrong.

"Maybe if had I been younger I would have reacted as you did and gone out and killed a few *gringos*, but I no longer have the strength and am cursed by the weakness of age, which makes me a coward."

"No," Balo said quietly as he began to regain his composure. "You are not a coward. Your years have given you strength and made you wise. Killing is not the answer. I know that now. My father and mother have been telling me that for years, but I was too filled with anger that I would not listen."

Balo's thoughts suddenly turned to his mother. She had suffered as great a loss as he had. Two of her brothers were killed by the *rinches*. Now she had to endure her son's *capricho*. His stubborn desire for revenge was now making his mother feel even greater anxiety with the possible loss of her son at any moment. Balo's father had tried to make Balo understand what his mother was feeling, but the thought of vengeance had blinded Balo to everyone else's feelings. It was only now, seeing another parent in agony over a lost child, that everyone else's positions had become clear.

Balo realized at that moment that the war had ended for him. It was causing too much pain for too many innocent people. Besides, it was a futile struggle. His father had been right about the power of the *Americano* Army. The money they had been promised to continue the with the war had been lost. The people's support for the war was quickly waning. Manuel's last message regarding Hoffman's news from Washington was likely to cut off their only source of support in México. Carranza was too eager for recognition and would cut loose the *revoltosos* the first chance he had of normalizing relations with the United States.

"*Perdón, señor*, but I do not even know your name," Balo said to the man with graying hair squatted in front of him.

"Francisco Perales, your humble servant," the man responded, with an outstretched hand.

"Baldomero Reyna," Balo answered, grabbing the hand of his new acquaintance as they exchanged smiles.

"*Señor* Perales, can I return to México with your family?" Balo asked Christina's father.

Señor Perales was surprised at the request and hesitated before answering. "*Po... pos* you are very well-known *se... señor* Reyna," *señor* Perales stuttered. "You may bring the *rinches* upon us."

"*No, papá*," Christina interjected anxiously. "He can wear some of Miguel's clothes. They will think he is a *campesino* like us."

Balo smiled at Christina's suggestion. He was flattered that she again came to his aid with her father. Her help was becoming a welcome habit, Balo thought.

"*Bueno*," said *señor* Perales, turning to Balo. "Christina is right. Do you feel up to the long walk?"

"*Sí, señor*," was Balo's simple response.

"Where in México do you come from?" Balo asked.

"From a small town called Pénjamo in the valley of México City," Christina answered.

"That is too far and too dangerous for you to travel to now," Balo told them. "We will go to Linares to my father's *hacienda*. He will provide food and shelter for all of us. I will persuade him to provide employment for you, as well, *señor*."

Chapter 20

The maid's movement in the kitchen as she prepared breakfast awakened Captain Hoffman. He got up and freshened up before going out to the dining area, where he found *señor* Reyna reading a newspaper and drinking coffee from a mug. *Señor* Reyna had arrived during the night, after Hoffman and Manuel had retired for the night. The old gentleman was an early riser, and despite his long ride from Linares he was up and about by five in the morning, as was his custom.

"Good morning, sir," Hoffman said as he walked into the dining room.

Hoffman learned that *señor* Reyna had a mastery and understanding of English but could only speak the language with much effort and a heavy accent. Hoffman had become somewhat versed in what was said to him in Spanish but could not respond except in English.

"Good morning, Captain, please join me for some coffee," *señor* Reyna said in Spanish. "We will have to wait for Manuel to wash off his cobwebs before we have breakfast."

"I heard that," Manuel interjected as he rounded the door into the dining room. He leaned over and kissed his father on the forehead. "I was up writing way past the time you arrived."

The maid walked in with a large bowl of mixed cantaloupe and watermelon. She brought each of them a plate and fork and returned to the kitchen, where she continued preparing the rest of the breakfast of *machacado con huevo*, a mixture of dried beef and eggs. Hoffman marveled at the hearty eating habits of the people of the border frontier. The fruit would have been plenty for him, but in these parts it was merely an entrée. These rural people had a history of working hard on their ranges, pastures, and orchards that they needed sustenance. They would often go until the *siesta* hour without eating again, so breakfast was an important meal.

"I read in the Monterrey newspapers that the war is going well," *señor* Reyna said. "The Carranza forces are driving the Villistas back in the mountains, and the first chief is consolidating power over the entire country. He has now returned to the Palacio Nacional. The *Americanos* and their South American allies appear ready to recognize and accept the reality on the ground," *señor* Reyna pronounced as he turned to Hoffman, waiting for a response.

"I assume your president is ready to help bring peace to México by lending support for President Carranza and withhold it from the bandit Villa?" *señor* Reyna asked Hoffman.

"The president has asked me to communicate to Mr. Carranza a proposal to bring peace to the border," Hoffman said as he put down his fork and wiped his mouth before speaking again. "Peace throughout Mexico is something that must be settled among Mexicans, without American interference."

"Peace would have come to México a long time ago but for American interference," *señor* Reyna said.

Hoffman ignored the old man's gibe, attributing the diplomatic lapse to a lack of sleep. Hoffman had decided before this meeting that he would limit his dialogue with *señor* Reyna to the matter involving Balo. On the broader issue of recognition, he would insist on taking that up with Carranza directly.

"I believe I can relay an offer from President Wilson that will be acceptable to you," Hoffman told *señor* Reyna.

"And what would that be?" *señor* Reyna asked.

"The president is prepared to instruct Texas authorities not to pursue Balo unless he comes into Texas," Hoffman said. "The president will not ask for his extradition, either. In other words, as long as Balo stays in Mexico, he will be free from American prosecution."

"That is a reasonable proposition," *señor* Reyna quickly responded.

"Ah, but wait father," Manuel spoke up. "Balo is free from American prosecution, but the rest of us must subject ourselves to American persecution."

Hoffman was taken aback by Manuel's comment. He had understood, from their earlier conversation in San Diego, that Manuel was OK with the president's offer. *Señor* Reyna looked at his son, waiting for him to say more.

"The deal, father," Manuel continued, "includes a proviso that all your family must leave American territory. In America, apparently, not only those convicted without trial but also their loved ones must be punished."

Señor Reyna let out a laugh. "Being banned from the north to México is not punishment, son," *señor* Reyna said. "It is a blessing."

Señor Reyna turned to Hoffman and told him the president had a deal.

"My family will return to México at the earliest convenience. The situation here has settled down enough that they should be safe," he said.

The older man then turned to his son Manuel and instructed him to return to San Diego that very afternoon and prepare for the return of his mother and sister. He also told him to get word to Balo and let him know he wanted to talk with him within two weeks in Linares.

"And what of the other half of our deal?" *señor* Reyna asked as he turned his attention to Hoffman. "Will your president recognize my president?"

"With all due respect," Hoffman said, "that is a matter I have to take up with Mr. Carranza directly."

"Fair enough," *señor* Reyna said. "You have held up my end of the bargain. If you like I will take you to México City to meet with the first chief."

"I would appreciate that very much," Hoffman said. He had never been to Mexico and did not even know in what direction to head to reach the capital.

"Then it is settled. We will leave right away," *señor* Reyna said as he rose from the table to prepare for the trip.

Hoffman and Manuel were left alone at the table staring at each other. Hoffman broke the silence. "I was under the impression the president's proposal was acceptable," Hoffman told Manuel.

"I told you it would be acceptable to my father, and it was," Manuel responded. "I, nor you, found it acceptable as a matter of fairness."

Hoffman sat without responding. He recognized that Manuel was right. The idea of guilt by association was repugnant to him. Manuel rose and began to leave.

"Don't worry about us, my friend, we will be fine," Manuel said. "You and I both know we live in a turbulent world ruled by imperfect men. We idealists must be flexible in order to rise to the challenges flawed circumstances present us."

***

As Balo walked towards the *río* behind *señor* Perales' wagon he noticed some crosses up ahead by the side of the road. Three crosses marked the place where three of his countrymen had met death. The roadways throughout the valley and northern México were sprinkled by the grave markings. His people believed in honoring the place where the soul had departed the body.

The caravan Balo was with was approaching the crossing at Río Grande City. Little did Balo know that his brother Manuel had crossed at the same place only the day before. Balo had persuaded *señor* Perales to go to Agualeguas and then to Linares. He needed to get some good rest and nourishment before they continued on to his father's *hacienda*.

Balo played the role of poor *campesino* as they approached the United States inspectors on the north side of the river. The inspectors were not really concerned with *Mexicanos* heading back to México. Their interest was to make sure no rebels crossed over from México. Balo was not surprised at the ease with which his group crossed the river. *Mexicano* inspectors were only interested in getting a *mordida* from those seeking entry. People like the Peraleses did not have much to offer, so some of the Mexican soldiers would try to extort carnal favors from their women. One soldier made a move on Christina but quickly found himself at the end of a rifle barrel that Balo produced from under his *sarape*. The soldier stepped back and let them pass.

Balo urged *señor* Perales to continue on to Agualeguas before stopping. If they kept moving, he told *señor*

Perales they would make it to his grandparents' home shortly after nightfall. The rest of the caravan stopped at Mier.

When Balo and his benefactors reached his grandparents' home he noticed a candle on in a second floor bedroom. Balo knocked on his grand aunt's front door next to his grandparents' house and when the elderly woman opened the door Balo reached for her waist and playfully picked her up.

"*Hola viejita*" he joked with her as he kissed her on the cheek. "You did not expect to be swept off your feet tonight."

"*Huerco sinvergüenza*," the old spinster said, mocking anger, "put me down you shameless *bandido*."

Christina and her family stood quietly on the street. Balo turned to them and introduced them to his *tía* Nachita and them to her. He asked Nachita why there was a light on at his grandfather's house and she told him Manuel was up there writing.

"Your father and a *gringo* man left earlier today for Linares but Manuel said he would depart tomorrow for San Diego," Nachita told Balo.

The thought that Hoffman had been in his grandfather's house troubled Balo but he did not dwell on it. His father was working on a plan to stop the fighting and get his family back in one piece. Balo could hardly blame him for that. Besides, Balo was ready for the same. He was tired of the fighting and the killing. The last few days with Christina had mellowed him even more. He had no doubt but that he was falling in love with this girl of modest means and confident character. She had no dowry to offer him but she made him feel at peace with her plain talking and caring ways.

Balo went next door and entered the house without knocking. He invited his guests in and stood in the middle of the *sala* and called out to Manuel. "*Tu que eres un gran poeta, ven aqui y te entrego mi escopeta,*" Balo recited in his best effort at rhyming. "For war no longer beckons me, to the arms of my mother I long to flee."

Manuel smiled, instantly recognizing his brother's voice. He put down his pencil and ran downstairs, composing his own verse as he went. "Who is that who talks of war and love, who is it that who summons me from above," Manuel responded. "*Sona como la voz de mi hermano el menor, que siempre aspiro ser una persona mayor.*"

Manuel reached the bottom of the staircase and the two brothers embraced in a strong *abrazo*. Balo forgot about his wound and released from the embrace with a wince.

"*Que pasa hermano?*" Manuel asked. "Am I too strong for you now?" Manuel noticed a bandage as Balo reached for his arm.

"I can still take you in a wrestling match, *hermanito,*" Balo joked with his older brother whom he towered over by several inches. "I just took a *rinche* bullet, but I'm all right."

Balo assured Manuel that his wound was not serious. He then turned and presented the Perales family to his brother.

"And this is my *doctora*, Christina," Balo told Manuel with obvious glee.

"And a pretty doctor she is," Manuel teased his brother. "I'm sure she heals with all kinds of medicine and treatments."

Christina blushed. She saw, over Manuel's shoulder, a girl enter the kitchen to began to prepare food. She quickly excused herself, saying she needed to help in the kitchen. Balo tried to stop her telling her she was a guest but she would have none of it.

"*Muy wapa*," Manuel teased Balo some more. "Not only a doctor but a cook. That is someone you should keep an eye on."

"Oh, but I am," Balo winked at Manuel.

"*Señor y señora Perales* please have a seat," Manuel said directing them to the dining table. "I always make coffee when I am up late writing. Please have some and rest until the food is ready."

Balo and Manuel excused themselves and went into another room to talk privately. Balo told Manuel about his wounding and how the Peraleses had cared for him, especially Christina. Balo did not even try to be coy about Christina with his brother. He told Manuel about his feelings for Christina and how he had talked her father into going to Linares with him. His plan was to get more time to get to know Christina and for her to see him as an ordinary man and not as a bigger than life leader of a revolution.

"You know Manuel," Balo said, "I have come to the realization that our cause is worthy but our tactics are flawed. Father is right. We cannot begin to match the power of the *Americanos*. Not even with all the money in México, much less with leftover Mexican troops and *vaqueros* untrained in war tactics. In the meantime, the very people we are trying to help are being slaughtered. Our enemy is a ruthless, vengeful foe.

"In the last couple of months I have seen too many innocent people killed, and for what? The *gringo* has only gotten more reinforcements from up north and now they are stronger than ever. Our people are being killed with impunity. They are being driven off their lands in greater numbers than ever.

"The old timers like *señor* Perales are right. The way to improve our station in life is through education. We must improve our people's ability to read and write and count. When they learn these things they will be better able to understand and combat the trickery and fraud the *gringo* commits. They will not be so easily fooled. The second part of *señor* Perales' equation is patience. Time will give us strength; it will increase our level of understanding; and it will increase our numbers. With numbers and understanding come power; economic power and political power.

"Finally," Balo said as he reached the end of his homily, "we must keep our faith in God. No good and noble people have ever been forsaken by God. People of faith always triumph over evil in the end."

Manuel smiled at Balo. He was amazed that his brother had taken all that his father and mother had been teaching him for years and attributed its wisdom to a *campesino* with no formal education. But those lessons did not require book learning. They were the lessons of life that one picked up through years of experience. What Manuel found even more remarkable was that he had not stayed to write poetry. He had been writing a lengthy tract on the same thesis. Somehow, Manuel thought, his intellectual treatment of the subject did not measure up to the simple lucidity of Balo's or *señor* Perales' words.

"Our parents will be very happy with your epiphany," Manuel said. "It will make it easy on *papá*, especially."

"What do you mean?" Balo asked.

Manuel explained the morning's exchange between Hoffman and their father.

"*Papá* wanted me to contact you so that you could report to him in Linares. I'm sure he thought you would give him trouble in accepting the *Americanos*' terms."

"Not any more," Balo said, resignedly. "A couple of weeks ago, maybe. A couple of months ago, definitely. But not now. To Linares is where I am heading on my own. I will stay for a good while, I suspect."

As he said this Balo looked into the kitchen and saw Christina with a *delantal* on, standing in front of a *comal* cooking *tortillas*. He imagined this scene in a couple of years in their own house, perhaps with a son or daughter tugging at her dress.

"I was going to write you a letter about all this," Manuel said. "You have saved me a lot of trouble. My mission now is to return to San Diego and tell *mamá* and Monica the news.

"That should not present a problem," Manuel continued. "Mother will be eager to have her family back together. Monica may be a little disappointed but she will not resist."

"Why so?" Balo asked.

Manuel explained to Balo that Monica and Hoffman had been exchanging letters and she may have developed a platonic interest in him. At first, Balo resented the idea but then he realized his sister too was entitled to love and happiness. What if it was with a *gringo*. Hoffman had proved to be an honorable man, Balo surmised. In the end, Balo believed his father would have more concern over his choice of a poor *Mexicana* then with Hoffman, who after all was of the noble class.

"I guess I will be the most put out," Manuel said with a smile. "The love of my life is a *Tejana* through and through. I'm not sure I can convince her to come to México, nor am I sure I want to."

"Love knows no boundaries, *hermano*," Balo told Manuel. "*Si es firme*, she will follow her man."

"*Nos estamos haciendo viejo carnal*," Manuel said to Balo. "We must be getting old talking about relationships that promise to make us settle down."

They both laughed out loud and walked to the dining room where Christina and her mother were setting the food on the table. After a good meal, Balo was looking forward to a restful night's sleep. The road to Linares and the future was still ahead and he wanted to get started early, rested, and well nourished.

Before going to bed, Balo asked Manuel for a favor. "Please get word to Cleto and my men that I have been wounded and have returned to Linares to heal and that I will not be returning to Texas anytime soon."

Manuel placed his hands on his brother's shoulders and assured him that his "big brother" would take care of it.

***

Hoffman and *señor* Reyna had arrived at Hacienda la Purísima in Linares in the middle of the night and had gone straight to bed. It was mid-morning before Hoffman awoke. To his surprise, *señor* Reyna was not yet up and around. Hoffman worried he might have taken ill since *señor* Reyna made it a point to remind everyone that he was an early riser. Hoffman washed up and went outside to get some fresh air. He was impressed at the apparent wealth that *señor* Reyna commanded. Equally impressive was that he had held onto his enterprise relatively unscathed by the revolutionary devastation all around it. Hoffman reviewed the scene as he walked into a courtyard. He could see a number of smaller but well-built houses just beyond the main house. As he walked out of the main house's fenced area, Hoffman could see large orchards of peaches and orange trees. Smaller clusters of fig, pomegranate, and avocado trees could be seen off to the sides of the larger orchards. Sprinkled here and there were small gardens, where the hacienda residents grew corn, sugarcane, squash, beans, sweet potatoes, green onions, and a number of other vegetables. Truly, this was a fertile region. Behind the smaller houses were small pens with pigs, goats, chickens, milk cows, and a couple of head of beef cattle. This hacienda appeared to Hoffman to be a self-contained operation. The cash crops seemed to be the fruit produce, mainly peaches and oranges. All the rest of the activity seemed intended for consumption by hacienda residents.

As Hoffman rounded the grounds, toward the rear of the *casa mayor* he encountered barns, sheds, and corrals where the horses, wagons, carriages, and other items of transport were kept and maintained. Despite its apparent wealth, Hoffman saw little evidence of modernity. Not one automobile or tractor was in sight.

"*Buenos días*," came a booming voice from behind Hoffman as he stood watching workmen tending to their chores. Hoffman turned and noticed *señor* Reyna sitting in an outside veranda having coffee and reading a newspaper.

"Breakfast," was all that *señor* Reyna said. Without Manuel to interpret, Hoffman and *señor* Reyna had hardly exchanged a word during their trip from Agualeguas to Linares.

"Good morning," Hoffman said as he approached the table where *señor* Reyna sat with a stack of newspapers on the floor next to his chair. Apparently he was catching up with the news that he had missed while he had been away. By the looks of it, *señor* Reyna had been reading for a while; reaffirming his contention that he indeed was an early riser.

"Leave, one hour," *señor* Reyna said to Hoffman, holding up his right index finger for confirmation.

Three days later, *señor* Reyna and Hoffman were at the Palacio Nacional in México City awaiting an audience with Carranza. The trip south had been uneventful. *Señor* Reyna had chosen to take a route away from a potential encounter with warring revolutionary forces, especially Villistas who were still making incursions from the Sierra Madre. The two had traveled by carriage from the *hacienda* to Linares proper where they had boarded a troop train that took them via Ciudad Victoria to the port city of Tampico. *Señor* Reyna carried papers from Carranza that gave him and his traveling party safe passage anywhere the Carrancistas controlled. Troop movements were common throughout the trip, but no skirmishes were encountered. People generally were going about the business of reconstruction. On the countryside they were busy tending to sheds, fences, and fields. In the cities, the air of renewal also dominated. Merchants were peddling goods, craftsmen were rebuilding structures destroyed by cannon fire, and children were filling the streets — some playing and others peddling goods to help their families eke out a living.

From Tampico, *señor* Reyna and Hoffman had boarded a second train that had carried them to the capital. México City was a much larger city than the American capital of Washington, D.C. It was much larger than any city Hoffman had ever visited. The level of human activity was much more intense than any of the places they had passed through on their way down. The signs of war were also more evident. The capital had been occupied by a succession of factions contending for control of the nation. Villistas, Zapatistas, and now Carrancistas had held the capital since the beginning of the year.

Remarkably, the Palacio Nacional had been spared of serious damage. Located on the eastern edge of the Zócalo in the city's center, the Palacio Nacional had been the seat of civil authority in México since the days of the Spanish viceroys. The Zócalo itself had been the center of the Aztec capital of Tenochtitlan even before the Spanish conquest. The Zócalo was a large open square surrounded by the seats of power and culture. In addition to the Palacio Nacional, on the north end of the square was the Metropolitan Cathedral and an array of national and municipal governmental offices bounded other sides of the square. Across the street from the national palace was the residence of the bishop to whom the Indian Juan Diego had revealed the miraculous imprint on his cloak of the Virgin mother of Jesus, whom the Mexicans paid homage to as the Virgen de Guadalupe. Nearby were the Aztec pyramids.

Hoffman was amazed by the beauty and history that abounded at this place. They had entered the Palacio Nacional into an open courtyard surrounded by two floors of offices. They had ascended a splendid staircase, gone through spacious corridors, and were now waiting in an ornate waiting room outside the president's office.

A Carranza aide came out from an inner office and escorted *señor* Reyna and Hoffman to where the president was waiting, sitting in front of an open window in a poorly lit office. Wearing his customary tinted glasses, Carranza greeted his friend *señor* Reyna with a limp handshake. Hoffman expected the two would embrace firmly as he had observed to be the custom among Mexican men. Speaking in Spanish, *señor* Reyna introduced Hoffman to the first chief.

"Good morning, Captain Hoffman," Carranza said as he put out his hand. "I trust you had a pleasant trip."

"Yes, we had gene..., uh, Mr. Carranza," Hoffman responded, unsure of how to address Carranza, who had not been democratically elected. Still, if their meeting went as planned, Carranza would be recognized as head of state.

"I have truly enjoyed your great capital city during our brief stay here. I hope to have some time before we leave to see more of it," Hoffman continued. "My mother would enjoy a memento from the cathedral."

"You are Catholic, Captain?" Carranza asked.

"Yes, sir," was Hoffman's short answer.

"Then, perhaps we can deal as men of God who seek only peace for all his people," Carranza said.

"Servando telegraphed ahead that you had an opportunity to meet with President Wilson and may have a message for us," Carranza quickly got to the point.

"Yes, Mr. President," Hoffman responded, turning to a more formal diplomatic tone. "President Wilson sends his warmest personal regards to you and your family."

Carranza nodded acknowledgement as Hoffman continued. "President Wilson is very concerned over the situation throughout Mexico, but he is troubled by the spillover of violence unto American soil. The situation in South Texas is especially worrisome."

"We appreciate your president's concern over México, but that is an internal matter that is being decided among *Mexicanos*," Carranza told Hoffman. "We *Mexicanos* may have our differences, but they are no more serious than what your country had during your civil war. There are those who like to call our troubles a revolution, but we had our revolution a century ago.

What is happening in México is a great civil war testing and sorting out ideas of governing and of the makeup of the Mexican nation.

"What is happening north of the Río Bravo is an internal matter for you Americans to handle," Carranza told Hoffman. "As much as it pains us, the Treaty of Guadalupe established the Bravo as our border. We would no more want to entangle ourselves in your problems than we want you to interfere in ours."

"On that point we have no disagreement, Mr. President," Hoffman answered Carranza. "The problem is that the raids in the Río Grande Valley have been traced to soldiers of the Constitutionalist Army stationed at Matamoros.

"Moreover," Hoffman said, "the perpetrators seek and receive refuge on the Mexican side of the border."

"Those issues we cannot address if we do not have the recognized authority," Carranza interjected, as he maneuvered himself into a negotiating posture. "If we were to be accorded the stature of a legitimate and sovereign power by your country, we would have to be responsive to your diplomatic overtures."

"President Wilson is prepared to recognize you as the head of the government of Mexico. In order to do so, he must be convinced that the Mexican people accept your leadership. A sure sign of that would be if elements operating clandestinely on the border would obey your command to desist."

"Let us be frank and direct, Captain Hoffman," Carranza said as he leaned forward. "I am prepared to close off the border to anyone wishing to cross it for illegal purposes. I am also willing to close the border to anyone wishing to enter our country while in flight from illegal actions. Those orders will be given when I have assurances that the United States of the North is prepared to accept México under my leadership, and accord us full diplomatic recognition."

Hoffman hesitated for a moment. He had been given the authority to make an offer but he did not feel certain that he could accept an offer and consummate an agreement. Hoffman concluded that he had put forth President Wilson's offer and Carranza had in turn conceded the points President Wilson had wanted to hear. In his mind, Hoffman concluded, an agreement had been reached. He hoped President Wilson saw it the same way.

"Then I believe we have an agreement," Hoffman said to Carranza extending his hand. "You have my word on it."

Carranza shook on the deal, aware that Hoffman might not be able to deliver. Carranza felt he had to trust Hoffman in order to move forward. Besides, Carranza reasoned, if Wilson reneged on the agreement, México would lift the curtain on the border and the raids would resume.

"To show good faith, I will issue orders immediately for the border to be shut down, except for legal movements of goods and people," Carranza said. "Additionally, I will direct that all leaders of the disturbances in the north side of the border will be arrested if they are found south of the border."

"Mr. President," Hoffman said, "we do not believe that General Nefarrate would be fully disposed to carrying out your orders. He seems to us to be overly inclined to assist in the assaults being perpetrated in Texas."

"As a new partner in securing peace and order between our countries, I will remove General Nefarrate from Matamoros and name a replacement with no ties to the people on the border," Carranza said.

"I must tell you, however, that General Nefarrate is not your problem. Reports I have been receiving are that your Texas Rangers are the source of most of your trouble. General Nefarrate has often commented that he can work with the American military, but the Rangers are another matter. They do not listen, obey, care for, or respect the law. They are racist brutes who have not endeared themselves to those they callously persecute. They are the true bandits your authorities need to be concerned with."

Señor Reyna nodded his head in agreement, while Hoffman winced at the lecture from Carranza. Hoffman, of course, knew that the Mexican leader was right on point.

"Regrettably, I have seen firsthand some of their work," Hoffman responded to Carranza. "That is a matter that

I will personally take up with President Wilson. I believe he will take the matter up with Governor Ferguson. You must understand that in our system, the states have much independent power, and their leaders are not always obliged to listen to the president."

The first chief smiled and replied to Hoffman that politics was politics everywhere, regardless of the system of government.

"The president, I am sure, has the tools at his disposal to persuade the governor to do what is right," Carranza said.

"There is one more thing. President Wilson has assured *señor* Reyna that the United States will not pursue his son for the indictment issued against him in Texas if he stays out of our country. Nor will we request his extradition. In short, we do not want him arrested, unless he violated your laws and then it would be a matter for Mexican authorities."

"*Señor* Reyna is a very old and dear friend," Carranza said, "and I know his son is a good man. I do not anticipate that he would be a problem."

Señor Reyna smiled in relief and nodded to Carranza in agreement and appreciation.

Carranza rose and extended his hand to *señor* Reyna and bid him a safe return trip. Carranza reflected on how lucky his friend was to be able to return to his *hacienda*. He told *señor* Reyna how much he yearned to be going back to his own *rancho* in Coahuila. Hoffman also stood and shook Carranza's hand in turn, telling Carranza that he would report to President Wilson everything they had discussed and agreed to.

As Hoffman and *señor* Reyna walked out of the Presidential Palace, Hoffman noticed a spring in *señor* Reyna's step and a beam in his face. He was clearly pleased with the meeting and could sense soon having his family back together in the home he had made for them in Linares.

"Leave in two days," *señor* Reyna said to Hoffman, flashing two fingers for emphasis.

Good, Hoffman thought. He needed the rest, and he would have a little time to take in the history and culture of the amazing Mexican capital.

Chapter 21

Hoffman had spent an entire day as a tourist in Mexico City and had not made it out of the Zócalo and its immediate surroundings. The cathedral had occupied most of his day. He had purchased an etching of the Virgen de Guadalupe from a street artist that he planned to take to his mother in Cumberland. He also purchased a bronze medallion of the Virgin that he intended to give to Monica if he had a chance to see her before she left San Diego for Linares.

Hoffman and *señor* Reyna arrived at the Tampico train station shortly after noon. As they waited for their train destined for Monterrey, they observed a large contingent of soldiers headed north up the coast to Matamoros. Hoffman learned that they were troops under the command of General Eugenio López, who was to replace General Nefarrate. Hoffman felt good that Carranza was living up to his word. It was a good sign, another plus for Hoffman's argument to President Wilson to ratify his own agreement with Carranza.

The rest of the trip to Linares was without incident. Hoffman accepted *señor* Reyna's invitation to spend the night and get an early start the following morning. He rose early and went looking for *señor* Reyna in the veranda. He found him as he had expected with his newspapers and coffee. What Hoffman had not expected was to see Balo sitting at the table with his father. He, too, was reading a newspaper.

"Good morning," Hoffman said.

"*Ah, buenos días, señor* Hoffman," Balo said, as both father and son looked up. *Señor* Reyna motioned to Hoffman to take a seat at the table. Hoffman sat and the two men continued reading. A servant came around and served him coffee.

"You will have to excuse us," Balo finally broke the silence. "It is a family tradition not to bother *papá* while he is reading his morning paper."

"I understand," Hoffman said. "I merely wanted to say goodbye and thank your father for his help."

Señor Reyna spoke to Balo in Spanish, who relayed to Hoffman his father's acceptance and his invitation to join them for breakfast.

"Where are you off to?" Balo asked.

"Today, to Brownsville," Hoffman said. "My ultimate destination is Washington, and I hope to make a stop in San Diego, as well, to thank your brother for his help."

Balo could not hold back a smirk. He knew the *gringo's* real purpose for going to San Diego was to see Monica.

Balo was resigned to that reality and to the knowledge that his sister at 34 was a grown woman and could handle the situation.

"Well you better hurry, because Manuel left here a week ago to settle matters in San Diego and bring my mother and sister back here," Balo told Hoffman. "But first you must have a good breakfast. You will need the nourishment."

Hoffman was astonished at Balo's friendly demeanor. *Señor* Reyna also looked up with bemusement on his face. The three men continued eating their breakfast in silence, until Balo spoke up again.

"Father, I would like you to meet a family I have asked to move into the house that old man Ibáñez used to live in," Balo said. "They were very helpful to me when the *rinches* shot me, so I knew you would not mind it if I helped them in return."

Señor Reyna quickly put his fork down and looked at his son with concern. Hoffman also put down his fork and stopped eating.

"You were shot?" *señor* Reyna asked.

"*Sí, papá,* but I am OK," Balo responded. "The *rinches* are not very good shots, unless you have your backs to them and are unarmed. When you are rushing them on your horse with your rifle a-blazing, they do not shoot too well."

Balo was clearly enjoying telling the account of his most recent encounter with the *rinches*. He smiled and relished in his sarcasm about the *rinches'* bravery. His father was not amused at all. Hoffman wrote it off to male bravado.

"Where did they shoot you?" *señor* Reyna asked as he looked over his son for signs of injury.

"On my arm, above my elbow," Balo said as he touched his left arm with his right hand. "But *señor* Perales' daughter Christina tended to me, and I am almost completely healed."

Hoffman pushed his chair away and announced that he really needed to be on his way. He thanked *señor* Reyna again and bid Balo farewell.

"I hope you fully recover from your wound," Hoffman told Balo. "I hope we all recover soon from the social wound this whole affair has inflicted on the people of South Texas."

"Time will tell whether it really heals all wounds," Balo responded.

Neither Balo nor his father rose to see Hoffman off. *Señor* Reyna had provided one of his carriages and a driver to take Hoffman back to the river at Camargo. President Carranza had supplied him with papers guaranteeing safe and unimpeded passage anywhere in México. *Señor* Reyna's business with Hoffman had been completed. He was more intrigued with his son's latest adventure than with Hoffman's departure.

"For someone who has been shot, you are very cheerful," *señor* Reyna told Balo. "Something tells me this

Christina may have something to do with why you feel so happy at being shot."

"Why is it, father, that you always know what I am thinking and feeling before I tell you?" Balo asked.

"Because you are my flesh and blood," *señor* Reyna told Balo. "Besides, I traveled in your shoes, on your path many years ago. The glow in your face and tenor in your voice are what I experienced when I met your mother."

"Well, then you understand exactly how I feel, because next to my mother, I have never felt this warm-hearted for anyone," Balo said. "But the love for my mother makes me feel warm and comfortable like a blanket in winter. *Lo que siento para Christina es como cuando uno chamusca nopal en el santo sol.*"

Señor Reyna chuckled at his son's simile. He was not sure what burning cactus pear on a hot day had to do with love, but he guessed that Balo meant that his fervor for Christina was a burning passion.

"You have your brother's gift for romantic prose," *señor* Reyna told Balo, unable to hold back a laugh at his son's expressions of love.

Balo told his father all about how Christina had treated his wound with an old *curandero's* skill. He told his father of their more recent days at the *hacienda*. Of the long walks through the orchards, where Christina would talk about the importance of family and Christian values. The softness of her voice betrayed the hardness of the life she had lived. And yet, she had not been embittered

by her experiences. Instead, she had learned and had
built up her strength to combat other trials that life surely
had in store.

"While life has many tragedies looming for all of us, it
also has many joys. One could not experience one without
the other," she had said. "How can one know joy without having experienced sadness? How could one know
the difference, if these two feelings were not compared?
Every low point in life filled with grief is eventually followed by one of life's high moments of delight."

She pointed to their recent experiences for proof. She
had been in the depths of sorrow after her brother's
death, but then Balo had come into her life, and now
her happiness soared above the clouds. Balo looked at
his own situation to reinforce her wisdom. He, too, had
been wallowing in doubt and despair about his life, cul-
minating in his wounding. But now he was more certain
than ever about the future, and it was through that very
wound that he had come to know his happiness.

"Let's go to old man Ibáñez' house so you can meet
Christina and her family," Balo told his father. "I want
you to ask his father for me for her hand in marriage."

Señor Reyna could not stop chuckling at his son's
enthusiasm and uncontrolled joy. He was glad Balo had
found someone to love. Hopefully, it would replace the
hate he had carried inside him for years.

"*Cálmate, mijo,*" *señor* Reyna said to Balo, trying to
calm him. "These things are not rushed into. We must

wait for your mother to return. Then we will have the Peraleses over for dinner and we will discuss your intentions. When it comes to love, it is always best to wait for the storm of passion to settle down before acting on one's desires. All will be done in the right way, at the right time."

"I will not change my mind," Balo told his father as if to preempt any thoughts he might have about dissuading him from his plans.

"I know you will not," *señor* Reyna said. "And I do not want you to. If this girl makes you this happy, I, too, want her in our lives."

No other words could have pleased Balo more. He had always secretly longed for his father's approval, and up until now, that had been given very sparingly and reluctantly.

"We will go meet them just the same," *señor* Reyna said. "I want to know what my future *compadre* can do to help us with the upcoming planting season. But before we go, we need to talk about the business with the *Americano* Hoffman."

Señor Reyna told Balo about his trip to the capital city of México and their visit with the first chief. He also told him about running into General Lopez at Tampico.

"You must give up your activities regarding the *Plan de San Diego* business," *señor* Reyna said to Balo. "The first chief will quickly put a stop to any assistance his army may have been giving the movement. The matter will soon come to an end, crushed between the *Americano* and *Mexicano* armies."

Balo's joy at once turned somber. He understood, agreed, and accepted what his father was telling him. Still, he knew of too many men and of too many innocent civilians who had died in the struggle. Had it all been in vain? Balo could not help but feel that the blood of all those people would be in his hands forever. The weeping of all their surviving family members would forever haunt his dreams.

"The fight is no longer in me father," Balo responded with a heavy sigh. "After all the years of hearing you tell me how senseless all this was, and listening to mother tell me to let go of my hate over *tío* Salomé and *tío* Poncho, I have finally arrived at a point in my life where I agree with both of you. It took a *rinche's* bullet that pierced my body and the caring of girl who pierced my heart to help me crystallize my thinking.

"The truth is that I was almost there when I got shot. I could see the *gringos* building up and reinforcing their already potent Army. We could deal with the cowardly *rinches*, but as you often told me, the *gringo* Army is too powerful. The other thing that brought me around to your position were the untold numbers of innocent people who have been killed as a result of our struggle. We no longer have the support of our own people. *Rancherias* are calling the *Americano* Army for protection. Thousands of *Mexicanos* are fleeing *Tejas* and returning to México. Many abandoning land that has been in their families for generations."

A tear flowed down Balo's cheek as he tried to fight the urge to cry. He sighed profoundly before resuming to talk.

"The worst thing, *papá*, is that I am responsible for all those deaths. I was the spark that kept the fires of death and destruction burning. How will I explain to my children this horrible responsibility?"

"You will not have to because it is not true," *señor* Reyna told his son, trying to comfort him. "You are not responsible. The *rinches* and unscrupulous *gringos* will be stained by the blood of all those innocent lives lost. It is they who will have some explaining to do. Regrettably, those without morals are incapable of comprehending their own evil. They will probably gloat to their children about the role they played in the 'bandit' war.

"You, my son, on the other hand, were raised to know the difference between right and wrong, between good and evil. We, but especially your mother, taught you that men must live by Christ's teachings if he is to receive salvation and redemption.

"I did not oppose what you were doing because your cause was wrong. Every *Mexicano* embraces the struggle for fairness and the freedom to live our lives as we choose and to the degree of success that we are capable. Your cause is right; it is your means that are wrong. And I, unlike your mother, who is a pacifist, do not oppose the use of force to achieve your means. What I saw as wrong was the use of violence against impossible chances. Your struggle was doomed from the start because your enemy was just as willing to employ violence, and they had the means to sustain their attacks and up the ante with atrocities on innocent bystanders."

Señor Reyna paused and reflected for a moment on what he was trying to convey to his son. He had never really had a political conversation with either of his sons. As a *hacendado* his focus had always been his orchards and how they could provide for a comfortable living for his family. But like any man, he held political beliefs. They primarily centered on that of a conservative businessman. Money was the real power in the world. The idealists believed that political freedom was the answer to man's social dilemma. But political power could not be had without first acquiring economic power, *señor* Reyna believed. Still, political power was something, and in many respects, it was easier to acquire if one had the right number of votes. It was clear to *señor* Reyna the pragmatist that his people had the numbers on their side if they could be molded into a political force.

"You know, my son," *señor* Reyna resumed with his counsel to Balo, "the change you seek can be achieved through non-violence. It may take time and the patience of learned men to lead the struggle, but you can use the system of laws in the north to get what you want. The right to vote is an important right that can be used to remedy many wrongs. The access to the courts is another important right that can be used to rectify the injustices you fight against."

These points rang true with Balo. He had discussed his concerns with Manuel before. Manuel had pointed out to Balo the same line of reasoning. In San Diego, Manuel had met Archie Parr, a state senator who had molded the *Mexicanos* into a political force. Many of the elected officials in Duval County, for which San Diego served as county seat, were *Mexicanos*. Manuel talked about others whom he had met, like J. Luz Saenz, who was born in a *rancho* near Realitos but now was emerging as a leader of the *Mexicanos* in Alice. Manuel had read about Francisco Chapa of San Antonio who was a close adviser of Gov. Ferguson. Manuel told Balo of the many *grupos mutualistas* that were working to improve the lot of the *Mexicanos* in *Tejas*. Balo, himself, knew of the *abogado* Jose Tomas Canales from Brownsville who had represented one of the *revoltosos* charged with murder. Canales represented Brownsville in the state capital, Austin, and had aggressively criticized the *rinches* and had asked that they be investigated.

"You are right, father," Balo said. "Change will come over time through the ballot box and the courts. But it will have to come without me. I have had enough with this struggle. I was motivated by revenge, and I have killed enough *gringos* to avenge *mis tíos*.

"Now I just want to get married, raise a family, and help you with the *huertas*. That is if you will have me as a junior partner."

His father smiled broadly and put out his hand.

"*Hecho*," *señor* Reyna said, and the two sealed the deal with a handshake and an *abrazo*.

Chapter 22

Hoffman had spent nearly a week in Brownsville, much longer than he had anticipated or wanted. When he arrived, the town was abuzz with reports that General Nefarrate had arrested Cleto. Many, however, were skeptical. They told of hearing from friends that Cleto was freely cavorting around Matamoros.

What was true was that a day after Hoffman's arrival, General Lopez had marched into Matamoros and relieved General Nefarrate, who had departed for points south. What was equally true was that some 125 of Lopez's soldiers had attacked and routed a group of raiders seeking sanctuary south of the river, upstream from Matamoros.

Every sign told Hoffman that Carranza was making good on his word. Hoffman knew Balo was out of action in Linares. Now Cleto was reportedly in jail in Matamoros. The rebel sympathizer Nefarrate was no longer in a position to aid them with spare troops, and his replacement, General Lopez, had cut off their sanctuary.

Upon his arrival at Fort Brown, Hoffman telephoned President Wilson and reported on his meeting with Carranza. He told Wilson that the Mexican leader had accepted the terms Wilson had proposed to put an end to the bloodshed in South Texas. Wilson seemed pleased but remained skeptical. He did not trust Carranza to keep his word. The president asked Hoffman to remain in the Valley for an additional week to size up the situation under the new rules agreed to by Carranza.

Hoffman was deeply disappointed by the president's order to stay. He was anxious to get to San Diego before Monica left for Linares. He knew that she was the woman he had longed for in a relationship. She was beautiful, smart, and well read, as well as a good conversationalist and an independent thinker. Yet, Hoffman had to face the prospect that he might never see her again. He knew, also, that even if he did get to San Diego on time to see her, it could be for the last time. His prospects simply did not look promising. He had done his job too well, and now he could lose what he wanted the most in life because of his success.

But Hoffman knew that President Wilson was right. Any diplomatic agreement, especially with a belligerent power, had to be verified. To Hoffman's dismay, a day after speaking with Persident Wilson, troops were called out to squelch another bandit raid.

The southbound St. Louis, Brownsville, and Mexico Railway train was derailed a few miles north of Brownsville by a well-planned attack by what was believed to be a band of 60 Mexicans. The insurgents had loosened and tied a wire to a rail on the track. They then hid in a nearby *resaca*, and as the train approached, they yanked the rail out from under the train, causing it to go off the tracks and upending several cars. When the dust cleared, four U.S. Army soldiers traveling to Fort Brown and the train engineer were found dead. The Cameron County district attorney, a former Ranger, the state health inspector stationed in Brownsville, and the train's fireman were badly wounded. The attackers escaped without a trace. The following day, however, local vigilantes had rounded up "suspects" and had swiftly executed them. The brief optimism that had swept Brownsville with General Lopez's arrival was quickly replaced with widespread fear and acts of brutality.

When they talked upon Hoffman's return to Brownsville, President Wilson had asked Hoffman to call him back after a week. That time had come, and Hoffman placed the call with great trepidation.

"Hello, Matthew," the president's voice came through the telephone after his secretary put Hoffman through.

"Good morning, Sir," Hoffman said in a somber voice. "I'm afraid I do not have good news to report."

"That's not news in itself," Wilson responded, his attempt at dry humor. "That is what I hear on a daily basis, I'm afraid. So give me your dose of bad news."

"Well, Mr. President, we have had another raid in the last week," Hoffman said. "We have lost four soldiers and a civilian. That tragedy was followed by the cruelty that all these raids engender. American citizens, in retribution, summarily executed a dozen or so local Mexicans."

"That is a tragedy," Wilson responded. "So many young and innocent people dying on American soil. Surely, many more will undoubtedly die in Europe soon. I do not believe I will be able to keep us out of the European war."

After a pregnant pause, the president resumed talking, asking a series of questions.

"Were any of Carranza's men involved?"

"No, Mr. President," Hoffman answered.

"Did the bandits seek escape across the river?"

"Not to my knowledge, Mr. President," Hoffman said.

"Is Carranza keeping his end of the agreement?" President Wilson asked.

"As far as I can tell he is, Mr. President," Hoffman said. "General Lopez has sealed off the border from escape and to infiltrators. He has some of the renegade leaders in custody."

Hoffman did not pass on the rumors that Cleto had been given a commission in Carranza's army and was allowed to make haste to Monterrey. Nor did Hoffman mention that Balo was enjoying the comforts of his father's *hacienda*.

"That is going to have to be good enough for me," Wilson said to Hoffman's surprise. "I can no longer maintain the numbers of troops we have on the Mexican border. We will need them in the European campaign.

"I will instruct Secretary of State Lansing to recognize the Carranza regime and to ask our South American friends to do the same. Governor Ferguson will have to restore order in his state as best he can. Hopefully that will happen soon, while our troops are still there to help."

"Let's hope for that," Hoffman responded. "I do not believe that the Texas authorities can control the situation without our help and Carranza's cooperation. Left alone, the Rangers will only make things worse. I believe you have made the right decision, Mr. President," Hoffman added. "The challenge in Europe will be much greater."

"Only time will tell, Matthew," the president said. "But for now, we must move on. You have completed this assignment, Matthew, and as I explained, you have done very good work. You may report back to your post at Fort Sam Houston as soon as you can make the arrangements."

"Thank you, Mr. President," Hoffman said, somewhat relieved. At the start his mission Hoffman had been apprehensive and concerned with earning the professor's approval. He started out as a late-blooming college student, but he was going back to San Antonio as a much wiser man who, in a few short months, had seen more of the real world than he had ever imagined. He was no longer concerned with gaining the approval of the old professor. Now he merely wanted for his efforts to result in saving lives. Wilson, too, had grown, Hoffman thought. The professor had been affected by the weighty problems of being commander in chief. Try as he might, President Wilson had come to realize that he could not control events thousands of miles away. The best the president could hope for was to manage events as they reached his office. He was limited in what he could do by the things he could not do.

Hoffman stayed an additional day in Brownsville after his talk with President Wilson. Despite his longing to return to San Diego and a hopeful encounter with Monica, duty commanded him to stay on and monitor how things were evolving.

Word had come that while some raiders who attacked the train had made good their escape to Mexico, several had been cut down in the middle of the river by General Lopez's men. Rumors persisted that Cleto had led the raid. Investigators at the Brownsville train derailment had found a note signed by Cleto. Also found were several white headbands with the inscription, "*Viva la Independencia de Tejas.*"

Though the information appeared conflicting, Hoffman concluded that Carranza was being true to his word. Despite the rumors, there was no indication that could be substantiated that Cleto was a factor in the latest raids. The note found at the scene of the train attack could have been dropped by the person Cleto sent it to. Cleto may have been trying to orchestrate affairs from across the river, but he did not appear to be directly involved. Hoffman believed General Lopez was also being faithful to the spirit of the agreement. He had removed Cleto from the action. He may not have been jailed as had been hoped for, but he was out of the picture, nonetheless. Some raiders had managed to get across the river. That was to be expected. It was a long and porous border. General Lopez could not be expected to have men at every foot of the river.

The movement, Hoffman concluded, was indigenous to South Texas. While rebels often depended on, sought, and received arms and sanctuary from Mexico, the heart of the movement was locally grown. With Carranza and Lopez denying the rebels assistance and protection, the rebels would not be able to sustain the fight. With their leadership removed to Mexico, it would not be long before the troubles would come to an end. Hoffman decided to return to San Antonio and his next assignment. But first he would stop in San Diego.

Chapter 23

Despite recent events and his own experience on the St. Louis, Brownsville, and Mexico Railway train, Hoffman decided to return to San Diego via that mode of transportation. When he arrived at Robstown, Hoffman transferred to the Texas Mexican Railway train to San Diego. Upon arriving at Alice, passengers were told that tracks between Alice and San Diego had been washed away by overnight flash floods. Railroad officials expected a delay of at least a half-day.

An agitated Hoffman decided to seek alternate means of getting to San Diego. He feared the delay would add to his risk of missing Monica. In reality, Hoffman feared that the Reynas may have left for Mexico several days before, but he was hopeful that they were still in town. Hoffman crossed the road by the depot and went to a hotel where he observed what appeared to be taxis. He asked the hotel clerk if there were any cabs that would make the 10-mile trip to San Diego. The clerk told Hoffman that a motor vehicle made the trip to San Diego daily and carried a number of passengers. It would be by within the hour.

Relieved at the news, Hoffman decided to have some coffee in the hotel's restaurant. He picked up a copy of the *Alice Echo* and looked for an empty table but there was none. A gentleman sitting waved at Hoffman to join him. He was a distinguished looking man, dressed in a suit that was somewhat out of place in this rough and tumble country that still imagined itself to be an untamed frontier.

"Please join me, Captain Hoffman," the man at the table said to Hoffman, who had a look of bewilderment because the man was a stranger to him.

"Thank you," Hoffman responded, as he took a chair across the courteous stranger and asked, "have we met?"

"No, we have not, but let's remedy that right now," the man said. "My name is Archie Parr."

"Pleased to meet you," Hoffman said. "I'm Captain Matthew Hoffman, but you already seem to know that."

"I make it my business to know everyone who comes into my county," Parr said. "There is very little that goes on in Duval County that I don't know about."

Indeed, Hoffman was aware of Parr as well. He came across his name often when he read the *Corpus Christi Caller and Daily Herald* for news of the Plan of San Diego. Hoffman read every news story regarding San Diego so naturally he had read about Parr and had surmised that he was the political leader of Duval County.

Hoffman frequently came across Parr's name in the Corpus Christi newspaper regarding political events. From the newspaper Hoffman had learned that Parr had been elected to the state Senate the year before in a highly controversial election. As a former Duval County commissioner, Parr was widely considered to be the political boss of Duval County. Manuel had told Hoffman that many of Duval County's elected officials were in fact citizens of Mexican origin. Parr had gained his political strength by earning the Mexicans' loyalty. He organized the Mexican population into a political force and using their greater numbers, Parr had won control of the county governing apparatus.

Still, the newspaper reported that all had not been smooth sailing for Parr. A cadre of Anglo landowners was challenging his power in court. They had asked the courts, and the courts had agreed, for an independent audit of the county's finances. The county courthouse had mysteriously gone up in flames two years before when a similar request had been made.

With his newfound power base in the Texas Senate, Parr had taken moves to weaken his opponents and strengthen his own power. The *Corpus Christi Caller and Daily Herald* reported that Parr had introduced legislation to split Duval County into two counties. This, the newspaper claimed, would give him twice as many political plums to hand out to his friends and supporters. It would also insulate his home base of

Benavides, in the southern part of the county, from the rich Anglos challenging his power who mostly lived in San Diego, which was situated in the northern half of the county.

Parr was serious looking, befitting his position. Hoffman noticed, however, that this urbanely dressed, slightly balding man with a gentle voice was more than met the eye. His handshake was firm, and his hands were those of a man who had experienced manual labor. While they drank their coffee, Parr shared his personal history with Hoffman. He said he had grown to manhood on the saddle. At an early age, he had become a working cowboy, and 40 years later he was still a cowman, managing his own sizable spread in Duval County. Parr said he had become a successful ranch man since coming to Duval County as a ranch foreman some 30 years earlier.

"This lad here is my son, George," Parr told Hoffman, as a young boy — not more than 15 Hoffman thought — joined them at the table. Even the young boy was somewhat familiar to Hoffman. According to the newspaper, he had been the subject of anti-nepotism legislation introduced in the state Legislature after his father appointed him as a Senate page.

"I have been told you have made several trips to San Diego looking into the so called 'Plan of San Diego,'" Parr said to Hoffman.

"That's right," Hoffman replied. "From the sounds of it, you do not seem to place much weight on this matter."

Parr smiled. "No, I don't place much weight on this so called Plan," Parr answered Hoffman. "The Mexican people around these parts are good hardworking citizens. They have no desire to return to Mexico. I know because many are my friends and neighbors. They are good people and are happy with their lives."

Even though San Diego was the namesake of the Plan under which the rebellion was being carried out, it seemed to be a minor player. Two locals had been arrested in connection with the plot, but they had been released on grounds that though they had names similar to suspected organizers, they were in fact unconnected to the Plan of San Diego. The Corpus Christi newspaper reported that residents of San Diego and Duval County dismissed the plot as lunacy. During recent celebrations for Mexican Independence Day, army troops from Kingsville had been sent to San Diego on reports that the celebration would result in renewed activity regarding the rebellion. The deployment proved to be needless, as San Diego residents carried on their annual fiesta without incident. Hoffman thought it curious that Mexican independence would be celebrated with as much or more fervor than July Fourth. But he reminded himself that at the time of the American independence, this part of the country was part of New Spain. Also, the area was part of Mexico when that country declared its independence from Spain. Since most San Diego residents were Mexican, it made sense, Hoffman surmised, to celebrate the event that truly gave them independence.

"How do you explain the daily raids being carried out all over the Valley?" Hoffman asked.

"Are you on your way back to my county?" Parr asked in return.

"Yes, I am," Hoffman replied, thinking it was curious how Parr referred to the county as his county. This was not said as if he was from that place, but rather as if he owned the county.

"Well, if you'd like we can give you a lift there and we can talk on the way," Parr said to Hoffman.

"I was waiting for the next bus, but I would like to get there sooner if possible," Hoffman said. "I appreciate your kindness."

"Think nothing of it," Parr said, patting Hoffman on the back as they walked to Parr's automobile. "It is my stock in trade to do favors for people. Why are you in a hurry to return?"

"I would like to see some folks before they leave town," Hoffman answered.

"Then we best be on our way," Parr said.

As they started out toward San Diego, Parr returned to Hoffman's earlier question.

"The troubles you have been reading about in the newspapers are exaggerated in order to sell papers. They have a tendency to make mountains out of mole-hills," Parr told Hoffman.

"I agree, one should not believe everything you read in newspapers, but I have seen much of these atrocities firsthand," Hoffman said. "And I have talked to many, both residents of the area and soldiers, who have also witnessed the violence taking place."

"Oh, I'm sure some of that is going on," Parr said. "But most of that is banditry or spillover from the trouble in Mexico. You have noticed, I'm sure, that most of these so-called raids are taking place along the border. Mexican bandits and so-called revolutionaries are the source of these problems, not our Mexican citizens."

Hoffman found Parr fascinating. He had a special knack of making you feel comfortable. His speech and manners were soothing, yet he was gratuitously dismissive about the things he disagreed with and patronizing about that with which he agreed. He colored his suspicions with the phrase "so called" and predicated references to people and thoughts he found agreeable with the word "my" as if he owned them.

"If the president would listen to my governor, this whole mess will be taken care of soon enough," Parr continued. "What we need is, first, more Army troops on the border to keep order, and second, for Mr. Wilson to make peace with Carranza. Order needs to be brought to Mexico before things will settle down in the Valley."

Hoffman could hardly argue with Parr. That had been his assessment and the view finally agreed to by President

Wilson. It was obvious that the senator was unaware of the latest developments, and although Hoffman had completed his mission, he felt an urge to continue this line of conversation with Parr.

"What about your Texas Rangers?" Hoffman asked.

"What about them?" Parr's retort came back quickly and with more than a tinge of acrimony.

"Governor Ferguson seems to believe that more Rangers can solve the problem," Hoffman replied.

"Well, he's dead wrong," Parr said crisply. Parr took a deep breath and paused. It was clear to Hoffman that Parr had been flustered and was trying to regain his composure.

"That is one thing Jim boy and I don't see eye to eye on," Parr finally spoke. It was common knowledge that Parr and Gov. Jim Ferguson were close friends and political allies.

"The Rangers are no more than a bunch of hooligans," Parr continued. "They are hired guns who owe their allegiance to big landowners like Bob Kleberg and Ed Lasater."

Kleberg was the owner of the famous King Ranch, and Lasater was a wealthy landowner in neighboring Brooks County. Lasater was spearheading the effort to audit Duval County's books, where Lasater also owned considerable land.

"The Rangers are a bunch of white trash who do not respect life or property, much less the rights of our

Mexican citizens," Parr went on. "They are a disgrace to Texas."

Hoffman was completely surprised by this type of talk coming out of the mouth of a South Texas Anglo. He was equally surprised that he agreed with every word this particular South Texas Anglo had said. From press accounts, Hoffman had made out Parr to be a corrupt politician and an ogre. But then again, the same press had glorified the vicious Rangers as the saviors of democracy and the protectors of freedom. Nothing could be further from the truth, Hoffman thought. Parr was right: The Rangers were hooligans whose primary concern was protecting the power and wealth of the Texas power structure.

"You may not have heard yet, but President Wilson has agreed to recognize Carranza as the legitimate government in Mexico," Hoffman told Parr. "Already, things on the border are quieting down."

"Well, that's good news," Parr said. "We will have to wait and see if it continues."

"While I agree largely with your premise that much of the troubles have an international aspect, I have also witnessed many transgressions against the civil liberties of American citizens of Mexican descent," Hoffman told Parr. "Not the least of which have come from the Rangers. Local lawmen and plain citizens, often acting as vigilantes, are also guilty."

"The answer to that is political action," Parr said.

"I believe we in Duval County have the answer and the model for others in South Texas to follow. I have marshaled my Mexican friends into a political force. They have paid me back with their votes and support."

Parr went on to tell Hoffman of his experiences with the Mexican people. Parr's first real contact with them was when, as a boy of 15, he had become a cowboy with the Coleman-Fulton pasture company. There he had been taken under the wings of the older Mexican *vaqueros*, who taught him everything he knew about working cattle and living on the range.

The *vaqueros* had taught him a lot more, Parr told Hoffman. They taught the young boy, who had been left fatherless at the age of 10, the value of loyalty. The *vaqueros* looked out for one another. Out on the range, one faced danger every day, and it did not matter whether you were Anglo or Mexican. At least it did not matter to the *vaqueros*, who were true cowboys.

Parr recalled an instance when he got word that his mother was very ill and he did not have enough money to go see her. The *vaqueros* pitched in and loaned the young Parr $20 to go see his mother. Parr had never forgotten that act of generosity. Ever since then he had considered Mexicans "his people." Parr learned Spanish and insisted that his sons do the same.

"In Duval County, while I run things, Mexicans are in charge of county operations. Our sheriff, tax collector, and justices of the peace are all Mexican,"

Parr told Hoffman. "We have no Mexican problem in Duval County."

Hoffman was thankful for having run into Parr. He had hope now that the future may hold some promise for South Texas. Hoffman had difficulty balancing Parr's public persona with what he had heard over the past hour, but he would rest his hopes in what Parr had said and not on what the press said Parr was doing. To be sure, Parr exhibited a degree of paternalism and raw political power, but he also seemed to have a grasp of the problem and the solution.

"Well, we're about to enter God's country," Parr told Hoffman as they pulled into San Diego. "Whereabouts do you want to go?"

"If it's not too much trouble, can you drop me off at the Reyna residence across the creek from the Catholic Church?" Hoffman responded.

"That is a good family," Parr said. "Manuel is a good man, but his brother is a hothead, as I'm sure you know."

"Yes, I am familiar with both of them," Hoffman said. "Manuel has been very helpful to me, so I wanted to say goodbye before I return to Fort Sam Houston."

As they pulled up to the Reyna house, it appeared to be deserted. Hoffman had a sinking feeling.

"It appears they may have returned to Mexico," Hoffman said. "With peace returning to Mexico, many families are returning to their homes."

George Parr, seated behind Hoffman, called out the window to a neighbor feeding his chickens.

"*¿Oyes, donde están los Reynas?*" the boy asked.

"He says they left only this morning to take the train to Laredo," George Parr told Hoffman.

"Well, with the train being delayed in Alice, they should still be at the train depot," the elder Parr said.

"Please don't go to that trouble; I have inconvenienced you enough today," Hoffman said.

"It's no trouble," Parr said. "It's only a short distance, and the depot is a good place to see my constituents."

As they approached the depot, Hoffman immediately saw the Reynas waiting on the outer deck. Their trunks were lying next to them. As Parr drove up to the depot, he told George to go out among the people and let them know that the train would be along shortly.

"Tell them we stopped to talk to the boys repairing the line and your father told them to hurry it up because people were waiting," Parr told George as he winked at Hoffman. They had not stopped anywhere along the route, but like a true politician, Parr was taking credit wherever he could grab it.

Parr came to a stop next to where Manuel was standing. George jumped off and ran into the depot to carry out his father's orders.

"*¿Que tal,* Manuel?" Parr said to Manuel as the car came to a stop in front of the depot. "I got a friend here looking for you."

"*Hola, viejo,*" Manuel said to Parr, as the they shook hands. "Where did you find this straggler?"

"He was stranded in Alice and seemed to be quite in a hurry to come down here to see you folks," Parr said.

"That wouldn't have anything to do with my *hermanita* would it?" Manuel asked as he nodded toward Monica, who was seated on a trunk next to her mother.

"Oh, so that's the way it is," Parr said with a smile. "Well, I'll leave you young people."

Hoffman got off the car and thanked Parr for the ride.

"I truly appreciate your kindness," Hoffman told Parr. "I was also happy to hear your thoughts on South Texas, Senator."

"It was my pleasure, Captain," Parr said.

Parr then turned to Manuel and asked him to tell his son "Choche" to take the train to Benavides and get a ride to Los Horcones from there.

"*Hasta luego,*" Parr said as he drove off with a wave at the two men.

"Well, my friend, you made it in the nick of time," Manuel said to Hoffman. "If the track had not been washed away, we would have been halfway to the border by now."

"I'm glad for the flood," Hoffman said to Manuel. "I truly wanted to see you all before you left."

"All of us?" Manuel teased. As he did, Hoffman noticed a young lady standing off to a side, quietly imploring Manuel for his attention.

"Matthew, I want to present you my new bride, Aurora," Manuel said as he reached out and pulled the young lady toward him. He told Hoffman that her parents would not allow her to go with him unless they were married and he had proceeded without his father's blessing or knowledge. Manuel said he would face his father when he returned to Linares.

"I told you about her the last time we talked," Manuel continued. "Well, believe it or not, because I am still pinching myself to make sure it all happened, but she agreed to marriage and to return to México with me."

"Only on a trial basis," Aurora interjected. "As soon God grants us a child, I will return to San Diego. My children will be born and raised in my home."

"*Seguro, mi amor,*" Manuel said as he pulled her from the waist against him. "By then everyone will have forgotten the recent troubles and I will be able to come back without notice."

Hoffman pretended not to have heard that last comment as he looked past Manuel and Aurora toward Monica and her mother.

"Why don't you go and talk to my mother and Monica while I go look for Choche to give him his father's message on how he should get home," Manuel said to Hoffman.

Hoffman moved on to where Monica and her mother were standing. He tipped his hat and greeted the older lady.

"*Bueno días, señora,*" Hoffman said in Spanish in an effort to impress *señora* Reyna.

"*Buenos días, señor* Hoffman," *señora* Reyna responded, surprising him with an embrace and a kiss on his cheek. She motioned Monica to came and interpret for her.

"She wants to thank you from the bottom of her heart for what you did for her son Balo," Monica told Hoffman. "She said she is finally getting her family back and she has you to thank."

"Tell her I appreciate her kindness, but your father had as much to do with that as I," Hoffman told Monica. "I, too, am glad that she has her family back, but I regret very much that you must return to Mexico."

After Monica translated to her mother what Hoffman said, he continued talking with her. The mother noticed the tone of the conversation had changed, and she discretely walked a few feet down the platform to her new daughter-in-law and left Monica and Hoffman alone.

"I hope you don't mind that I brought you a gift from Mexico City," Hoffman told Monica as he pulled out the medallion of the Virgen de Guadalupe from his shirt pocket and handed it to her.

"Thank you so much. It's beautiful," Monica said as he handed it back to Hoffman and turned so he could place it around her neck. Hoffman was taken by surprise but clumsily managed to put the necklace on Monica.

"I shall always treasure it," Monica said to Hoffman.

"I am glad you like it," Hoffman said as he struggled to find a way to tell her everything he had rehearsed on the way up from the Valley.

"I am also glad I was able to get here in time to give it to you in person," Hoffman said. "I was afraid you would be gone by the time I got here."

"With Manuel's decision to get married, we were delayed so that Aurora's parents would have an appropriate amount of time to consider his marriage proposal," Monica told Hoffman. "Then we had a small wedding and a *fiesta* afterward."

"It sounds very romantic," Hoffman commented.

"Well, Manuel has a poet's soul, but God knows father was not as pleased," Monica said.

Señor Reyna did not approve of a hasty wedding without him having had the opportunity to properly ask for Aurora's hand. He had not even met her parents. Moreover, *señor* Reyna was not sure how he felt about his son marrying a *Tejana* who spoke more English than Spanish.

"But father will get over it," Monica continued. "This is a quickly changing world, and he, like all of us, must be prepared to accept change."

"That is true," Hoffman said. "But not all change is good. We must jealously hold on to those customs that add character to our lives."

"Such as what?" Monica asked.

"Such as the importance of family in our lives," Hoffman responded. "It may sound odd coming from me, but I believe your father has a point about what is appropriate courtship."

"Oh, my," Monica said, mocking surprise. "No wonder my father speaks so highly of you. You think more like him than his sons."

"I'm flattered," Hoffman said. "Having admitted my medieval tendencies in the area of courtship, I must now depart from my chivalry and be forward. Monica, I must tell you that I am at a loss knowing that you are returning to Mexico so soon. I had hoped we could get to know each other better."

"I, too, had hoped for that," Monica said. "I know you may be surprised by my answer. I certainly am, but I have never met an *Americano* such as you. You are different."

"I'll take that as a compliment," Hoffman responded.

"You should," Monica continued. "You do not feel threatened by us, nor do you show disdain for our ways. In fact, you show a genuine affection for my people."

"I must be honest," Hoffman responded. "My affection is especially pronounced when it comes to you. As some of my elders in Maryland might say, I have been smitten."

"Smitten?" Monica asked with a puzzled look. "What does that mean?"

"That I am infatuated, in love," Hoffman said shyly.

"Oh, I see," Monica said with a smile. "Since we have so little time I must be honest, too."

Hoffman tightened with fear of rejection.

"I, too, have been smitten," Monica said to his surprise.

Just then, Hoffman heard the whistle of the incoming train. Apparently the track had been repaired.

Hoffman felt bold as he realized time was running out. He reached out and held both of Monica's hands.

"What are we going to do about this?" Hoffman asked Monica.

"We will let God direct us," Monica answered. "If it is our destiny, then time will take care of what will happen. If our feelings for each other are true, they will endure until things are sorted out."

"I don't know where I will be off to when I return to San Antonio," Hoffman said. "I fear I will be sent to Europe once we enter the war."

"That is your duty as a soldier," Monica told Hoffman as she squeezed on his hands. She had been excited when she first saw Hoffman get off the car. She had never seen him in his uniform. He was a striking presence in his officer dress greens. "You know where I will be. You have been to my home. You will know how to find me when the time comes."

"Pray for my safety and that the war will end quickly," Hoffman said as he realized the time had come to start boarding the train.

Manuel came back and said a quick farewell to Hoffman and began loading their belongings, while *señora* Reyna waited on Monica.

"I will pray for you and for a quick peace," Monica said as she looked deeply into Hoffman's eyes. "I have to believe that God brought you into my life for a reason. I cannot believe that he would take you out of it now.

I know you will be back, and I will be waiting. In the meantime we will write to each other."

Monica handed Hoffman a letter with instructions on how to mail letters to her in Linares.

"You are a gentleman with old-fashioned beliefs about courtship, so I will resist my urge to kiss you goodbye," Monica said. "Besides my mother too believes in the courtship rules, and she is staring at us quite intently."

"I will settle for the thought that you wish to kiss me as much as I wish to kiss you," Hoffman said to Monica as tears welled up in his eyes. "I can promise you I will not be able to hold back the next time I see you."

With these words, Monica pulled her hands away and turned to join her mother and board the train. As the train pulled away, Monica, standing behind her mother, who was waving at Hoffman, could not resist the temptation, and she blew her soldier a kiss.

CPSIA information can be obtained
at www.ICGtesting.com
Printed in the USA
FSOW01n1216210515
7331FS